Praise for

i woke up dead at the mall

"A feel-good novel about being dead? Only in this quirky, even romantic story." —*Kirkus Reviews*

"Sharp, snarky." —*The Bulletin*

"Humorous and offbeat." —*SLJ*

"What I didn't expect from *I Woke Up Dead at the Mall* was a streak of quiet loveliness that quickly elevated it for me . . . I really enjoyed every part of this book: the quiet romance, the rich characters, the magical realism, the comforting idea that we can cycle through and start all over again, a little smarter for what's happened before." —*Book Riot*

"Such a fun read. . . . I had chills and tears." —*Kidliterati*

i woke up dead
at the mall

i woke up dead at the mall

judy sheehan

EMBER

Text copyright © 2016 by Judy Sheehan
Cover art copyright © 2016 by Olga Grlic

All rights reserved. Published in the United States by Ember, an imprint of Random House Children's Books, a division of Penguin Random House LLC, New York. Originally published in hardcover in the United States by Delacorte Press, an imprint of Random House Children's Books, New York, in 2016.

Ember and the E colophon are registered trademarks of Penguin Random House LLC.

randomhouseteens.com

Educators and librarians, for a variety of teaching tools, visit us at RHTeachersLibrarians.com

The Library of Congress has cataloged the hardcover edition of this work as follows:
Sheehan, Judy.
I woke up dead at the mall / Judy Sheehan. —First edition.
pages cm.
Summary: Sixteen-year-old Sarah wakes up dead at the Mall of America only to find she was murdered, and she must work with a group of dead teenagers to finish up the unresolved business of their former lives while preventing her murderer from killing again.
ISBN 978-0-553-51246-5 (hc) — ISBN 978-0-553-51248-9 (ebook)
[1. Dead—Fiction. 2. Murder—Fiction. 3. Mall of America (Bloomington, Minn.)—Fiction. 4. Mystery and detective stories.] I. Title.
PZ7.1.S5Iam 2016   [Fic]—dc23
2014044042

ISBN 978-0-553-51249-6 (trade pbk.)

Printed in the United States of America
10 9 8 7 6 5 4 3 2 1
First Ember Edition 2017

To Mom and Dad,

who have moved on, but who left me

with a lifelong love of stories

i woke up dead
at the mall

chapter one
i feel dead inside

I woke up dead. At the mall. Still dressed in the (hideous) mango chiffon bridesmaid gown I was wearing when I died. My hair was still pulled back in an elaborate ponytail that was meant to look windswept, but trust me, it would have survived a tsunami. This proves that if you use enough product, your hair can endure things the rest of you can't. My shoes sparkled in the light. My french manicure was unchipped. I was surrounded by waves and waves of mango chiffon.

Isn't this perfect? I had actually kept my mouth shut, opting not to tell the bride that I'd never be caught dead in mango. Now here I was. Dead. In mango.

I knew without even a tiny flicker of doubt that I was dead, but I didn't want to know it. (By the way, that's my specialty: knowing things I'd rather not know.) And just for the record, I didn't have the white-light-and-loved-ones-coming-to-welcome-me-because-death-is-a-wonderful-thing transition to the afterlife. Oh no. It felt like I was on a malfunctioning ride at Six Flags and the staff had abandoned us in an electrical storm. I rose up, up, up and took a sharp turn to the right, then a big drop, then a loop, then suddenly rose up again, going faster. So yes, my afterlife started with motion sickness. Nice.

And now I just wanted to slow down the rushing river of panic that was flowing through my veins. FYI: mango chiffon will make you sweat more than usual.

The place was crowded with the ever-so-typical mall suspects: crying toddlers, frazzled parents, laughing teenagers, exhausted store employees, and overweight mall cops. I waved my hands in front of one of the cops and shouted, "Hey! Can you help me? Please!"

He yawned and checked his phone. Why? Because he couldn't see or hear me. Why? Because he was alive and I was dead.

High over our heads was a multicolored star with these words stretched across its middle: MALL OF AMERICA. (Which is in Minnesota. I never ever once considered that the afterlife was in Minnesota. Did you?)

New York City was where I lived and where I died before my time. And you could say that Manhattan is a giant mall, with subways in place of escalators. This was my first Minnesota visit, and so far, sorry, no, I was not enjoying it. I stayed on my brown modular bench, in my ugly dress and shoes, rocking back and forth, holding myself together at the elbows. It seemed like the thing to do. There were roller coasters off in the distance, so the rumbling sounds of passing conversations were punctuated with high-pitched screams, which was sort of perfect. Keep screaming.

But then the screams stopped. The crowd thinned out. I

watched the shoppy shoppers head home to face their buyer's remorse.

And now is the time to say that this mall was huge. It was ridiculous. It was stupid big. It was like a massive, fake, shiny city. The bright, patriotic Mall of America sign was like a colorful North Star. There was a kiosk with a cheerful and insanely complicated map. So this place was four stories tall, a million miles wide, with approximately three billion stores. Plus roller coasters.

There was a big TV screen above the map, which suddenly lit up and blared an ad for *CBS This Morning*. It was loud, bright, and absolutely terrifying. I stared at it like it was a roaring dragon. But it stopped midsentence as the lights began to dim all around me. One by one, the escalators stopped moving.

The mall turned sort of dark, but it wasn't empty. It still had me.

Off to my right, I saw something move. A person. No. Two people. No. Three. They were walking toward me. Slowly and at an even, steady pace. A chill zapped me from my spine to my skull.

"Hello?" I called out. "Can you hear me? Can you see me?" I stood up and got a better look at them. All three were youngish, all staring off into the distance as they walked toward me. Closer and closer.

"Hey!" I shouted. "What do you want?"

They didn't speak a word but kept coming closer. So. The thing to do when you're scared for your life (assuming you're actually alive) is to put on your best tough New York voice and yell, *"Back off!"*

And then run like hell.

The escalators were stopped, but I leapt upward, two steps at a time, to the next level. I mentally kicked myself for not watching any zombie shows when I'd had the chance as I turned and saw two more, walking along on this level. I leapt to the top floor, with nobody following me. They just kept walking, as if they hadn't noticed me. Youngish, spaced out, silent. Were they everywhere?

I stood in front of a darkened multiplex and asked, "Now what?" right out loud.

The deep, hard silence all around me was interrupted by a *click-clack click-clack* coming from the escalator. I spun around and caught sight of a pair of truly unfortunate shoes, worn by a cheerful young woman speed-walking toward me. She wasn't a slow-walking zombie. And. She could see me.

"Hi there!" she said, confirming that yes, she really could see me. "They were having some very big sales today or I would have found you sooner. You picked a busy day to die, missy!" She had sparkling blue eyes and blond hair braided over her head. She was dressed in a bright blue polyester suit that made her look like she was applying for an internship at Me So Corporate, Incorporated. Her shoes were like horses' hooves.

"Welcome!" She clapped her hands in delight. "I'm Bertha!" She looked like she was my age, but she sounded like a cartoon grandmother, with a faint Irish lilt to her voice. (And who names their kid Bertha? Doesn't that qualify as child abuse?)

"So then. You're Sarah. And you're really rather dead. But you didn't move on, did you now? No siree! You're a bit stuck, aren't you?" She kept answering her own questions as she

4

took me by the arm (please don't invade my personal space) and guided me into a narrow hallway. (BTW, when I was alive, I never let anyone guide me into a narrow hallway.)

"You have unfinished business, Sarah. You were murdered, and you're a bit upset about it." She said this as if she were saying, *Oh, you spilled the milk, but don't cry over it, okay?*

"Um, wait up, there, Bertha," I said, taking my arm back to its rightful, solitary place. "I wasn't murdered. If I really am dead, I died from *food poisoning.* It was accidental."

"Oh dear me." Bertha sighed and led me to a side exit marked AUTHORIZED DTTW PERSONNEL ONLY. ALARM WILL SOUND. She pushed past as if she had all the authorization in the world. And after all that warning, we just ended up in a Bed Bath & Beyond.

"Aren't you just a bundle of unfinished business!" She took my hands (!) and sat me down on an ugly ottoman, while she sat on an even uglier one.

"What does DTTW mean?" I asked, already dreading the answer.

"Dead to the World," she explained patiently. "The living can't come in here. They can't even see it."

(Sorry I asked.) "I may be dead, but I'm not *murdered-dead.* That's completely worse," I reasoned (sort of unreasonably).

Bertha had an air of I-know-everything-oh-you-poor-fool. "You were poisoned, Sarah. Murdered. Killed. Slain. I'm quite certain of that."

"But I didn't have any enemies. Nobody would want to kill me," I insisted. Because I was right.

She started to say, "And yet, someone did," but I cut her

off. "Okay then. Who killed me?" I asked. "And why? It makes no sense. Why would someone kill me?"

Bertha just smiled some more at me, which became more and more infuriating.

"It's so nice here!" she replied. "This mall has everything. The living don't notice the dead here, what with the bright lights and the sales and free samples. Most malls are haunted. Did you know that? The Boy saves this extra-big one for New Yorkers. Rather a tough town, isn't it? We get our fair share of murder victims."

The boy? What boy? I looked around, but Bertha kept talking. It was as if this were a long, memorized speech (badly performed) and if I interrupted her, she'd have to start over. And nobody wanted that. She cleared her throat, crossed her feet at the ankles (so ladylike), and clasped her hands in her lap.

"I'm here to help you let go of your old life. All that attachment, all that connection. You have to say goodbye to it all." She leaned in a little closer, and I thought she was enjoying this. "And here's how you'll do it: you'll get to revisit a day from your life. You'll go to your funeral, and you'll work with me and your fellow dead to let go of your old life."

"What, like group therapy for the dead?" I smirked, trying not to throw up in my brain.

"Yes! You've got the idea," she declared, totally missing the fact that I was mocking her. "And if you can finish the stuff that has you tied to the living world, then off you go to your next life! Isn't that lovely?"

"What if I can't?" I just had to ask.

She touched my arm (!) and answered, "You will. I'm really

6

good at this!" I didn't believe her. I thought she could tell. "Let me take you up to our floor. We have our very own stores, separate from the living! Isn't death such fun already?" And with that, she directed me past an elevator on the side wall of the store. She was a little too good at dodging my questions. (And if we were going upstairs, why didn't we get in that elevator?)

"But what about my murderer?" I asked. "What happens to him? Or her? Or them?"

Bertha shook her head and half-smiled. "You're asking all the wrong questions, Sarah."

Funny. These seemed like pretty good questions to me. But before I could respond, she clapped a white bracelet onto my wrist like a handcuff. It changed to a dark crimson red when it came in contact with my skin.

"Why did it turn red?"

"Because of *you*," Bertha explained. "You're not ready to move on. Your unfinished business is flowing through you like blood used to flow through your veins. I'll be watching that bracelet closely. When it loses its color, you'll move on."

She hurried onto an escalator, and I hurried right behind her.

"How long does that take?" I asked. "What's the average time?"

"It's entirely up to you," she said. (Don't you hate that kind of answer?)

"How do I finish my unfinished business?" I asked.

"I'll help you. I'll be your death coach."

"My what?" I asked, even though I'd heard her. I just couldn't believe her.

"Your death coach!"

"My what?"

"Your death coach!"

"My what?"

"Your death coach!"

I toyed with the idea of seeing how many times I could get her to repeat it, but then I dropped it when we reached this new floor. We were in the upstairs of the Bed Bath & Beyond, looking out on a whole new floor of the mall. This one wasn't on the map. Bertha rompy-stomped forward in those shoes. (Oh, those shoes!)

"Well, look at you! You died in such a fancy gown! A touch too elegant for everyday, don't you think?" she said, which immediately made me question her taste level. (This dress was a faux Alexander McQueen, if McQueen had suddenly lost all of his talent.) And yes, I knew that she was changing the subject. "On our floor, you can take whatever you want. It's not shoplifting, it's just *taking*!"

There they were again: those quiet people, walking slowly through the mall, just like the ones I had seen before on the lower floor. They walked at that same slow, even pace. It was sort of hypnotizing. But I turned my attention back to Bertha.

"Why are they walking around like that?" I asked, pointing to the people around us.

Bertha's expression changed from bright to nervous/controlled/badly-acting-another-memorized-speech.

"They're mall walkers. A bit like zombies but minus the aggressive tendencies," Bertha explained. "That's what happens to you if you fail to move on. They're stuck in a sort of dream state, trapped in their own awful memories." She shuddered as a sad girl with straw-colored hair stepped past us.

8

"Why don't you wake them up?" I asked.

"They have to wake themselves. They have to choose something different. Never underestimate the power of free will, Sarah." Bertha shook her head, staring after the girl. "Poor things. They suffer so. . . ." She turned her attention to me, revving up her energy. "You mustn't become like them. Do whatever you have to do and *move on.*"

Bertha fished through a huge briefcase that might have belonged to a little girl dressed up as Business Lady for Halloween. She handed me a sheet of paper with printing on both sides and a measly little golf pencil. Before I could read any of it, she said, "And it would be oh so helpful if you would complete this questionnaire for me. It will help *me* help *you.*"

"Does anyone know who murdered me? And why?" I asked, but she ignored me. Maybe I should have pushed her harder, but I couldn't. Death started to feel like rain settling on my cheeks. It was here, no escaping it. And soon, I knew, my skin would be soaked. I shook my head slowly.

"I've got three other fairly recent arrivals, just like you. You'll meet them tomorrow. All of them were murdered, all of them are young and not quite over it. My specialty!" Her energy level made me wonder about her caffeine intake.

"Okay. Fine. If you won't tell me who murdered me, can I haunt my family and friends like a ghost and find out who did this?"

Bertha's voice turned hard. "No. You mustn't even consider that. People who go back and haunt the living get stuck there. They watch the living go on without them, forget about them, grow old and die. But the ghosts remain, roaming the earth forever. Powerless and useless."

It felt as if the mall had just grown ten degrees colder. The knot of fear in my head was sort of like brain freeze. I didn't think my day could get any worse after dying all alone (in this dress), but it had.

Bertha looked down at her sad shoes. "You'll see your family at your funeral and say your *final* goodbyes then. We don't haunt the living. We let go, and we move on."

"Are you completely and totally sure that I was murdered? Really?" I repeated it louder, harsher, but she waved me away, which I hated as much as I hated having my personal space invaded.

"I'll meet you and the others tomorrow at our Staples store, after breakfast. You should take a bed in the Crate and Barrel for now. That serves as the girls' dormitory for you and your roomie! Well. Good night!"

She started to click-clack away, but I called after her. "Okay, if you won't tell me who killed me, at least tell me what I should do now."

She sighed, and it looked like she was trying to remain upbeat while dealing with a fool.

"Shop! Help yourself to whatever you need or want. Food, clothing, books, and so on. Crate and Barrel has some lovely throw pillows. You may be here for . . . a while. Oh. And everything is free."

Welcome to the Mall of the Dead.

chapter two

fill in the blanks

My Bracelet Is Red
Like the Lipstick on a Movie Star

DEATH QUESTIONNAIRE

Please be completely honest in your answers so that your death coach can help you to move on. We don't know what you did back on earth. We only know how you died. We don't know when you're lying. But you do.

Please note: You will not move on to heaven or hell. Heaven and hell are back on earth. Your mission now is to return there.

Name: **Sarah Evans**   Age at Death: **16**

  1. As I review my life, my greatest regret is:

    a. Something that I did
    (b.)Something that I didn't do
    c. Something that I left incomplete when I died
    d. I have no regrets

2. Thinking of my most recent birthday:

    a. I got everything I wanted
    b. I wanted more
    (c.) I didn't care about gifts
    d. I didn't celebrate it

3. I would prefer to:

    a. Return to the kind of life I was living
    b. Start over in a completely different life
    c. Keep exactly what I want from my old life and throw away the rest
    (d.) Undecided

4. Here's what I will miss most about being alive:

    a. Food
    b. Sex
    c. People
    (d.) Other: _Everything. But nothing specific._
                    Never mind.

5. This was my favorite place on Earth:
    Washington Square Park, near the fountain,
    especially if a good band is playing. Or my
    bedroom, in my bed, under the covers.

6. This was the worst thing I did in my life:

<u>After my mom died, I told my dad that</u>
<u>he should have taken better care of her</u>
<u>and that I hated being stuck with him. He</u>
<u>cried for an hour. To be fair, I was only</u>
<u>seven years old and really sad.</u>

_____

_____

7. This was the best thing I did in my life:

<u>It's a tie: When I was little, I helped out</u>
<u>a pregnant lady and maybe even saved her</u>
<u>life. Sort of. That's tied with the day</u>
<u>that I died, when I put on the world's</u>
<u>ugliest mango bridesmaid gown, smiled, and</u>
<u>made the last day of my life all about</u>
<u>somebody else's happiness. And I meant it.</u>

chapter three

help yourself
to unlimited stuff

When I was alive, I didn't really care all that much about clothes. Well, I cared a medium amount. But right now, I had an urgent need to stop looking like a walking slice of fruit. I began exploring the stores available to me.

Our floor (the Floor of the Dead?) surrounded the dizzying mallverse below. I leaned over the railing and peered into the semidarkness. The roller coasters off to my right were fast asleep. Looking around this top floor, every store was brightly lit and fully stocked. But there were no cashiers, no salespeople or customers. The only people I saw were those slow-walking ones who didn't speak, and they never went inside any of the stores.

I took a small wheelie suitcase and roamed the stores, seeking the necessities of life. Or death. I headed directly into Anthropologie. Hello, soft dark skinny jeans. Hello, pale blue cotton V-neck T-shirt with no words on it. Good-bye, uncomfortable, ugly, unnatural gown. Hello, strappy sandals. I don't mind (too much) that you show my mango pedicure. Goodbye, old-lady pearl earrings. Hello, dangly silver wires. Hello, big, shiny trash can. Would you like a whole lot of mango chiffon?

I was starting to feel like myself again.

Now that I was dead, could I see my mother again? Where was she? Why didn't she come greet me? I looked around as if she might be sneaking up behind me. It was a little hard to realize how much I ached to see my mom. I needed her now, more than ever.

"Mom," I whispered. "We're both dead now. Please come see me? Please help me?"

Thinking about her, I was suddenly bursting with a million questions about life, death, afterlife, God, war, ghosts, reincarnation, karma, heaven, angels, Mount Olympus, my hamster, my cat, recycling, to be or not to be, and why good things happened to bad people. I was dead. I could have the answers to everything. Tomorrow, with Bertha, I could unlock the secrets of the universe. At the Staples store.

At Ulta, I unleashed my hair from its windswept prison. I found a brush that promised to promote shine and health in my hair. The giant mirror magnified my face to the tenth power, which is always terrifying, so I flipped it around to life-size.

What a very normal, alive activity this was. I let myself fall into a trance as I brushed and brushed. I even started humming a little bit, which helped break the huge block of silence that surrounded me. I studied the reddish-brownish straight-as-a-pin hair that I inherited from Mom. My skin was littered with a few faint freckles that you had to be thisclose to me to see. My eyes were a grayish blue/bluish gray. I stared at my reflection and brushed. Who killed me? Why? How? And did the police catch them already? (Please!)

Backing out of the store, I bumped into a young woman who was one of the mall walkers I had seen before. She had long straw-blond hair and was wearing a baggy oatmeal-colored dress.

"Sorry," I said. But she just kept walking, staring straight ahead.

"Okay then!" I shouted. "Great talking with you. Catch you on the next lap."

She didn't even slow down. Just kept walking.

I sat down on a bench and watched the mall walkers. The next person to pass by was a woman dressed in an embarrassing Goth Girl outfit. Black hair, lips, nails, clothes, and enough eyeliner to circle the globe. Oh, honey.

"Hey!" I shouted. "How's it going?"

She didn't slow down either. Next up was a guy dressed in some kind of wizardy/*Game of Thrones* robe, but I let him keep walking. There was a long, oppressive silence. But then I saw him. A boy. Fresh-scrubbed, like a kid who lived on some wholesome farm. But his face held a stony sadness that took my breath away. He kept coming toward me.

"Hey!" My voice was unrecognizably deep. It felt like sandpaper in my throat. "Just keep walking! Okay? Keep walking!" But he stopped, right in front of me. His vacant eyes fixed on me. Sort of.

"What?" I asked him, as if I were daring him to utter a single word.

The zombie boy's mouth dropped open, just like *The Scream*. His mouth got so big, I sort of thought it might reach the floor. But then he let out a small cry, followed by two words: "No . . . more . . ."

He looked up to the ceiling as his face turned to ash. Then his body, his arms, his legs, all dissolved into ash. He was, ever so briefly, a sculpture of ash suspended in the air. And then the ashes dropped to the floor. He was gone. The air smelled faintly like someone had just blown out birthday candles.

I wanted to scream-cry-run, scream-cry-run, scream-cry-run. But I didn't. I closed my eyes. Tight.

I wanted my mom. I wanted her to hug me and tell me that everything would be okay. Wow. I hadn't let myself long for her in so many years, and now it felt like the need was reaching out from the deepest part of me and taking over. I squeezed my eyes shut tighter.

Maybe when I opened them, this would all be some fever dream and it would be over. I'd be back at the hotel, with my dad and Karen hovering over me, smiling in relief that I was back with them. It would be like that last scene in *The Wizard of Oz*. Everyone was worried about me, but now I was okay.

I opened my eyes and looked in every direction: mall, mall, mall, mall. One huge damn mall. So I closed them again. Obviously this place was way more dangerous than Bertha had let on.

"Murdered." The word flashed like a beacon inside my head. Murdered. Why? Who? Why? I spoke out loud but very quietly. "I want to get out of here. I want my dad. I want my life. I want my room. I want my music, my stuffed animals, and my phone, and everything else. I even want pop quizzes and paper cuts. Help. Please."

I wasn't exactly praying. Just talking. "Mom. Mommy? Are

you out there somewhere? Can you hear me? Please, please help me."

Bertha's words ricocheted in my skull: I had to finish the unfinished business of my life. Then again, my life was nothing but unfinished business. I was unfinishable.

Whatever had been sustaining me so far disintegrated. The breathless shock of the new (dead) world I inhabited took a damn breath, as something inside me fell away, fragile as a robin's egg, and I let myself tumble into tears. It was a deep, hard cry that rattled my shoulders, jackknifed my knees, and sliced me in two. I was dead. Someone had hated me enough to kill me. I felt as thin and lost as that boy who had just turned to ash.

The sound coming from me was a kind of keening, terrible song. Eventually I formed the word "help." Not very loud, not very clear, but on and on. Help, help, help. I have no idea how long it took me to figure out that someone was sitting next to me, whispering, "Shhhhhh. I'll help you."

I felt a cool hand on my left shoulder. It belonged to the straw-blond girl.

"I'll help you," she said. "I'm awake now. Can you take me to Bertha?"

I jumped to my feet and let out a small scream. The other walkers kept walking, but this one was smiling at me. I stood there, openmouthed and stupid.

"Who are you?" I asked, and yes, I did sound scared. "What do you want?"

"I'm Alice," the girl said. "I just want to sit down." And she did.

"I'm Sarah," I answered.

"You just died. Is that right?" she asked. She looked extra-happy to be sitting. So I nodded and sat down too.

Alice didn't seem dangerous. She seemed pretty tame.

She was staring at the stores around her as if she had just landed on a space station.

"I'm fine. Really." I used my best fake I'm-an-electronic-device voice so that I sounded more together than I felt.

Alice was a bit dreamy, staring at her surroundings. "The last time I was awake, this was a shopping mall. But it seems bigger now. Shinier. I don't recognize any of the names."

"The last time you were awake?" I asked. I didn't need to fake calm anymore. I was calm. And curious.

"I died a long time ago. I've awakened twice before. This time I really need to move on. I need to"—her eyes searched the stores, as if they carried the right words—"*get over it.*" Those were the words she settled on. "I have to *get over it all and move on.* This walking is the worst thing in the world, believe me."

(Here's what I didn't say: I just saw one of the mall walkers burst into ash, so the walking part might not be the worst thing in the world. I didn't say that because she looked way too fragile to hear it.)

I finally took a moment to really look at her. She should have been a figure in some tea-colored picture from Ellis Island or a PBS show my dad would want me to watch.

"When did you die?" I asked.

She smiled knowingly. "I died in 1933. And Bertha died twenty-two years before me."

"You died in the Great Depression. Bertha has been dead for over a century. I died today. We're all here at the mall," I said, just needing to work with some big, fat headline facts.

19

"Would you mind if we went to the girls' dormitory?" she asked. "I've been walking since 1999. I could use a rest."

✻ ✻ ✻

The mall was dark and dreamlessly quiet, simulating night-time, I guess. I wondered if it would do this darkness thing every night. Alice stopped in Talbots and bought (well, *took*) the most awful granny nightgown I've ever seen. Inside Crate & Barrel we made our way past patio furniture and found a collection of beds with an excessive number of blankets and throw pillows on top of them. Did Bertha put them there?

"Perfect!" Alice exclaimed. She was pulling back the covers on a four-poster bed and settling in. "I've always loved sleeping here," said Alice.

"Why?" I asked.

"No nightmares," she replied. "We dead have no dreams of any kind. And after my long, walking nightmare, this is just what I need: it's like a little taste of death. Or at least what I used to think death would be like."

Okay then.

"Good night, Sarah!" Alice called out, half breath/half voice. "Sleep well."

I'd never been good at falling asleep in strange places. And this was by far the strangest place I'd ever been. So here I was. In bed. Awake.

Closing my eyes, I stared into the darkness before me. To be or not to be. To sleep, perchance to dream.

At the mall.

chapter four

my so-dull life

(please feel free to skip ahead. nothing to see here.)

This has to be some kind of mistake. No one would ever want to kill me. I wasn't that interesting.

I wasn't good. I wasn't bad. I wasn't tall. I wasn't short. I was that blurry face in the crowd shots. "Have a great summer" was written a hundred times in my yearbook. And that is exactly what I wanted. Here's what I didn't want: to be different, special, weird, odd, or in any way abnormal. Wish granted.

My parents made a lot of money when my dad invented the super-big plastic lids for Starbucks. Hey, somebody had to invent them. After that, they had so much cash that they didn't need to work anymore. But Dad loved work, so he and Mom started a consulting company for other people who wanted to invent stuff. (Are you totally bored yet? I am.) And guess what? That business made a ton of money. They were just money magnets. Dad used to joke that he was the brains but Mom was the magic. The clients all liked her best. And so did I.

Mom was truly magical. She always seemed to know

what I was thinking before I thought it, and she knew what was going to happen to me. She scooped me away from dangers with lightning speed. When she came to my pre-school to volunteer, I showed her off to everyone like she was a movie star. She was pretty. She was kind. She smiled by default.

On my first day of kindergarten, she took a set of Hello Kitty bandages, gave each kitty a little kiss, and then stashed them in my backpack.

"In case you get hurt today, these already have my kisses to make you feel better," she explained. Sure enough, at recess I skinned my knees bloody. Through my tears, I insisted that the nurse use the Hello Kitty bandages, the ones with Mom's kisses on them. How did Mom know that I'd need them? She was magical.

Me, I was a little kid. I ran around Washington Square Park. I played piano. Blah blah blah. Okay, here's one exciting thing: when I was six years old, I woke up from a dream where I saw a lady in a green coat waiting for a subway, but she was wobbling and starting to lose her balance. She was in danger and just about to fall onto the tracks when I woke up.

And then that day I saw a lady in a green coat, waiting right near Mom and me on the subway platform at West Fourth Street.

"She's going to fall," I said to Mom. She looked kind of confused, so I said it again, really loud. "She's going to fall!" Lots of people heard me.

Sure enough, the lady started wobbling, just like I knew she would. And two guys and a teenage girl grabbed her as she started to lurch forward. They caught her. It turns out she was pregnant, with a really big belly. But instead of thanking the people who saved her, she yelled at them for being too rough. Go figure.

That night at bedtime Mom hugged me extra tight. "You knew. When that lady almost fell, you knew. Sometimes I know things too."

"You do? Is that part of your magic?" I asked.

"I don't know if it's magic," she half-laughed. "And it certainly doesn't happen all the time. But it does happen. I call it the Knowing. Have you known things before, sweetheart?"

I sat up in bed, ready to release my one tiny secret to my favorite person in the world. "Yes! I knew when Sam was going to fall off the monkey bars, but I was too scared of him to say anything. And he fell," I confessed.

"And he's okay now," Mom assured me. "I knew when that big client of ours was going to tell us some very bad news. The Knowing is a gift. And you got it from me."

It was nighttime, but hearing her say that made me feel like I was bathed in sunshine. I got this Knowing thing from her. We were connected, and we always would be.

"Do we get to know everything in the whole world?" I asked, not sure if that would be good or bad.

"Sorry, no. For me it's just something that comes and goes. It was stronger when I was a kid." She spoke as if she were just figuring that out now. "I wonder what changed."

We knew things. Sometimes. We had the Knowing, Mom and I.

I didn't understand it completely. I still don't. But that night I thought it was great.

Of course, it wasn't always great. In fact, sometimes it was

23

terrible. I knew when my favorite teacher, who was pregnant, was about to lose the baby, and I couldn't stop crying because I knew that it had already begun and she wouldn't be able to stop it.

Sometimes, the Knowing gave me a really bad stomachache, so Mom would cradle me in her arms and sing very quietly so that only I could hear her. She loved the Beatles and made sure that I heard every album while I was a baby. That night she sang "Blackbird."

And then this happened: It was a Tuesday morning in summer. I was seven years old, and I woke up knowing something very bad was about to happen to Mom. I could hear glass shattering, metal screeching. I ran out of my room, leapt downstairs, and found Dad sipping coffee.

"Where's Mom?" I asked.

"She's meeting with our new client. Apparently they like her better than me!" He half-laughed, but that changed in a blink. I proceeded to throw the biggest tantrum of my life, and I was never really a tantrum thrower.

"I don't understand, sweetie. What's wrong?"

"Get her back! Now! *Right now!*" I screamed. I pounded his chest. "Call her! Get her home! *Now!*"

He reached for the phone, maybe just to calm me down. But it was too late.

Mom was in a taxi that was stopped at a red light. The light turned green and the taxi started to go. But some asshole in a Hummer was running his red light and slammed right into the taxi. Right into the passenger seat. Right into my mom.

She was broken beyond repair. She lingered for a few days.

Dad took her off life support. She lasted for one more day, and then she left.

I stopped talking. I cried. I made sounds but no words.

That night I dreamed about her so intensely, so vividly, I swore she was there in my room with me. She felt real and solid as she tried to console inconsolable me.

"I'll always be with you," she promised. "One way or another."

"But I bet you won't be here when I wake up," I thought. But I still wasn't speaking. I dreamed about her the next night, and the next, and the next. She was my secret, private Dream Mom, cradling me in her arms and singing to me. I looked forward to sleep every night, just so that I could hear her sing "Blackbird" one more time. I had her all to myself. So I let myself speak at long last.

"Will you come back every night and visit me?" I asked her, fully expecting her to promise that she would.

"No, sweetheart." She kissed my forehead and smoothed my hair. "I have to stop this. I have to move on."

I went silent once more, locking my arms around her as if I could keep her there forever.

And then I woke up.

Everyone we ever knew was at her funeral. Everyone loved my mom. I stood in a corner, mute and miserable. I clutched a folded piece of paper against my heart. Eventually Dad stooped down and spoke softly. "Sarah? What have you got there? Is it something you want to say or maybe sing for your mom? You could do that if you want."

Had he been spying on me? The paper held a song that I had written for her. I couldn't write my own music, but I rewrote the words to a Beatles song. Mom had loved them, and now their music sort of belonged to her. The whole room went silent except for a few quiet sobs. I walked over to the coffin, where a plastic-looking version of my mom was laid out in a pale pink dress. I placed the poem next to her hands, turned, and broke my silence with him.

"This is your fault. You should have taken better care of her. She shouldn't have been in that taxi. And now I'm stuck with you."

I watched my words pierce him and slice him in two. And I still hate myself for doing that to him.

He cried and hugged me and said, "You're right."

That night she didn't appear in my dreams. She never came back again. The Mom part of my life was over. We were disconnected.

Losing her the second time was even more painful than losing her just once. And I got to have that second round of pain because of the Knowing.

And just like that, I hated the Knowing. If it couldn't save Mom, what good was it? All it ever gave me was a stomachache and a broken heart. Was it going to torture me again and again until my own unexpected death came along?

No.

It needed to end along with my mother's life. If it started to rise up, I shook it off, thought of a song, thought of something else, anything else. I was like a left-handed kid learning to write with the right hand. It was hard, but I hung in there and sent it far, far away.

Okay, so. Fast-forward a bunch of years. Why, there's Sarah. Doing schoolwork, being polite, watching from the sidelines, and being blurry. Does she have any close friends? A boyfriend? Does she ever play her music in front of anyone? (Don't waste your life on such stupid questions.)

She doesn't magically know things, save lives, have fun, or sing Beatles songs in her dreams with her mom. If she thinks she starts to know something, she pushes it out of her brain and throws it as far as she can. And you know what? That works. That feeling inside her goes quiet. She becomes someone else. It isn't easy, but she does it. Done.

All that time, Dad was working, working, working, working, working, working, working.

Enter Karen. Dad met her at a work conference last year. She was a bit of a Midwestern dork with questionable fashion sense. But very nice. Warm. And a fantastic cook. Her family had made a pile of money in health supplements. She was kinda sorta melting the polite frost that was our father-daughter relationship. Global Warming Karen even invited me to be her bridesmaid after Dad proposed. And I was sort of honored, not to mention happy about the way life was getting better for us.

Okay, so. Fast-forward to the last day of my life. (If only I had known that it would be the last one.) Dad wore a penguin-friendly tuxedo. Karen wore a traditional wedding gown, which was bright, bright white with pearls, lace, sparkles, and puffs. It looked like the dress that would be chosen by a child who eats too much sugar.

At the reception everyone talked about new beginnings, and I felt this amazing flame of hope light up in my solar plexus. Maybe this was that Knowing thing—but in a good way. I even contemplated singing at the reception (thanks to an illicit glass of champagne that I'd swiped from the dais). But I restrained myself.

I danced. Me. Dancing. Wow. Who knew? Everyone was having fun. I thought about Mom, and it felt like she was maybe nearby. And she was happy for us all, I think. So I was happy too.

And then this happened: someone was watching me. I could feel it, like heat on my skin. I turned to look in the direction of the heat, but all I saw was some guy in black and white, disappearing into the kitchen. Probably some waiter. So what? I just wanted to dance.

Oh, but I couldn't. A heavy shadow fell over the day. I started to feel this pain, a sharp-knife, sick-to-my-stomach kind of pain. And I didn't want to ruin everyone's good time, so I slipped out of the reception and upstairs to my hotel room. I got a whole lot sicker. It was torture, and I was a prisoner in my own body. So you'll understand that I felt almost relieved when an oppressive sleep began pushing me down, like I was at the bottom of the ocean. I fell asleep on the bathroom floor.

And I woke up dead at the mall.

chapter five

you'll never walk alone

So it turns out that when dead people sleep, they sleep reeeeeeeeeeally deep. That first night at the mall I slept like someone had drugged me, then clubbed me, then made me watch golf on TV.

It was all great until something ridiculous happened. I had a dream. About Mom. I was breathless with joy. In the dream I was back in my room, at home, just like a living person. Mom was the magic (Dad was right about that), so I felt her presence before I saw or heard her.

Seeing her made me feel safe and complete. She smiled and I melted a little. She took a breath, ready to speak. I recognized her voice as easily as if we had just spoken yesterday. Mom. Right there, right next to me. Mom. And I kind of stopped breathing. She smiled so sweetly, it tore a hole in my chest. I think I gasped when I tried to start breathing again. I held my arms out to her, just like when I was a little kid, because right then I was. She folded me into her arms. She smelled like soap and honey. I hugged her tight enough to crack some ribs.

"Sarah," she said gently. "My little girl. Why did you have to die so young?"

"I didn't want to die," I answered as I started to cry, and it felt as if my face were sparking with fire. "Somebody killed me. Do you know who it was?"

She smiled at me with the wisdom of the world in her eyes. "I'm much too young to know such things," she said, rubbing my back like she used to when I was little. "I'm sorry I had to leave you like I did. I've missed you so."

She hugged me tight, wrapping me in the scent, the feel, the world of her. If only I could stay there.

"How can I be dreaming?" I sniffled, and she rose and backed away. "Wait," I called to her. "I'm not supposed to dream. That's what Alice said."

"Who's Alice?" Mom asked. "Is she dead too?" She kept backing away, sort of fading around the edges.

"Mom, where are you going? Please don't leave me! Not again!" I cried. "Please, Mom. Stay? For me?"

"Do you want to move on?" she asked. I nodded a vigorous *yesyesyes,* unable to speak.

"Then don't tell them you dream." She faded a little bit more. "Dreams like this one keep you attached to your old life. After I died, I dreamed that I came to see you and sang Beatles songs to you."

"Mom, that actually happened. You did come see me. I remember it!" I was shouting now; she was barely visible.

"The living are always in danger, Sarah. So just let go and . . ." She was speaking, but I couldn't hear her anymore. Her voice was muffled, hazy tone.

"Mom? Come back? Please? I miss you!" I said to the empty space before me.

"Hey! Dead girls! *Wake up!*" A booming voice interrupted my dream.

Mom was gone. Or the dream of Mom was gone. Wow. The dead aren't supposed to dream. But I did. Had I just done something wrong? Something illegal? And did it show? Should I hide it? Or was it too late, and I was already busted?

Now here I was, squinting in the bright lights of the mall at a curvy girl with streaks of orangey blond in her long dark hair. She had to be the roomie Bertha had mentioned.

"Hiya, stupid new girls. I'm starvin', and I'm going to the food court without you!" she announced.

Eyes fully open now, I saw that the main event with her, really, was her outfit. She was dressed like she was going to the Trashy Oscars. She wore diamonds in her ears, on her neck, and on both wrists, and she looked like she meant it. Her dress was a turquoise pastel floral thing with layers of fabric that danced in the air around her. She wobbled on perilously high heels.

She smiled, sorta kinda posing for us. Obviously she felt pretty. Oh so pretty.

"Wow," I said wearily, then pointed to her outfit to add, "That's a lot of look."

She lost her smile, turned on her heels, stumbled a bit, and left.

"*See* ya! Wouldn't wanna *be* ya!" she shouted over her shoulder. Her walk in those heels was unstable, and I was worried about her. A little.

"Food," said Alice. "The dead have their own food court. We can eat whatever we want. We don't have to pay, and we can never get fat."

That was all she needed to say. We made a mad dash for the food court and a mountain of food that might have killed us, if only we were alive.

✻ ✻ ✻

Bertha actually squealed with delight when she saw Alice enter Staples.

"Ooooh! This is going to be fun!" Bertha exclaimed, hugging Alice, then speaking, then hugging again. "Alice is awake, everyone! Oh, Alice!"

Alice's face was tomato red with embarrassment. The curvy girl was still posing and now smiling in the direction of two boys who had just entered the store. One was a lanky guy who was totally and completely bald. He had large, pale-blue moon eyes, set in a sort of pale-pink complexion. He was smiling and carrying a king-size Snickers bar. His face beamed as bright as the sun.

"Another Snickers bar? You're so crazy!" The curvy girl giggled in what may have been an attempt to flirt with the bald boy.

The other guy was pretty tall, with chocolate-brown hair that fell over hazel eyes. He pushed it back. It fell. He pushed it back. It fell. He had a crooked grin, angular features, and sort of amazing shoulders.

I actually may have flinched when I first saw him. He

looked me in the eye for a couple of long moments. And then we both looked away. Sparks. I know.

This was not like me. At all. When I was alive, I may have found the occasional boy or TV vampire good-looking, but none of them made me flinch or gasp or lose my train of thought. I'd never had this reaction to any guy—and I went to a private school where some of the boys worked as underwear models. They came from serious money, where the families spent generations perfecting the gene pool so that nobody ever got a zit and everybody had amazing abs. They strode the world like Photoshopped colossi with spray tans.

But this guy looked completely normal. So why was I ridiculously and painfully aware of how much I was blinking?

"School is in session," he said in a low voice that only I could hear. He was a side commenter. Just like me. Wow.

Bertha gestured for us to settle into the hard plastic chairs that she had arranged in a semicircle. So yes. I sat next to him. And he sat next to me. And I managed not to make a fool of myself. Yet.

"Some of you have been here for a little while, so you know one another. But a few new arrivals have joined us, so let's all go around and introduce ourselves." Bertha didn't wait for an answer but gestured to Alice, who waved shyly.

"Hello. I'm Alice. I lived in Hell's Kitchen. Many years ago. I died at my job, I was . . ." She gulped, flushing red once again. "I was thrown to the ground. I died from a head injury." She touched the back of her head gently. "I have unfinished business with my murderer . . . and my parents. . . ." I thought she was going to say more. But the curvy girl spoke next.

"I'm Lacey. I lived on the Bowery on the Lower East Side. And you wanna know how I died? I got pushed from the top of a building. I flew through the air and landed on the ground. My neck snapped right in two. I died like *that*!" She snapped her fingers, and I wondered if her snapping neck had sounded like *that* too. "And I don't have a ton of unfinished business. I just wanna see the guy who killed me get what's coming to him."

"No guarantees on that," Alice said, so quietly that she seemed to be talking to herself.

The bald guy went next. "Harry." He smiled at us all. He looked young, but his voice was deep, making him sound older. "Upper West Side." He pointed to his bald head. "Cancer." He shrugged, as if it were all too obvious.

Bertha gave him a sideways look. "But, Harry, did you *die* of cancer?" she asked pointedly.

Harry nodded, caving in on something. "Right. No. I got killed, just like everybody else," he conceded. "I spent way too much of my life being sick. It wasn't fair and it kind of sucked. And that's my unfinished business."

I should have been next, but Bertha skipped over me and called on the guy to my right. The one I was trying not to pay too much attention to.

"Nick?" she prompted.

He smiled. "Well, that gives away half my story: I'm Nick." I let out a little laugh at that. "Are you ready for this?" He looked me in the eye. "Gunshot wound. To the chest." He held his hands over his heart. "I didn't stand a chance."

He looked at me, through me, and I held my breath.

"What about you?" he asked me. "How did you end up dead before your time?"

I answered him. What I mean is, I didn't answer the group, I just answered him. Nick. With the hazel eyes and the hair that fell over them. And the shoulders.

"I'm Sarah. I lived in the West Village, and I died from food poisoning." Ew. As soon as I said it, I wanted to take it back. Was everyone (Nick?) picturing me in full-on food poisoning mode? Ew.

"Sarah," Bertha spoke softly. "Try again, please."

I had no idea what to say. Nick did a comically fake cough as he said the word "murdered." Bertha scowled at him, which made me like him even more.

"Okay. Sure. Let me start over. I'm Sarah. Someone must have poisoned me, but I really can't believe that because, honestly, nobody knew me well enough to want to kill me."

That last statement cut too close to my heart and left a catch in my throat. My face was hot. But Bertha kept her smug beam aimed at me.

Lacey let out a slow whistle. "Maybe you should go to the Comfortable Shoe Shop. I'm betting there's going to be a lot of walking in your future."

Lacey was hard to like.

chapter six

get back to where you
once belonged

"You must move on," Bertha (Captain Obvious) said for the billionth time. "And if you all manage to do so together, you'll start a whole new life, and you'll have the chance to meet and maybe even grow up together next time around. Doesn't that sound lovely?"

Actually that got mixed reviews from me. Just being honest.

"In a few days you'll be attending your funerals." Alice let out a long sigh. Her funeral must have been ages ago. "Except, of course, for you, Alice. Your funeral was . . . well, it was what it was." Bertha's face turned crimson. "I—well—I don't know what more to say about that."

"And how often does *that* happen?" Nick whispered to me. We smiled at each other, then looked at the floor. Still, I wondered: what had happened at Alice's funeral?

"Nick?" Bertha spoke sharply. "Did you have a question?"

"No. I have a million questions," Nick replied. "Who made all the food we just ate? Where did the stuff in the stores come from?"

Ha. I hadn't even thought to question any of that. Nick's mind was so different and intriguing. "Are we ghosts? Are you the one in charge here?" He started to ask more, but Bertha cut him off.

"Nick. I appreciate your intellectual curiosity," she said, oh so insincerely. "You only just died today, so I suggest that you pace yourself. There is much to learn, and I'm sorry, but there are some things you simply can't know. But I can answer this one: no, I'm not in charge. The Boy is." Nick tried to ask, "What boy? Who's that?" but Bertha steamrolled over him with words, words, words.

"Each of you will revisit a day from your life," she chirpy-chirped. "Take your time making this choice, as this is a big decision! Pick a nice day, but not a day that's too heartbreakingly wonderful. Remember, you must"—Nick and I looked at each other and mouthed the words with her here—"move on!" (Oops. She saw us and scowled, which made Nick laugh.)

"This event is known as your Thornton Wilder Day!" Bertha waited to see if we could make the connection. I did. I remembered that scene because I played Townsperson Number Seven when our school did *Our Town* last year. I did a lot of walking and nodding. Great part. I was brilliant in it.

Once again Nick was bursting with questions. "Can we change stuff? Can I go back to the day I died and end up not dead?"

"No! You can't change anything about the day," Bertha explained. "You'll watch yourself, but you won't be able to interact with yourself or anyone else. You only do this once, so choose well."

"I already know what day I'll choose," Harry said with a wide grin.

"Give it some thought anyway!" Bertha urged. I think we were getting on her nerves. "Sarah, you'll go on your Thornton Wilder Day while the others are at their funerals, so consider your choice. Your final arrangements were a bit delayed due to the autopsy."

Out of all those words, the one that slapped me right across the face was this: *autopsy.* I'd had an autopsy? Oh great. Was everyone (Nick?) picturing me naked on some table somewhere, being sliced and emptied and explored? *How lucky am I?*

"Is the autopsy—the thing—all over? Do the police know for sure that I was murdered? Couldn't it have been an accident?" I insisted.

Bertha sighed. "Forget about the police. *I* know for sure. And the sooner you accept your fate, the sooner you'll move on. Sarah, you're just as murdered as everyone else. No more, no less. And you don't hear the others complaining!"

"Because we're all happy we were murdered," Nick side-commented to me.

"What was that, Nick?" Bertha busted him. "Another question?" But he gave her that grin, and I had to wonder how often it had gotten him out of trouble when he was alive.

"I was just saying," he began. "It's a little easier for us. We know how we died, and who did it. It must be tough for Sarah."

I think my face went a little bit pink when he said my name.

"My murderer was at my funeral," Alice added. "And it only made things worse."

"The Boy sends you to your funeral to say goodbye, to let go," Bertha declared. "And besides, you're a ghost. You can't call the police or get anyone arrested, so what's the point? This is why the Boy—"

"Come on! Who is this boy?" Nick called out. "And who made him the boss of me?"

Alice gasped. Lacey snorted a little laugh. Harry said, "Ha!"

"I think we all want to know," said Nick. He sat back, relaxed, like he was waiting for a show.

Bertha clucked and sighed. (Hate that!) She searched the air for the words to speak. Here's what she found: "It's a title. The Boy is not exactly a boy."

I groaned. She wrote the letters

B

O

Y

on a whiteboard. And then she added words to each letter.

Boss

Of

You

"The Boy is not *a boy*—not a male child. The Boy is the gathering of the collective wisdom of humankind," she explained. "The good, the bad, the kind, the cruel—it's all there, and it is in charge of you. We are not ruled by someone *outside* of ourselves. The Boy is the best and worst of us, ruling us."

There was a massive, heavy, weary, ominous pause.

"I have no idea what that means," Nick said.

(Good. Neither did I.)

"It doesn't matter. Here's what you need to know about the Boy," Bertha said, and I think we all leaned in a little. "Humanity is not all that wise or mature—as a species. Think of the world you just left—the one that killed you. *We are children.*"

And our mission was to get back to that world as soon as we could. Really?

chapter seven
do you see dead people?

Harry absolutely insisted that we go downstairs and move among the living. And Harry was sort of irresistible.

"They have roller coasters!" he crowed. "What are we doing up here, being all dead? Boring! Let's go *live*!"

We stood in a row, peering over the railing from our top floor. We were so close but so far. We studied the living below us, twisted and mixed together in a crazy pattern. Harry began to lead us toward it all, and we all followed, except Alice.

"No!" she said with a small cry. "I don't like to be among them. It's too much. That's what sent me over the edge last time. They're so alive, but they have no sense of it, no appreciation. They just want to buy things and argue. It's unbearable."

Nick gave her a hug. "I'll look out for you. I won't let anything bad happen to you. I promise." But Alice shook her head.

"Look. I really *need* to go there," Harry said. He was staring longingly at the crowd. "I was so sick for so long, I just want to see some of this life and stuff, I want to hear it and be around it." He returned his gaze to us. "That's my unfinished business out there. I got cheated out of so much life while I was alive."

Lacey took his arm and smiled at him sweetly. "What are we waiting for? Let's go."

That's how Lacey, Harry, Nick, and I left Alice upstairs and made our way to the land of the living.

✳ ✳ ✳

When I was alive, I was able to move among the living like a ghost. So you'd think that being dead at the mall would be easyish for me. Or at least, *I* thought it would.

Living people were loud, loud, loud. Especially the children. The adults walked around with odd, worried faces and didn't seem to realize how they looked. Not one of them could hear their children calling to them until the kid yelled at least seven times. We slipped through them with shocking ease. Nobody saw us, heard us, or gave any sign that they sensed we were there.

Lacey critiqued the fashion choices around her. "Now, *that's* an ugly shirt!" and "Um, yeah, nobody is falling for that comb-over!" and "Where'd you buy that? Forever Ugly?" She got louder as she decided that she was hilarious. None of the living heard her. (And I wished that I didn't, either.)

"Don't let Lacey scare you," Nick whispered in my ear. "She's all talk."

"I know!" I answered, a little more defensively than I should have.

At Harry's request, we went directly to the roller coaster, which was part of a whole cluster of rides. (Did I mention that this place was kind of big?) We filled the empty seats at the back of the ride, and if people could have seen us, we would have looked like two couples on a double date. Lacey threw her arms up in the air and shouted, "WOOOOOO!" for the entire ride. Harry looked at her and at the life all around him and laughed.

Nick and I sat right behind them, silent as, well, the grave. We slowed to a high climb, with a big drop awaiting us. I shut my eyes and held on tight, bracing for (second) death.

"It can't kill you." He shrugged. "Nothing can kill you!" And then we all screamed as we plummeted forward and finished the ride. My legs were shaky as Nick helped me out. But Lacey and Harry stayed in their seats.

"Again, again, again!" Lacey cried, and Harry clearly agreed.

"No way!" Nick protested. "That thing's a death mobile!" He wasn't a very good liar. We all saw that he loved the ride, but he knew that I didn't. With Nick covering for my cowardice, we slipped into the crowd of the living.

"Thank you," I said.

"This is all part of my charm," he said with a straight face. "I get us off the ride before I'm the one who gets sick. Works every time."

That charm was real and very much alive. I would have loved to bask in it for a while, but that was when the first weird thing happened.

There was a toddler having a total meltdown over by the bumper cars, and his mother had no clue how to make his piercing shrieks stop (please, please make it stop). Nearby, three other mothers were tut-tutting and gossiping about her.

43

"If she can't control that child, she shouldn't bring him out," the tall mother said as the shorter two nodded.

"People used to do that to my mom," Nick said quietly. "I always hated it. If I was even a little bit less than perfect, they blamed her." The little half smile usually on his face was gone. He looked grim.

"They're just being mean," I agreed. And in a louder voice, directed right at the tall mother, I said, *"And if they're such mother-geniuses, why don't they go over and help her?"*

And just like that, the tall one blinked hard, turned, and went over to the meltdown kid and his mother. She didn't act like she had heard someone tell her to go. She just went. As if she had come up with this new thought completely on her own. She knelt down and spoke to the toddler.

"Whoa," Nick whispered. "What did you just do?"

Before I could give the obvious "I have no idea," the mother of the meltdown toddler began to screech at the tall mother:

"Who asked for your help, lady? Mind your own business!" With that, she yanked her son sideways onto her hip and carried him like a football away from all the rides. He temporarily stopped screaming and seemed to think that this was a fun ride.

I backed away. Did I do that? Did I communicate with that obnoxious tall mother? How? I retreated all the way to one of the big map kiosks.

Nick followed me there and looked back at the rides, the mothers, the kids.

"She heard you. What was that?" he asked. "Sarah, that was weird."

44

"No. I don't want to be weird." As soon as I said it, I wanted to take it back. Only a weird person would say that.

Nick tried and failed to swallow a laugh. He put one hand on my bare arm, which suddenly took all my attention. His hand was warm against my cool skin. His hazel eyes held some kind of gold flecks, scattered like stardust. If he was laughing, he wasn't laughing at me. That was clear. His laugh was infused with kindness, and it worked on me like truth serum. I wanted to tell him everything about me.

But just then Harry interrupted us. He and Lacey had abandoned the rides and made some new discoveries.

"Legos!" he shouted over the crowd. "Let's go. Legos!" He was pointing to an obscenely large Lego store. We circled around a mini Lego Park. There was a cluster of Lego tables, occupied by Lego-building children. They ignored the giant Lego robots, tigers, and trees looming above them and focused on their own little plastic pieces. It was a Lego zoo.

Harry was blissed out. Lacey was blissed out watching Harry be blissed out.

"I loved Legos when I was alive. I made really cool things with them. And I could have built a whole *house* with this many Legos," Harry proclaimed as he turned left, then right, taking in the Lego wonder of it all. "Wow."

I tried, really tried to focus on Legos, but it wasn't easy. Nick stood next to me. I hated being so aware of him and his presence. But I was. I couldn't help it. He gave off a kind of energy that a dead guy shouldn't be able to generate. I wanted to turn to him, face him, talk to him, listen to him. He was so inevitable.

"Okay now. It's just us, so talk to me. Did that woman hear you?" asked Nick, a note of admiration in his voice.

"I don't know. I wish I knew. But I don't know," I answered. *(Idiot, idiot, idiot!)* I gave up trying to have a conversation with Nick just yet.

A group of children abandoned their table of Legos, and Harry stepped right up, ready to build something stupendous in their absence. But when he touched one, his hand passed right through it. He tried again, focusing on just one stray Lego. But he couldn't touch it, couldn't hold it. Couldn't play. Being dead wasn't all fun and games.

And for a second there, I thought he was going to cry. He bowed his head. "Oh. Of course."

Lacey rushed to his side to comfort him as a new collection of children swarmed the table and began to demolish everything that had been built there. Harry watched them enviously.

Here's the second weird thing that happened:

One little girl stood apart from the other kids. And I swear, she was looking right at Harry. Her mouth was open, and her eyes were wide.

She saw him. She did. And she was terrified.

"Go on, sweetie. Go play!" her mother urged her. The other kids all seemed fine, but the girl stared at Harry and shook her head. She was the picture of dread as her big eyes filled with tears.

"Harry," Lacey loud-whispered. "She can see you. Get out of here. *Now!*"

Harry looked like his heart might break. All he wanted was to play, and he ended up scaring a little girl. Not fair. The mother (who didn't see Harry at all) took her daughter by the hand and dragged her to the table, saying, "You'll never get anywhere in life if you don't develop decent social skills!"

Why did I rush over to the table? What did I think I could do there? I mean, I knew for sure that I would never have done this when I was alive. I stooped down next to the frightened girl as Harry and Lacey retreated.

"Legos are fun," I whispered to the girl. She took a breath and reached for a stack of red plastic bricks.

"Did she see you?" Lacey asked Harry. "Did that kid see him?" she asked us. "She looked really freaked out. I think she saw him!"

"Maybe," Harry replied. "But she's okay now."

She was. She was even starting to talk with some other little kids, and maybe that satisfied her mother's need to see her daughter's decent social skills. Lacey clapped. "Harry, you're special! She saw you!"

Nick opened his mouth, and I knew he was going to say something about me being heard. But somehow he knew I didn't want him to say it. *Please don't put me in the spotlight. Don't say what you're going to say. Please.* He stopped. He understood.

Harry half-smiled at us, but his blue eyes looked a bit bluer.

"I changed my mind. I want to go upstairs, where we can do things. And eat," Harry suggested. The melancholy in his voice tugged at my heart. We left without another word.

chapter eight

we are the stories
we tell ourselves

Food was the best thing ever. If I were alive, I'd eat and eat and eat and let myself get huge. I wouldn't care. I loved food.

We all officially loved our food court. I had waffles with bacon and ice cream for dinner. (Don't judge. And by the way, delicate little Alice ate a brick of cheese, popcorn, and a Cinnabon roll. So there.)

"Harry can be seen by the living!" Lacey said for the hundredth time, devouring a pile of chicken wings. "He's special!"

Nick gave me a big-eyed cartoony look, pleading with me for permission to reveal that the living could hear me. Maybe it was my old instinct to hide in the crowd, camouflage myself like one zebra in a big, fat herd of zebras. There's safety there. So I slowly shook my head. *Please don't tell them.* And he got it.

"It was a fluke," Harry insisted.

"So, Sarah. You're being all chopped up on some slab, huh?" Lacey asked me, chewing with her mouth open. "Who are the suspects? Who were your enemies?" She grinned, putting her high-heeled feet on a second chair. The stilettos stuck outward like weapons.

"Maybe it wasn't an enemy," Nick offered. "Maybe it was a spurned lover. Broken hearts make people do crazy things. Did you spurn many lovers while you were alive?"

(Should I be flattered that he assumed there were lovers for me to spurn?)

"No," I said, and I suddenly felt so stupid, so empty. Shouldn't there be at least one brokenhearted boy back on Earth, pining for me? There wasn't. Lacey was sneering as she shook her head in pity.

"I still wonder, who makes all this food?" Nick's question rescued me from the awkwardness of the moment. "I wish they'd add some shitake mushrooms to the stir-fry."

Lacey blinked in confusion. "No. I won't eat anything named after shit," she said with some finality. Nick didn't laugh. Because Nick was a good guy.

"Well. I love mushrooms," I chimed in. "But I'd have to pass. Mushrooms were the last thing I ate before I died. At my dad's wedding."

Lacey was so excited, she nearly spit out a chicken wing.

"Your dad got remarried?" she sat up, dropping her feet to the floor. "You're so stupid. The wicked stepmother did it. It's so obvious. She killed you to make room for her own kids."

"She isn't wicked—she's wonderful. And she doesn't have kids, and we got along great. I don't know, maybe the caterer was a psychopath who wanted to kill some random person?" It didn't sound very likely. I knew that.

"Nice try," said Harry. "But we're all in this place for a

reason. We were young New Yorkers who were murdered. And murder is pretty personal."

He sounded so ridiculously casual, like, *Oh hey, I was ordering coffee, and they were all out of soy milk, but that's okay, because they had two percent milk, and I'm not lactose intolerant. And by the way, we were all murdered. The end.* Really?

"You had cancer," I said. "Who would kill somebody who's already that sick?"

"Do you really want to know?" Harry asked the group. Yes, we did. And that's how it all ignited. Our Death Stories.

HARRY AND CANCER AND LIFE

Harry's first battle with cancer was when he was five years old. He was not a saintly sick boy. In fact, he'd be the first to tell you that he was a total brat. He yelled at everyone, especially his parents.

When you're five, life is supposed to be fair. But cancer was so *unbelievably unfair,* Harry had to rail against it. It didn't help that he had been the middle child of three, who constantly fought for his toys, his place on the sofa, his song in the car, his choice of game, his anything.

He did not want cancer and would happily have given it to either of his brothers, if only he knew how. Chemo made him sick, bald, weak, dizzy, and tired all the time. One fine afternoon, he fixed the bald problem by painting his head with permanent marker. He added Count Chocula eyebrows. It was a look.

But then it passed. He was done. Cancer-free. The laundry-marker toupee faded, replaced by real hair. But his bratty behavior had become a habit. Besides, it worked.

When Harry was nine years old, he figured out that everyone caved in to him because he was loud and because he was Cancer Boy. Not because he was right. This discovery didn't make him angry. But it did make him cry. He looked at himself like he was a character in a movie, and he didn't like what he saw. It wasn't easy, and it wasn't all at once, but he managed to stop being a huge jerk. And he started to enjoy his cancer-free life.

And then the cancer came back. He was fourteen this time. Old enough to know that life wasn't fair. He wasn't a brat anymore, but he did cry sometimes. Doctors carved out his organs. They poisoned him with chemotherapy and fried him with radiation. But the cancer kept winning.

When he was seventeen, he sat his family down. "There's nothing more to do," he told them. "No more surgeries, no more treatments. You have to let me go." His mother wept. His father sobbed. His brothers cursed cancer's existence. Harry hugged them. "I don't want to leave you. I love you guys. But I think I kind of have to go." Harry's brothers dissolved into a puddle. And Harry cried too.

The doctors didn't put up a fight. They knew they couldn't save him, so they granted his wish:

to die at home, not at the hospital. His mother slept by his side. She measured every inch of his suffering. Pain was his constant companion. When it overpowered him, he could click a button to summon morphine. It quieted the pain and clouded his mind.

And then came the day when he was too weak even to click. The cancer was in his bones, and it held him prisoner in a cage of pain there on that bed. He felt his tears fall back into his ears. That was the only body part that didn't hurt.

His mother caressed his cheek and dried his tears.

"No more pain, sweetheart. No more." She clicked the morphine button. She clicked it again. She clicked it a lot. "Oh, my little love. My boy," she whispered. "Be at peace now, Harry. I love you so."

Dad stood by her side. "I love you. I'll always love you," he said.

His mind escaped into a fog. Then his heart. Then all of him. All done, all gone. There.

chapter nine
infinity beer

"Wow," Nick said to Harry. "You suffered. A lot."

"I know, right?" Harry said in a lighthearted voice. "Oh, and check it out. I died bald, and I'm still bald in my afterlife." He laughed, shaking his fist at the sky. "Thank you, universe! Boy! Whoever! Way to go!"

"Are you kidding?" Lacey asked. "Bald makes you look like a badass!"

"Technically," Alice said with some caution, "your mother killed you."

"Yeah." Harry nodded. "She was a good mom. I *reeeally* needed to go."

"I'm glad you're not sick anymore," Lacey continued. "I hate being around sick people. Me, I died like I lived," she said with a sneer. "Partying."

And without anyone asking, Lacey told us her Death Story.

Lacey grew up on the Bowery. She was an only child, who was uninvited from all of the neighborhood playdates, one by one by one, because the wimp parents of other kids couldn't handle her amazingness. Her favorite words were "Mine!" "No!" and *"Shut up!"* As she got older, she grew tired of spending so much time with her stupid parents. She got herself a circle of followers who knew, out loud and unquestionably, that *she* was in charge.

Lacey loved her life. She loved her clothes, her shoes, her makeup, her jewelry, her room, her phone. She didn't love school, but she got by. Even the teachers knew better than to mess with Lacey too much. It was never worth the loud, relentless argument that she could produce at a moment's notice. Everyone at school followed her on Twitter and took it as a sign of cool if she allowed them to be among her many Instagram followers.

Her tenth-grade boyfriend was pretty good. His name was Jorge. She decided to have sex with him right away, just to get it over with. It was okay, but really, what was with all that sweating and pushing? Lacey wondered what all the fuss was about. Still. Lacey and Jorge became a fixture at school.

Jorge was a wrestler, but the school's favorite sport was basketball. He should have known that eventually Lacey would trade up. In the middle of eleventh grade, right before Christmas, Lacey broke up with him. When they returned to school after the break, she was madly in love with a point guard named Manuel.

Lacey was so damn happy, she couldn't stand it. Everyone admired her, respected her, obeyed her. Including Manuel. And now, finally, at the advanced age of seventeen, she understood why the world was so crazy about sex. Manuel luxuriated in her body in ways that Jorge never had. She couldn't wait to be alone and naked with him. Oh, Manuel, yes yes yes.

But then she went to that party, over spring break. Everyone was there, and the apartment was packed and noisy. There was a keg, which made Lacey feel like they had infinity beer. She could have as much as she wanted. Unlike with some girls, beer didn't make her fat. It just made her luscious. And happy. And loud. And even bolder than usual.

"Poor Jorge," she said. He was sitting alone on the sofa in the middle of the party, nursing a red plastic cup of beer. He looked miserable. Lacey felt her claws come out. "You should get a woman," she advised him.

He watched her without moving his head, just looking up from under his eyebrows. She gave him a lot more advice, most of it about how to please a woman sexually, and all the annoying things he should stop doing. "That licking my ear thing was *gross*!" She was really loud now. "You don't know *nothing*!" Everyone was watching her, listening to her. She wished she had a microphone. They laughed and hooted. Jorge didn't move.

Eventually Lacey joined the group that had migrated to the roof for more space and more air. Wow, she had had a lot of beer, and a shit-ton of Doritos. She and Manuel made out for a while, but her stomach was bothering her.

"I'll get you more beer, baby," he whispered. His breath tickled her ear.

She stood up, a tiny bit unsteady. But okay. She craned her neck to the right. Through the mist, she just barely saw the glittering lights of the Brooklyn Bridge. They made her smile. She liked things that sparkled.

"Yo, bitch!" Jorge growled behind her. Not very loud. She turned carefully. She was near the edge and just drunk enough to need to be careful.

"You talk too much," he said. She was about to belch in response when suddenly he shoved her. Just one clean push on the shoulder and she was flying. The belch escaped her lips in place of a scream. It took several long seconds to land, but not long enough to really enjoy the view. She landed on a car hood, setting off the alarm. A broken neck. A lot of blood. A last glimpse of sky, hoping for a sparkling star. But it was cloudy that night.

Lacey seemed to be amped up on anger. She got up from the table and walked around. When she returned, her face was red, especially her nose. She slammed a fist on the table. "That asshole thinks he can just kill me? *Me?* I was supposed to rule my world. I'm not supposed to be dead. I wish we had Internet here. I guarantee you that Twitter is exploding for me right now. I wish I could see. And you wouldn't believe the things I'd post about him. He can't end me."

But he did end her. And someone ended me. And Harry. And Nick. And Alice. Someone ended all of us, and all I wanted right now was a private place to cry for an hour or a day. I didn't want to be over. Not yet. Not like this.

"My funeral is going to be awesome," Lacey decreed. "Everyone misses me like crazy." Her voice cracked as she said "crazy." A big tear rolled down her cheek. She sniffed loudly. "And I wanna haunt Jorge's trial. They'll all make him pay for what he did."

chapter ten

sea life and see life

It was official. I dreamed. I wasn't supposed to, but I did. Don't tell anybody.

At first, this dream was about those mall walkers. They were doing their walking thing, but this time they whispered the word "she" over and over again. "She she she she she she!" After a while, it almost sounded like a rainstorm. But then the dream changed, because that's what dreams do.

Now I was in Washington Square Park. It was the middle of the night, and the park was lit up with blue, silver, and deep green. I stood dead center (ha ha) near the fountain. There was a man roaming around the park sort of aimlessly. He reminded me of the mall walkers. He wore a shabby, wrinkled suit and a hat. He came a little too close, looked into my eyes, and screamed. The sound of it could shatter bones and teeth. I turned and ran. He went in search of someone else to scream at, and I gravitated back to the fountain.

"Be careful," said a gentle voice just to my right. Mom. Mom once again, here in my dreams. I let out a kind of squeaking sound as she hugged me.

"Oh, Sarah," she whispered in my ear, and managed to pull away far enough to look at me. She smoothed my hair in that motherly way. "We need to stop meeting like this!"

"Mom? Are you really here?" I wanted to say more, but my throat was choked with tears. "Am I going to keep dreaming about you?"

"The important part of me is here." She pointed to my heart and added, "Always. But you're sort of conjuring me up. Like a dream."

"It's because of the Knowing, isn't it?" I asked. "It's the strand that connects us. This is the Knowing rearing its ugly, useless head."

"Wow. What happened to you?" she asked.

"I died," I answered, and Mom tried very hard not to laugh at me.

"No, I mean what happened while you were alive? After I left?" she asked. "Remember when you saved that lady in the green coat? I wonder how old her kid would be today. Did you ever save anybody else?"

"No. I couldn't save you, Mom. And after that, I just didn't want to know things anymore. Besides, the Knowing was just some kind of torment. It wasn't a gift."

"Sweetheart, that's a bit childish. The gift wasn't perfect, so you threw it away? Really?"

I had never thought of it that way and deeply hated hearing it from her.

"Listen to that voice inside your heart and bones," she

59

whispered. "It's still there. The Knowing." I stayed very still and listened. It gave me a stomachache, just like old times. Mom wrapped her arms around me. "You know now. You know: your dad is in danger."

"What do you mean? What kind of danger?" I asked.

"Death danger. It's all around him, like the sky," she said.

She was beginning to fade, and for some reason she was half-smiling at me.

"See? This is what I hate about this Knowing thing. It's incredibly frustrating. Why is he in danger? How? And what am I supposed to do about it? I'm already dead."

And I woke up.

✷ ✷ ✷

The mall wasn't open yet, so I took myself downstairs, into the dark and quiet living world. When I was alive, my dreams were not this disturbing. I blamed the mall. And Bertha. And her shoes.

The quiet of the place was almost oppressive, so I sang softly to myself. Just to fill the silence. When I was alive, music was my bf, my bff, and my chief consolation. Music still felt like my most vivid connection to Mom. Dead Mom. So I sang the same songs she sang to me in my dreams just after she died.

Blackbird singing in the dead of night . . .

"Hey!" A gruff voice shouted out, scaring me so hard that I froze in place. It was a security guard. He was super tall, with a

60

lantern jaw and a belly that spilled over his belt. His voice was deep and oversize.

"Somebody out here?" he asked, looking all around, at me, through me, past me.

"I'm here," I said tentatively, then louder. *"I'm here."*

He looked around again. I held my breath for a bit, and then I said, "Can you hear me?" He squinted in my direction. He'd heard me.

"You're kind of a cop," I began, more to myself than to him. "I mean, you're a mall cop, and that's still a cop, right? Look, I need your help. You see, I was murdered in New York City, and . . ."

He checked his watch.

"I'm losing it," he mumbled to himself. "Again." He shook his head and walked away.

"I'm here." My voice choked. "I'm Sarah Evans. Can you hear me? Can you call my father? His name is Charlie Evans. He lives in Manhattan. Please! Can you see if he's okay?"

He stopped and looked back in my direction.

"Hello?" I called in a voice that sounded a lot younger than it should have. "Charlie Evans. Just check on him? Please?"

But he lowered his head and mumbled, "Why does everybody on the night shift go loony?"

And then he was gone. I let the silence of the mall wrap around me like darkness.

"Sarah? Is that you?"

I jumped, flinched, twisted, and generally made a fool of myself when Nick's voice shouted to me, *"Come to the aquarium! It's cool!"*

Dead girl walking with a thumping heart ready to burst out of her chest. That was me.

There was a big sign pointing to the Sea Life Minnesota Aquarium, and when I looked in that direction, I saw a blue-green light in the distance. (And dead people should always go toward the light, right?)

"Okay!" I shouted back, trying to sound like he hadn't scared me half to death. (Half to life? How do I use that phrase?)

There was a big metal gate blocking my way, and it was locked. I stood there feeling stupid and awkward, wondering how to get in. After a while, Nick called out, "You're dead, Sarah. Just pass through the gate."

Of course. Sure. Obviously. I pushed my hand against the gate and felt a strange sensation. It was a bit like brushing my hand over a woolly sweater.

My hand was on the other side of the gate. It itched. I stared at it and thought for a split second that I might have to spend eternity like this. And then I passed all the way through it.

Wow.

The aquarium was so enormous, you actually walked through it like you were inside a massive undersea tunnel, with the sea life all around and above you. The blue-green sweetness was enticing. Anyone who was suddenly surrounded by its beauty would instantly have to whisper, "Oooh." And there was Nick.

"Hey." He grinned, looking away as a massive sea turtle drifted by. "Can't sleep?" he asked. I nodded.

He sat down on the floor, maybe to get a bigger picture of

the sea life that floated over our heads. I was still just standing there like a complete idiot. He smiled that wicked grin and invited me to sit down across from him. (Walk three steps, Sarah, and sit down without being stupid.)

"You've already been murdered, so you've probably been through the worst thing already. What are you so worried about, Sarah?"

(Great. He could tell that I was worrying. About *sitting down*.) Never fear. I managed to sit across from Nick. Our legs bent at the knees, looking like fake mountain ranges.

"They can hear you," he said. "Living people can hear you. Can we please talk about that bit of weirdness?"

"I'm not sure if anybody really did hear me," I began, but Nick shook his head and pushed his hair out of his eyes.

"Did that mall cop hear you just now?" he asked. I shrugged uncomfortably. He focused on me so absolutely, I felt like a creature under a microscope. Oh, to change the subject/focus, please. "It's okay, Sarah. I won't tell anyone. Not if you don't want me to."

I believed him. There were some people you could just look at and know they were telling the truth. That was Nick. There was something solid and old-school about him. My mom and dad would have liked him.

"I think maybe he heard me a little," I conceded. "When I was singing."

"What is it about you, Sarah? You look sort of familiar to me, but I'm sure we never met when we were alive. I definitely would have remembered you."

Oh, and I would have remembered him. Absolutely.

"Isn't it amazing that we both ended up here, dead, together, at the same time?" he asked. I searched for a word stronger than "amazing," but I gave up. "I'll tell you a secret: Bertha almost sent me away from the mall when I first got here."

"Why?" I asked, a tiny bit panicked at the thought that he could actually leave this place.

"It's because of the way I died. After she read my questionnaire, she said that I could have gone to some spa instead of the mall. It ended up being my decision. Apparently free will is a big deal."

"Wow. A spa would be . . . ," I began, but I stopped myself from saying anything that might make him reconsider his very good decision to be here. At the mall. With me.

"What's your story?" he asked.

I made myself smile. "I don't have one." There. True fact.

Nick edged toward me, and I resisted the urge to make a quick and clumsy exit. I stayed. He smelled good, sort of like a tree in a rainstorm. (Why was I feeling my pulse in both hands? By definition, I had no pulse.)

"I'll tell you mine if you tell me yours," he whispered. His breath was soft and sweet.

On the floor, in the dark, Nick wove a magic spell over me while a shark passed above us, its face frozen in a tragic frown.

NICK'S DEATH STORY IS A KILLER

Nick never knew his father, and that was fine by him. Based on what his mom said, the guy was a deadbeat. "We should never have ordered that second bottle of wine. That's how I ended up knocked up," she would say sometimes, then realize that she needed to add, "But I'm glad I had you, Nicky."

His mom dated a string of bad boyfriends. She didn't see it, but everybody else could. The landlord would shake his head and say, "Another loser. How do they all manage to find her?"

Nick learned early on to stay under the radar around those boyfriends, at school, anywhere. He was sort of invisible, which meant that he was safely lost in the crowd. Medium grades, medium social life. There was safety in his anonymity.

But that changed when he was just a skinny thirteen-year-old boy. He came home to find that the latest bad boyfriend had made his mom cry, so Nick punched him and told him to get lost. Bad boyfriend punched him right back. Nick was in pain, but he didn't cry. There was a purple swelling on his cheekbone, which made him look tough.

That day, the boyfriend left for good. And Nick's inner superhero was born.

Now Nick began to stand out from the crowd, finding solutions to every problem. Sometimes he was kind of reckless, calling out bad drivers, people taking up two subway seats, and rude bicycle messengers. He embarrassed his friends and made his mother nervous.

Nick learned to cook. And we're not talking

microwave burrito or mac and cheese. He started out making comfort food, aimed at healing his mother's occasional broken heart. But he learned how to experiment and improvise. He enjoyed one-upping famous TV chefs. The thing about the kitchen was this: it played fair. If he combined ingredients that he liked, and cooked them long enough, but not too long, the kitchen rewarded him with pure joy.

In his junior year he met Fiona. Or rather, he saw her. A lot. She was an A-plus student (compared to his lengthy B-minus track record, because he never thought that future chefs required amazing report cards). She played varsity volleyball. She was president of the Drama Club. Nick was determined to get to know her. So. He auditioned for the school production of *Our Town*. He didn't get the part, but he managed to kiss Fiona in the audition. And she took notice.

Their first date was on a warm spring night. He took her to a hipster coffee place downtown after dinner and a movie. They stayed out much later than she was supposed to. Life was so damn sweet.

The guy who mugged them was short. He was sweating, and his voice was thin. He seemed more scared than Fiona or Nick. His hands shook. Maybe that thick metal gun was too heavy for him. Nick stood in front of Fiona, who didn't want to be protected.

"You don't scare me," she hissed at the guy.

"Okay, okay, everybody stay calm." Nick used his most soothing voice. "Here's the money. Here's everything. Just take it." He was talking directly to the gun. It made the hairs on the back of his neck stand up. His inner superhero knew that this gun contained the Nick version of kryptonite.

But then the guy went for Fiona's necklace. And she wasn't going to give it up.

"Oh please," Fiona said. "What are you going to do, shoot us?"

The guy sort of grunted and raised his gun a little higher, a little more forward. Nick grabbed Fiona's arm and pulled her as they tried to outrun a bullet. Or die trying.

"Ohhh!" Fiona cried.

That's the last thing Nick heard, if you didn't count the gunshot. He wasn't sure if he heard that or not. Maybe he heard his own head hit the ground. Maybe.

I was stunned into silence. We both stayed there, all quiet on the floor, letting the story settle around us, connecting us.

"Fiona didn't die?" I asked.

"Apparently not," he answered, looking around for her. "Nope."

He cleared his throat and looked away. I started to figure out that telling your story was a big deal. Nick was struggling to recapture his breath, his voice, his cool. His mask of charm and funny side remarks was gone, and here was a sweet, sad boy who missed his life and didn't want to cry in front of me.

"You were brave. You were a good guy," I said, but he shrugged, not ready to speak yet. He stretched sideways out on the floor and focused on a small school of blue and yellow fish overhead.

"You should try this view," he said at last, his voice sort of tight and strained.

I did. I lay down on the floor next to him. It felt like a big deal.

"I wish I could still be there, be a good guy," he said at last. There was a painfully long pause before he spoke again. "I wasn't ready." He didn't finish that sentence. He couldn't. I wanted to reach out to him, but he cleared his throat, shaking off the emotion.

"That spa place," I began. "Would that be your reward for saving Fiona?"

"But I was just trying to get us away. I didn't mean to die in her place. I didn't mean to die at all." His breathing was slowly easing back to normal. "But I hope she's okay. I hope she has a long life."

I'd never be able to explain why I was so drawn to Nick. And I'd never be able to deny it. Something about the glint in his eye or the ready smile made me nervous and totally relaxed all at the same time. I could say anything to Nick. And maybe saying it would make it better.

"What will you choose for your Thornton Wilder Day, Sarah?" he asked.

(When people said my name, it felt super-intimate.)

"I think I'd pick something really random from when my mom was alive."

"Your mom is dead?" Nick sounded shocked. He propped

himself up on his elbow and looked down at me. "I can't even imagine that. Okay, that's it. Come on, tell it. Now. Tell me your story, Sarah."

(Oh, he just had to add my name there at the end, didn't he?)

HERE'S WHY MY STORY ISN'T A STORY

My story is that something in me stopped, ended, shut down, and died the day we buried my mother. It wasn't just that I missed her. It's that I changed in some really fundamental way. And that was my choice. I think. At first I blamed Dad for letting her die (as if he had power over life and death). And then I blamed him for not fixing things between us. He threw himself into his work and let me drift away, like a girl alone on a raft. Mom and I had connected in a way that most people couldn't. And now that it was over, I wouldn't connect at all. That was the story I told myself. And I repeated that story *all the time*.

But when Karen joined our lives, she got him to stop working for five minutes and notice me. I started to tell myself a whole new story, and it was like the best gift ever. We laughed. We cooked. We went ice-skating and fell down a lot.

Or maybe it was the worst gift ever. Because now I knew what I had been missing all those wasted years. Now I saw that Dad had been sad and wonderful all that time. And that he loved me, even if he had to struggle to find a way to say it. My life was worse than unfinished business. It was unstarted. And then I ate toxic mushrooms and died.

The end. Of me.

Yes, I know. That was the heavily edited/important-stuff-left-out version of my story. How was I supposed to tell Nick all about my mom and me and the Knowing stuff? I didn't understand it myself. So I said nothing about the Knowing, or about running away from it. Then again, if anyone could tell that I was hiding something, it would be Nick.

He was on his side, leaning close enough now to read the freckles on my cheeks. I turned and held his gaze, which was not as easy as it sounds. The scent of trees and rainstorms was intoxicating. He looked at my mouth, and then at my eyes, then back at my mouth. If you've ever seen a movie, you know what that means.

"No, no, no, no, no, no, no! Absolutely not!" Bertha's voice shattered the moment and scared all the fish. We both jumped and sat up in a flash. I instinctively shifted my body away from Nick.

"What in blue blazes do you think you're doing?" she asked. "Have you gone completely insane? *You absolutely, positively will not start a romance in the afterlife.* I unconditionally forbid it. No."

"We were just talking, I swear," Nick answered for us both.

"Romances in the afterlife are practically a guarantee that you'll get stuck here. A guarantee!" Bertha's voice was strained and shrill. Very unattractive.

"We weren't starting a romance. Sarah and I are just friends," Nick said in a reasonable, calm voice. He sounded a little bit amused at the very thought of starting a romance with me. Like that would be crazy. Who would do that? (Oh God, really? *I'm a complete idiot!*)

"Just go. Just get out of here." Bertha shook her head as she spoke. "Nick, go get ready for your funeral."

Add that to the long list of weird-ass sentences I never expected to hear.

chapter eleven

thornton wilder
was right about everything

*My Bracelet Is a Flaming Shade of Coral,
Like the Sunset in a Bad Painting*

The next morning there would be funerals for Nick, Harry, and Lacey. Alice and I helped ourselves to a breakfast of bacon and chocolate chip cookies. Please continue with the not-judging thing.

I was about to ask Alice where the food actually came from, when Nick showed up, wearing a dark suit with a bright white shirt and dark tie. He looked crisp and smart. I smiled at the sight of him. "Ta-da!" he proclaimed. "Yes, I look sharp, but you should have seen Harry. His funeral started early. He thinks they did that because he was always an early riser."

Lacey arrived just after him, wearing a red satin gown with a neckline cut almost to her navel and a side slit that rose as if trying to meet it. Her left boob kept popping out, which was distracting. She had added on so much jewelry, she clinked and chimed whenever any part of her moved. This was also distracting. And yes, this was how she chose to dress *for her own funeral.*

Nick grinned at me, and just in case I thought there was some special connection between us, he turned and gave the same grin, same twinkle-in-gold-flecked-eyes look, to Alice and to Lacey. There was no special secret message, no invitation to start an illicit afterlife romance. This was simply his face, and I needed to get over it. I had imagined the whole thing. Me = idiot.

He and Lacey both seemed pretty excited, as if they were on their way to a big party just for them. And okay, yes, they sort of were. But still, it was weird. Lacey was too excited to eat. Nick ate enough for both of them. He put together some kind of exotic fajita, and I suddenly wished that he could cook for us all.

"So. Nick. Tell me." Lacey eyed him up and down. "Who killed you?"

At Lacey's command, Nick and I both told our Death Stories. But here's the thing. In this version, we cut them down drastically. Nick revealed next to nothing about his mother, her bad boyfriends, and how he was her protector. As he told the story, he avoided looking at me, and I noticed that his skin was slowly turning red. My conclusion: he wasn't all that comfortable lying.

My story took less than two minute to tell because, surprise, surprise, I revealed as little as I possibly could. Lacey looked incredibly impatient while I talked. And then I realized that she hadn't asked me for my story. I had just volunteered it. Oh well.

I looked at Alice, and maybe she knew that I was going to

ask how she died or what her funeral was like, because she clumsily hurried to ask a question of the whole group.

"Have you all chosen your Thornton Wilder Day?" Alice asked.

I'd been ninety percent decided. "Yes. Hey. What day did *you* choose?" I asked. Ha! I'd managed to ask her *something* about her mysterious life and death. So there.

"I chose the day that I was born," she replied. "Before Ma and Da were too poor, before they had so many children and so many troubles. I thought it would be sublime."

I could tell from her voice that it was less than sublime.

"The birth itself was hideous. It was painful and bloody. And my father was off at his local. I didn't see him there at all. My mother wept. But when it was done, she kissed me and held me close. I was hers. And she was mine."

Alice bowed her head. "Choose wisely," she said in her small, still voice.

"Hello, everyone!" Bertha called out gleefully. She was decked out in a bright blue suit with massive shoulder pads. Big ones. That's all I can say about that. Words fail. Oh, and she had someone with her. He was tall, tan, and chiseled-looking, with perfectly streaked blond highlights. A life-size Ken doll.

"We have a new young man who just died today!" Bertha announced. "His name is Declan!"

"Hey." Declan nodded at us all and struck a pose. And then another pose.

Lacey let out a quiet "whoa." Which we all heard.

"Do you have a Kiehl's here?" he asked Bertha. "I really need some skin care products."

"In a moment," Bertha answered, then turned to me and sang out, "Sarah, good news! We've got your autopsy results. You were indeed poisoned. *And* you were drugged with a potent sleeping pill, which ensured that the poison could finish you off before you could seek medical attention."

Murdered. Definitely. Murdered, murdered me. I felt myself shrink a little, as if this confirmation that yes, I really was murdered, had diminished me somehow.

"It's okay, Sarah," Nick assured me. "You're in good company, remember?"

True. But still. "Do the police know who killed me? Do you?" I asked.

"Sarah, I'm so sorry." Bertha's voice sounded strained. "But if you don't already know who killed you, you never will. Stop asking about it, stop focusing on it. Move on."

Declan looked at me, then looked at me harder, then did a sort of cough/laugh/choke thing to himself. I checked my teeth discreetly for chocolate chips.

"Alice, I wonder if you could help Declan settle in, explain what's what?" Bertha asked. Poor Alice looked as if she'd rather eat a mouthful of bees than be alone with this pretty boy. But she looked at the ground, rising silently and obeying Bertha's request.

"I can help," I volunteered.

Declan laughed the worst, most fake-sounding laugh I'd ever heard. And I'd heard a few. Private school, remember?

"Wow. Hey. This always happens to me. Girls fight over me. Guys too," he explained to Bertha. "I was an actor. Maybe you guys saw my commercial for eczema cream?"

Maybe I had. He had a kind of generic-handsome-guy familiarity to him. But nothing like what I felt with Nick. Which I would stop feeling immediately, please.

Bertha nodded at Declan with an extra dose of tolerance, then turned to me. "You should stay here, Sarah. I'll come for you next."

The fact that we all watched Alice lead Declan out into the mall just added to her self-consciousness. I tried to look away, but Declan had a lot of swagger. A. Lot. Poor Alice.

"Lacey? Nick? Are you ready?" Bertha summoned our attention back to her. Lacey practically jumped out of her seat. Bertha led the two of them away.

I could still hear the click-clack of her shoes (really, were they shoes, or were they a cry for help?) and her babbling of instructions and advice. I heard Nick's voice cut in.

"I forgot something. I'll be right back!" he shouted.

Bertha made indignant noises and a crack about how "it's unseemly to be late for your own funeral!"

I stood up to see what Nick could have forgotten, but then he came dashing into the food court and right up to me. He quickly wrapped one arm around my waist, which felt incredibly intimate. With his other hand he touched my face, brushing my hair aside.

And then he kissed me. Just a little. He looked at me, as if asking for permission to do that again. Yes. I melted into this second kiss, breathing him in, feeling his arms tighten around me. I was weak and strong, giddy and completely sane, all at once and maybe for the first time ever.

Our bodies were aligned and electric, just like all the songs say they should be. For a dead girl, I felt pretty damn alive. I draped my arms over and around his shoulders and leaned in to this kiss. So did he. Yes.

"Sarah," he said, finally letting go, a faint smile in his eyes. And then he was off to his funeral.

Yes.

chapter twelve

thornton wilder
was wrong about everything

In the last scene of *Our Town*, Mr. Wilder has dead Emily re-visit her life and proclaim that it's all too beautiful. But. She only said that because (a) she died of natural causes, and (b) she didn't stay for very long. Oh sure, it started out all kinds of pretty for me. But then I realized and accepted for absolute sure that I was murdered. And then I figured out who killed me. And then it got worse, if a situation like that actually can get worse.

Bertha was skeptical when I told her that I wanted to re-visit my last birthday. "Why that one?" she asked, with super-size worry in her voice.

"If I went to a day when my mom was alive, I don't think I could handle it. What if I saw myself be mean to her?" I be-gan. Bertha nodded. In spite of her approval, I went on.

"My last birthday was a good day but not a big deal. I didn't have a party or anything. As birthdays go, it was pretty low-key. I went to study at a coffee shop and met up with the Math-letes. Did some homework. Ordinary stuff."

That didn't win Bertha over. I kept going.

"That night, I went out to dinner with Dad and Karen. We ate at a place way out in Brooklyn that Karen had raved about, and the food was amazing. And that was when I first noticed that things really were better between my dad and me. And that was thanks to Karen. It was a good day. I felt . . . hopeful."

Bertha looked super-skeptical. "Your funeral will take place tomorrow. Perhaps you should stay here at the mall and choose your day later?" she proposed.

"This is the day I want," I insisted. "After all, I died from food poisoning, so it just makes sense that I'd like to revisit a really spectacular meal."

That did it. Bertha undid her worry face. Now if we could just do something about those shoes.

✳ ✳ ✳

We walked at a brisk, click-clack pace along our floor of the dead to the Bed Bath & Beyond elevator. I felt a jumble of excitement in my fingers and toes. I dodged around the mall walkers and realized that Bertha was studying my face pretty closely. Could she see Nick's kiss lingering there? Did I look too happy? Did she have some way of knowing that I had dreams? I tried extra-hard to look neutral and normal. (A throwback to when I was alive.)

"Um, a question for you," I said to Bertha, to change the subject before it could even start. "What does it mean when one of the mall walkers becomes a big cloud of dust or ash or something?"

Bertha stopped walking. "Who told you about that?" she asked with an icy tone of accusation in her voice.

"Nobody told me. I saw it happen," I answered, slowing down and gesturing for her to catch up with me. She did. Finally.

"It happened right in front of you?" she asked. "You *saw* it?"

"Yes, that's why I'm asking." I was losing patience. "What does it mean?"

"It's bad. It's very, very bad," she said as we resumed walking. "It means that the individual in question has given up. They're gone and they'll never be back."

"What? That's not fair!" I protested. "Why?"

"Sarah, you still don't get it. It's all about free will. If this person decided it was hopeless, then, well, it became hopeless, well and truly." Bertha's voice was sort of singsong.

We entered the elevator in Bed Bath & Beyond. I tried to push the button, but my finger went right through it. I tried again and Bertha sort of laughed at me. Which I didn't enjoy.

"You can't make contact with the material world," she said as she pushed the button. "But I can."

The elevator bumped into motion, and I muttered one more "Not fair." As the elevator bumped to a stop, Bertha took my hands in hers.

"I hope that you see it all. Keep your eyes open," she told me.

"I will. I promise."

✳ ✳ ✳

I shut my eyes right away. Tight.

(Okay, keep your eyes open. Don't cry. Don't cry. It's all

too beautiful, but don't cry. Open your eyes. Look. Listen. Be here now.)

Home. I was home. Where I wanted to be.

There's no way Dorothy could have gone to Oz and then come back to Kansas and played that scene. Oz must have been just a dream, because she couldn't simply wake up and hug Auntie Em and smile for her close-up. She would have shaken and fallen and cried out and called out, unable to find the English language. She would have rooted herself in the middle of her own particular world and owned it. Like I did. Funny noises escaped from my lips. I didn't take a step, but I did reach out for things, point at things and stare hard at everything within my sight.

Home.

I watched myself, Living Sarah, in bed, half asleep/half awake. I remembered that feeling. I remembered wishing that I could have more sleep. I watched myself try to push the morning away. The morning won.

My eyes blinked open. I groaned and fell back against my pillow. Watching myself there, I could feel the memory of cotton against my skin. I had that sense of sunlight piercing its way into my brain, beckoning me to life. Right about now I'd be thinking about the day ahead. What was on my mind that day? Was I worried about something? What was so important? Living Sarah groaned and rolled over in bed.

(I laughed at my sleepy self. Get up. Go. See the world in all its hideous glory.)

Say it with me now: There's no place like home. There's no place like home. There's Dad. My dad.

He was making breakfast for me, quietly singing (off-key) to himself. It was the Beatles song "Birthday," and his version was almost unrecognizable. Clearly I didn't get any musical ability from him. Oh. And he was dancing. Awkwardly. And I would have given anything and everything just to tell him how much I loved him and his lack of musical talent.

I roamed the house and witnessed things that Living Sarah missed. (In an instant, I felt like she was someone else. Not me.) She was upstairs taking a marathon shower. I drifted back upstairs and through the bathroom, enjoying the feel of steam passing through me and the flowery, fruity, soapy scents of absurdly lovely bath products.

My bed was rumpled, my room chaotic. There was a stack of half songs on my desk. (I only ever wrote half songs. That is, I wrote my own words to someone else's melody, usually—okay, always—the Beatles.)

I sat. I breathed. I kept my eyes open. I drifted back downstairs to Dad.

He was sitting at the table, writing a note inside a birthday card for me. I peered over his shoulder:

"My Dear Sarah," he wrote. And then he stared at the card. It took him the better part of a half hour to write this little note. He struggled over each word, forming the letters with great care.

"It's such an honor to be your dad. It's remarkable to see how quickly you have become this beautiful young woman, possessed of amazing talents, grace, and infinite possibility. The world is at your feet. Thank you for allowing me a front-row seat to the marvelous story of your life. I can't wait to see what's in store for you."

His face was bright with joy and hope. I forced myself to push aside the fact that his daughter had just a handful of months left on this earth. Don't. Think. About. Death. Not now.

When Living Sarah (finally) came downstairs for breakfast, she breezed through the card in less than ten seconds, hugged him, and said, "Awww. Thanks, Dad." She sounded sincere. I might have tried to slap her if she had been rude. And she looked sincerely rushed. She inhaled some toast and bypassed everything else.

"So, what do you think?" Dad asked as he sipped his coffee. "Presents now, or presents later?"

Living Sarah covered her mouth demurely as she spoke with her mouth full. "Has to be later. I have to go to Think Coffee."

Oh yes. Think Coffee, the politically correct NYU coffeehouse hangout with free Wi-Fi and overpriced vegan baked goods. I spent a lot of time (and money) there when I was alive.

"Ah, delayed gratification," Dad said. "A sure sign of maturity."

Living Sarah smiled as she packed her laptop, notebooks, and school stuff into a backpack. "Welcome to my mature life," she said. "I have to finish my American history paper. Civil War."

"Spoiler alert: the North wins," Dad said. And Living Sarah half-laughed.

"Also, I promised I'd meet with the Mathletes. Impressed?" she asked, snagging a swallow of orange juice.

Dad sighed. "Yes. Always." And he lifted his coffee cup in a salute to his daughter. "Remember your eighth birthday, when we had that bowling party and your whole third-grade class came? That was so much fun."

Living Sarah froze. "Dad. Please tell me you didn't invite my high school class to the kiddie lanes at Bowlmor. Please." (I laughed at her. It was so easy to remember that flare of pure fear at the humiliation I was imagining.)

"No, no. I was just remembering. Birthdays do that to me," he explained. His face was smiling but wretchedly sad at the same time.

Living Sarah noticed. She reached over and hugged him (thank you!) and said, "It was fun. You did a great job. And it was the first one without Mom."

Dad choked up just a little. Living Sarah noticed (good girl!) and said, "Do you ever feel like she's here? Like she's watching over us?"

Dad nodded. "Oh yes. A lot. I feel like she's nearby right now."

Living Sarah said, "Me too."

"Oh, you guys," I said softly. "You're killing me."

✳ ✳ ✳

I was expecting to see my fellow Mathletes as a group of socially awkward yet endearing peers. They weren't at the forefront of school popularity, so they must have been nerds, right? What was I thinking?

Living Sarah was relaxed and funny in their presence, and they were the same as they discussed an upcoming Mathletes competition. After they concluded their math business, they hung out in the noisy café, paid too much for cupcakes, and left Sarah to her studies. So far, this was pretty much the tame, nice-nice day that Bertha wanted me to choose.

The café was jammed with weary college students who needed a coffee IV. The music switched to a thumping reggae beat and the energy of the place ramped up. I had been keeping my focus on Living Sarah, not on the anonymous jumble of faces and voices all around us. She opened her laptop, plugged in her headphones, and became her own planet in a crowded, noisy galaxy. She worked dutifully away at her paper on the Battle of Antietam, where 3,654 people died.

She should have looked up.

I did. And my entire universe capsized. I was now in the land of infinite impossibility. I let out a small cry and reached out to the sight before me.

At the next table the manager of the café was interviewing a candidate to pour coffee. Was this guy qualified to pour coffee? Did he have the right people skills for coffee-pouring?

It was Nick. He was two feet away. Nick. Living, breathing, grinning Nick was trying to get a part-time job pouring coffee. It was inexplicable.

"Sarah!" I shouted. "Take off those damn headphones and *look at him*." She typed a pithy insight about Antietam. Great.

"Nick! Nick, look over here!" I yelled. He kept his focus and his crooked grin trained on the manager. They were shouting to be heard over the crowd and the reggae playlist. "It's me, Sarah!"

I crouched right next to Nick and studied his face, his carefree smile, his shoulders. At that moment I couldn't remember if it was impossible to change the past or just something Bertha and the Boy didn't want us to do. And right then I didn't care. I was on fire with desperation. I would make this happen. I must.

"Please! Nick! Go meet that girl! Right there!" I pleaded with him, as he nodded politely and attentively at the manager. "Don't go out with Fiona. Go out with Sarah. Go to her dad's wedding with her. You could both live. You could both survive. If you *just meet each other!*"

(Please, please, please, please, please, please, please! Please. Just let me have this chance to live past sixteen. Please, please, please. I don't want to die. I want to have a life, and I want Nick to be part of it. Please, please, please, please.)

Living Sarah never took her eyes off that damn screen.

The café manager stood up. "Well. We'll let you know," he said as they exchanged a handshake and a nod. Nick sat down, looking defeated.

"Nick! Look at that girl right there! Talk to her! Save both of your lives!" I shouted as hard, as loud, as I could. Even the living were having trouble being heard over the din.

Just then Nick looked over at Living Sarah. He studied her face for a few long seconds. He smiled.

But then he stood up and left the café without saying a word to her. She never looked up, and he never looked back.

I turned to Living Sarah and said, "You're an idiot."

chapter thirteen

knowledge is power

How many times had Nick and I been in the same room at the same time when we were alive? Did we ever ride the subway together? Did we go to the same movies? Did we sit by the fountain in Washington Square Park and fail to see each other through the sparkling water?

I started to follow him outside, but I couldn't go. I couldn't travel that far from Living Sarah. When I tried, it felt like I was pushing up against a thick pane of glass. *"Nick!"* I shouted after him, but it was pointless. I sat on the steps and watched him turn a corner and be gone.

After way too long, Living Sarah emerged from Think Coffee and walked up Mercer Street in the exact same damn direction that Nick had just gone. "Oh come on! Sarah!" I shouted. But she was listening to her music, rushing for home, for dinner, for the last few months of her life, and for her ugly, violent death.

That's right, Sarah. Hurry up. You don't want to be late for all that.

We were in Brooklyn, where all of the living people at this table were about to have Ethiopian food. Dad and I hadn't tried it before.

"It's kind of like soul food. You'll love it!" Karen exclaimed. "And if I'm wrong, I know where to get the best pizza outside of Italy." She ordered for the table.

(Okay, so breathe. Let go of the Nick sighting. This is nearly the end of your Thornton Wilder Day. Enjoy how happy everyone is. Remember the delicious food. Breathe. This matters. This. Is. Good.)

She raised her glass in a toast and said, "Thank you. Thank you both for allowing me to share in this special day. I can't tell you how overjoyed I am to be here and to say happy birthday, Sarah!"

We all clinked glasses (I had ginger ale, thank you). Karen nudged Dad and said, "Go on. Give her a sip of champagne. Just a taste won't hurt anything!" She giggled.

Dad looked around the restaurant as if the police might be waiting for him to make just this kind of mistake before they pounced. But Karen smiled, and Living Sarah blink-blinked in over-the-top innocence. Dad laughed and passed her the champagne.

I remembered that moment so clearly. It felt as if I were filling myself up with tiny helium balloons, getting ready to float away. And I remembered liking the sensation.

"That's enough!" Dad said, and took the glass back. Karen and Living Sarah shared a conspirators' giggle. (Being alive was so sweet.)

★ ★ ★

Ethiopian food is excellent. Try it, if you ever get the chance. It arrived as one big communal platter of foods, arranged in dollops over a massive round flatbread. You tear off a piece of bread and dip it into one of the foods arranged on top. It's a meal and an activity. And it made us all so happy. I found myself wishing that the food court had Ethiopian food, or that Nick could make some for us, as I drifted in and out of the conversation.

Good food. Good people. It should have ended there. I would have felt all happy and satisfied with the day. No, I couldn't get Living Sarah to meet Living Nick and change both of their fates. But I could come to terms with it all and take one more step toward moving on. I could. Eventually. I smiled as Living Sarah opened her presents. Earrings! Gift cards! A book! Thank you! It was all so painful and lovely at the same time. I think that's how it was supposed to feel. And if it had ended right then, that's how it would have felt.

But the meal came to an end, and Living Sarah left the table for the restroom. Dad brought the check to the front to pay. And then I knew.

Karen had killed me. My wicked stepmother had killed me. Fairy tales are true. Lacey was right. My life was turned inside out.

Allow me to explain:

Dad kissed her and left the table. When he turned to walk away, leaving her alone at the table, her smile dropped like an anvil. She was a different person now. Her mask was removed and I was seeing the real Karen for the first time. She sneered, sighed, and rolled her eyes as she watched him walk away. Okay, yes, secretly being a bitch just made her a bitch, not a killer. True. But as soon as he was gone, she began eating mushrooms. The food that killed me. The food that she claimed to hate and avoid. She picked them out of Chinese food whenever we ordered takeout. She plucked them off of pizzas. She made it very clear that she would never, ever eat "the dreaded *shroom.*" That was a lie.

When Karen and Dad were putting together the wedding menu, she made a big, magnanimous deal about allowing mushrooms on the menu. "Marriage is about compromise," she explained sweetly. "You two should have what you want." I felt kind of victorious. I bet Dad did too. And isn't that what a good con artist does? They make you think that the whole awful idea was yours. She maybe even batted her eyes when she said it.

Karen killed me. But why? It was clear that she had this planned for quite a while. Why did she hate me that much?

I turned to watch Karen smile, her mask now firmly in place, as she reunited with Dad and Living Sarah. They were walking toward the exit, heading for home. Inching me one day closer to my awful death.

"Hey." My voice just barely escaped my throat. "You guys! Karen's a liar! She's going to have poison mushrooms at the wedding. She's going to kill me. *Get away from her!*"

They didn't hear me, of course. And now Bertha was by my side.

"It's time to go, dear," Bertha said. I reached for her and threw myself into her arms. I cried against her shoulder in shaking, painful sobs.

"Help me!" I tried to say.

"Oh no," she whispered gently. "My poor Sarah. Was it too painful? Was the day too important?"

When I could finally speak, I said, "They were all important."

Bertha was watching a different scene at the table behind me.

"Why is Declan here?" she asked. She pointed to an attractive busboy. He gave a friendly nod/salute to Karen—he seemed to know her. But she shook her head briskly and turned away into the night, looking just a little bit pissed off.

Declan watched her go. He looked a little hurt, a little confused, but then he fixed his hair and everything was okay. For him.

chapter fourteen

beautiful people are an
endangered species

"Where is Declan? Where is he?" I was storming through the mall. Bertha struggled on her little legs to keep up with me.

"Sarah! Please! This is a matter for the Boy!" Bertha called out. "Please do not consider taking justice into your own hands."

I found him at Ulta. His face was painted with a green mask, and he was filing his nails. (Did he have any idea he was actually dead?)

"Let me handle this," Bertha insisted.

"What did you do?" I asked Declan.

"A pore-minimizing mask," he explained. "You should do it too. Seriously."

I thought my head was going to explode. I groaned and stepped away for a second. Bertha took Declan by the hand and sat him on a stool by the counter.

"Declan, dear, we need to understand what role you played in Sarah's life." She sounded like she was explaining algebra to a kindergartner. "And in her death."

I spun around and shouted, "Hey! Didn't you have to fill in that questionnaire? Didn't you have to say the worst thing you ever did? How did you answer that? What did you write?"

"I wrote . . ." Declan eyed the floor as he answered. "I wrote that I told this actor friend that he looked good in taupe. That was a lie. He looked terrible in taupe, but I convinced him to wear taupe to every audition. It really messed him up. I'm still so ashamed."

Okay, so now I fully understood the level of stupidity I was dealing with. I took on the same tone that Bertha had. I spoke . . . very . . . slowly.

"Tell me about Karen. Karen Blake," I said.

"Okay. Don't freak out at me," he began.

"Karen!" I ordered him.

"Karen. Yeah. She was going to get me set up in LA." He turned to Bertha and explained, "I belong in LA. They'll really get me there."

"Start at the beginning," I said. And he did.

Actually, Declan decided to tell us his life story, all about the trials of being beautiful.

DECLAN'S LIFELONG TRIALS OF BEING THE BEST-LOOKING PERSON IN THE ROOM

He was a beautiful baby. A stunning toddler. A perfect (looking) child. He never experienced any "awkward years" in adolescence, like ordinary humans do.

It's not easy looking this good all the time. Oh. You wouldn't know. Sorry . . .

Being born this good-looking was sort of a curse. No, a burden. It was a burden, and he carried it. I mean, look around you. How many people are really, seriously beautiful? How many have sculpted bodies, amazing skin, great hair, and faces that the camera loves? See? Not that many.

Beautiful people are an endangered species. Like dolphins or unicorns. It's a thing. Look it up.

He graduated high school last year. Sort of. And now he worked out, waited tables, and kept auditioning. His parents, who were only okay-looking, just didn't understand the responsibility he owed to this gift. They wanted him to get a real job. But real jobs are for ugly people, and real careers are for the ones who are just plain *plain*. So. He didn't talk to them all that much.

Sometimes he appeared in off-off-Broadway plays, but he got bored saying the same lines every night. He dreamed of getting enough money together to move to Los Angeles. That was where he belonged.

"Tell me about Karen!" I interrupted, trying to bring his story to an end, please, soon.

Karen was a little older, but she really took care of herself. She talked like she was rich, but she lived like she was poor. Which was weird. Anyway. She knew a lot about health foods. And Los Angeles. And movies. And food. And sex. They met at the gym. And Declan soon discovered that she was really, really, really flexible.

(EWWW!)

What? Anyway. She helped Declan get a cater-waiter job. She was getting married. Again. She'd been married like twice before already, both times to older guys.

The second husband ran a health supplement business, so maybe that's how she kept herself looking so good. But after he died, she found out that the business was almost out of money. So she went looking for a new husband. One with some money. Now that's a positive attitude!

Declan got a look at the new husband-to-be. He needed to moisturize, that's for sure. Anyway. Karen arranged for Declan to have the easiest job of the whole catering staff. He had to wait on the dais table that was just for the bride and groom and the groom's daughter. Done. Easy. And he was going to get paid as much as everyone else. Sweet!

And he didn't question it when she asked him to give a big portion of mushrooms to the groom and then little bits to everyone else. They were almond mushrooms? Almondine mushrooms? Whatever.

Oops. He might have given a little too much to the daughter, but she seemed to enjoy them. A lot. She really wolfed them down. Even ate some of her dad's mushrooms. Oh, and the pill that Karen dropped in the groom's champagne? Declan was ready to bet that it was Viagra for the old dude's wedding night. He laughed when he saw the daughter drink it. What would it do to a girl? He watched her dancing. He watched her leave. He spent the rest of the evening on the sidelines, quietly doing exercises that would firm his butt.

That was a good night.

"You killed me?" I asked, barely able to summon any voice at all.

"No! No!" he insisted, the green goo on his face now dry and cracking. He looked like Yoda with cheekbones and highlights. "I could never play a villain. I'm just not the type. There's no way I could kill you."

"Yeah, I'm thinking those were amanita mushrooms. Highly poisonous," I explained with the milligram of patience I had left.

"But I didn't know! It's not fair to blame me when I didn't even know," he whined, and something inside me crumbled a little. It was all too easy to believe that Declan knew nothing at all. About anything.

"Didn't she come from a wealthy family?" I asked. "That's what she told us. They made a fortune in health supplements."

"The second husband was in health supplements. But she was kind of broke when I met her," he said. "She always told different stories about her family. I just thought she was being creative."

"Declan. Karen killed me," I said, and he gasped in response.

"Are you sure?" he asked.

I was sure. "She's a liar and a murderer."

"Whoa. See, here's the thing," he explained. "When I heard that you died, I asked her what happened. I was all, 'What happened?' She was really pissed off when you died. And you know, she looked way older when she was angry."

"What did she do?" I asked.

"She asked me a bunch of questions about the wedding, and about you and the food and the pill. But then she stopped talking about you. She promised me she'd come through with the connections in LA. And she fed me a nice lunch. And then I died."

He paused for a second, a small realization dawning in his vacant eyes. "Hey, wait a minute. I think she killed me too."

"She's going to kill my dad," I said.

"Whoa," Declan whispered. "Um. Am I in trouble? Am I going to hell?"

He was asking Bertha, but I didn't let her answer. "No," I said. "She fooled us all. You didn't know what you were doing."

Declan collapsed in the world's biggest sigh of relief. And I felt a tiny bit sorry for him. Poor dim Declan.

"Sarah." Bertha spoke at last. "Now you know who killed you. Leave the rest to the police."

"But what about my dad?"

"Let earthly justice prevail," she insisted.

I pictured Karen in an orange jumpsuit. (Not pretty.)

chapter fifteen

people suck. really. and maybe that's the best they can do.

Alice and I were alone in Crate & Barrel as night fell. There was no sign of Lacey. I should have worried about her, but I was too busy worrying about my dad. In a way, I liked worrying about him. It saved me from looking back on my life and all the times I ignored him, was rude to him, or just didn't care if he was around. I cared now. A lot.

"I need to save him," I said. Again. "I need to stop Karen. Can I go back and haunt her and scare her to death?"

"No! Absolutely not!" Alice said with way too much force. She was a little self-conscious about it, and continued in a smaller voice. "The dead used to be allowed to haunt, but it went wrong too often. Too bad you're not an angel," she said sort of absently. "I met a girl who became an angel. She died when she was hit by a trolley car. She pushed a total stranger out of the way and died saving him."

"Wow. So there are angels," I said.

"Of course," she said, as if I were a simpleton. "When the

story of her death came to light, Bertha sent her out of the mall."

"Where do angels go?" I asked.

"Well. She went to the spa," Alice replied. "And now she can help the living and the dead." The spa. That was where Nick might have/could have gone.

"Wait," I said, trying to form these words. "Does that mean that Bertha is an angel?"

Alice nodded and giggled at the blank confusion on my face.

"How did she die?" I asked.

"She was in a terrible fire at the factory where she worked," Alice explained. "There were lots of girls crowding out the door. Bertha made sure that her little sister got out first. She gave up her chance and perished in the fire."

(I played that tale in my head like a movie, but it was too awful to watch. I shook it away. Note to self: try to be nicer to Bertha.)

"If she's an angel, could she help save my dad?" I brightened up. "I died in his place. Does that make me angel material?"

Alice shook her head, saying, "Sarah, maybe he's better off dead. He's lost his only child, and he's married to someone who doesn't love him." And then, in an impossibly small voice, she added, "There are worse things than death."

"My funeral is tomorrow, and I need to do *something* while I'm there." As I spoke I latched on to my little secret: sometimes the living can hear me—at least here at the mall they can. Perhaps I could speak to him at my funeral. My plan was hatching.

"It's quite a thing," Alice said. "To see them bury you, say goodbye to you forever. And to see the one who killed you still breathing, eating, drinking, shitting, lying."

I held my breath and then ventured a question. "Your murderer really went to your funeral?"

"Yes. They always do, if they can," she said. I could hear the venom in her voice as she said his name. "Joe O'Hara. He was a filthy man, a liar and a murderer."

"Would you tell me your Death Story?" I ventured. Alice took a moment to collect herself, smoothing down her dress and her hair. When she was fully composed, she began.

ALICE'S DEATH AND TRAGIC FUNERAL

Alice was the eldest of five squirming, squabbling girls. When she was nearly finished with third grade, her mother informed her that she'd be staying home now, helping with the wee ones. And Alice did.

Her father sold bathtub whiskey (not gin) to make ends meet during Prohibition. It took the finish off the tub, but it put food on the table. Mother told stories of life back in Ireland. Life there sounded harder but prettier.

And then came the crash of 1929. Suddenly, no one had money for anything, and the Great Depression settled over them like an endless night. When Prohibition ended, things got even tougher. Meals got smaller.

"A loaf of bread is only a nickel," her mother would say with a sigh. "But who has a nickel?"

The little ones were getting older and could look after themselves. Alice wasn't needed around the house quite as much.

"We've got a plan for you, my lovely," her father announced after breakfast one day. Alice's heart fluttered in her chest. School? Could they be returning her to school? Books. Pictures. Friends. Boys. They swirled in her imagination like leaves in the wind.

"You've got a job," he said proudly. "You're to be a wage earner. The biscuit factory downtown needs girls with small fingers to help with the machinery. The foreman is old Joe O'Hara from our parish. We shook hands on it last night. Done and dusted."

Alice hesitated, thinking of the difference between what she was supposed to say and what she wanted to say. She made the wrong choice.

"I don't like Joe O'Hara. I don't want to be in a factory. Please don't make me."

Her father rose slowly, not betraying the swell of anger in his chest. He liked to do that for dramatic effect. He stood over his daughter, stroked her hair, and then raised the back of his hand, unleashing its full power against her cheek. Alice was on the floor, her face alive with pain.

"You won't talk back to me, Miss High and Mighty. You need to earn your keep."

He walked out, dignified and righteous. Her mother rushed to Alice's side and said, "Why do you make him do such things? You should know better."

Alice left home by herself the next morning, taking the trolley from Hell's Kitchen to downtown, then walking along the cobbled streets. She didn't like to travel alone in the city. It always made her feel like prey that had been separated from the herd.

Joe O'Hara took her hand into his greasy mitt and said, "I'll show you around."

Alice only heard half of what he said over the deafening machinery all around her. His bushy mustache and odorous cigar blocked his words even further. The space was vast but dark, hot, with an acrid smell that burned her nose.

"This way." He opened a door tall enough to allow a giraffe to pass through and gestured for Alice to climb the well-worn stairs. Stepping into his cramped office, Alice squinted to see an oak desk that was too big for the small room, a few chairs, and not enough light. It smelled like a diaper that needed changing.

"And now, my dear," he said as he moved in close. Too close. Alice's survival instincts were fully awake. She tried to duck around him, but he planted himself against the only door, the only way out. She pushed against his barrel chest, crying out like a small cub.

"No fuss, no fuss," he instructed. His breath was foul and inescapable.

She kicked him in the shin, but she was aiming higher. And he knew it.

In a fury, he threw her to the ground, and her head slammed against the corner of his desk. She tried to hold on to consciousness, but it didn't want to stay in this terrible place. It slipped through her fingertips and toes. It left, it lifted, it flew. She didn't die right away. But she did die as he pawed at her underthings.

Her funeral was a small, shabby affair. Joe O'Hara told her parents that Alice had clumsily slipped down the stairs and clocked her head, even though he had warned her to be careful. He even tried to save her. It was her own fault. Everyone believed him and blamed Alice for visiting such grief upon her poor parents. He gave her father five dollars for his troubles. In his eulogy, the priest tut-tutted at Alice's inability to hold on to the gift of life.

Afterward, Joe O'Hara lingered a moment in the church vestibule, so Ghost Alice leaned close to him and screamed, *"Murderer!"* over and over, louder and louder. He went pale, looking all around. He didn't see her. But he heard her.

"Jesus, Mary, and Joseph," he whispered. "Forgive me."

"Never!" Alice screamed. And Joe O'Hara ran away.

chapter sixteen
hello, cruel world

According to Alice, the dead don't dream. But I was dreaming up a storm. So my dreams must have been that awful Knowing, that terrible, special gift, surging into my head and my heart. That night I had my least favorite dream so far.

At first I was in the mall, surrounded by the living. They were so noisy, I stood still, covering my ears, squeezing my eyes closed tight. Sensory overload. When I opened them, the mall was empty and pretty dark. But, of course, the mall walkers were there. They still kind of scared me, even though we had some important stuff in common: they all seemed to be somewhere near my age, and, hey, they had all been murdered too. But their silence and their slowness creeped me out.

I uncovered my ears and found sound all around me instead of the usual thick silence. Each mall walker was talking, but to no one in particular. As they passed me, I overheard them. I didn't want to. Believe me. The Goth Girl was saying:

"I tried to tell him I was sorry, but his hands were tight

around my throat. No air. No words. I was scared. It hurt so bad. But then I faded away. I tried to tell him I was sorry, but his hands were tight around my throat. No air. No words. I was scared. It hurt so . . ."

The next person to pass was a boy, maybe fourteen years old:

"And if I stayed down, they'd get bored and stop kicking. My head felt big and cloudy. My stomach was on fire. They kept kicking. My head played white fireworks in the clouds. I thought about how to outsmart them. Play dead. And if I stayed down, they'd get bored and stop kicking. My head felt big and cloudy. . . ."

The next person was a boy who was tall and skinny as a broomstick:

"They lied. They said I'd be safe here. I want to get out. I'm so hungry. My tongue feels huge in my mouth. When's the last time they gave me food? I want food. They lied. They said I'd be safe here. I want to get out. I'm so hungry."

I looked up and around and their despair swirled around me. I could feel their misery prickling my skin.

I woke up.

✹ ✹ ✹

Funeral Day. I didn't have much of a plan, but this was it: sometimes, the living could hear me, or at least they could get a sense of what I was saying. (I think.) So I would tell Dad to get out of there, to call the police, to go see a doctor, to stay at a hotel under another name until Karen was behind bars.

I had to use what talents I had. Oh. And keep the plan a secret from Bertha. Obviously.

I sat up in bed and saw that Lacey was still missing. As much as I wanted to focus on me and my funeral and my murder and my dad and me, me, me, I fell into a big vat of worry for Lacey.

"I'm not sure that Lacey came back at all," Alice said.

"Do you think she got stuck back there? With the living?" I asked. I pictured Lacey, drenched in diamonds and red silk, haunting Manhattan, one boob forever popping out.

"I wouldn't wish that on anyone," Alice whispered, her voice sounding as pale as her face. "We're safe here at the mall, even if we get stuck mall-walking. At least I got to wake up and try again. But if you get stuck back there, you're really stuck. And you go quite mad."

"She's here somewhere," I insisted. "She must be."

"Meanwhile, Bertha will never let you wear casual clothes to your funeral. You must change, and quickly," Alice instructed.

Fine. We dashed over to Anthropologie, where I slipped into a respectable dark blue wrap dress that seemed funeral-friendly. I still wasn't sure why Bertha wanted us to dress up for an event where we were invisible, but okay. As Alice and I walked out into the mall, I noticed something sparkly up ahead.

It was a silver-gray trash can. There was a diamond bracelet dangling from the opening. I peered inside and saw the bloodred dress that Lacey had been wearing the day before. It was littered with the rest of the diamonds.

"What does this mean?" Alice asked.

"I have no idea," I said. "But it can't be good."

✳ ✳ ✳

Lacey wasn't at the food court. Neither was Declan. But Nick was there. Locking eyes with him felt almost dangerous. My skin temperature skyrocketed. I sat down next to him, and he grinned as he took hold of my hand under the table. This was the most delicious secret. Tiny shooting stars exploded in the air around us, but only we could see them.

Wasn't it nice to have something so sweet and joyous to help me rein in the torrential energy coursing through me? I could wait, hold on to Nick, and then unleash it at my funeral.

"Did you have nice funerals?" Alice asked Nick and Harry. I'm pretty sure neither of them saw my hand, Nick's hand, or the Technicolor fireworks.

Harry stood and stretched. "I think it's safe to say that my funeral was the party of the year!" He was glowing like someone in love. Seriously. "They sent me off in style. Music, stories, crazy pictures, and videos. It was magnificent."

"But you're so young," I said. "Come on, everybody cries when it's a funeral for a kid."

"Sometimes," Harry said. "But there was a lot of laughter too. My parents would cry, but then someone would tell a story about me, and then they'd laugh. I laughed too."

He gazed off into the distance, maybe replaying the scene in his mind. "I tried to hug them. I tried to tell them I was okay. It sort of felt like they got the message."

"You were a good son," Alice said.

"Eventually," Harry said, with a sort of Mona Lisa smile.

"What about you?" Harry turned to Nick. "Was a good time had by all?"

Nick grinned. "According to the New York *Daily News,* I was, hmm, how did they put it? 'Calm and courageous.' And they ran a pretty cool picture of me." Nick pretended to be dodging a crowd of fans. "No autographs, please. I'm just an ordinary dead guy."

Harry elbowed Nick. "Oh yeah? My funeral was so big, they had to hold it in the school auditorium."

"Well, hey, if you give the people what they want—*they all show up,*" Nick replied.

Harry laughed hard. "Low! Very low, dude!"

I hesitated, but I just had to ask, "Harry, did anybody . . . see you?"

He shook his head. "No. I'm pretty sure that would have been kind of awful. Things are different here at the mall, don't you think?"

I took that in. If Harry couldn't be seen at his funeral, could I be heard at mine? I brushed the worry aside. My funeral was a mission. And I must not fail. The echo and importance of those thoughts made me drop Nick's hand.

✻ ✻ ✻

Declan escorted a girl into the food court. He looked as blank and pretty as ever, but she was unrecognizable.

"Look who I found!" he said, and then left her with us and made a frozen yogurt run.

I didn't recognize her at first. Lacey was dressed in soft flannel pajamas with pictures of puppies all over them. She wore no jewelry or makeup. I hadn't realized just how much makeup she usually wore. Now, bare-faced, sad and true, she looked like a heartsick twelve-year-old with oversize boobs.

Her funeral must have been some kind of disaster.

"Don't ask her about her funeral," Declan warned as he returned. "It sounds like it sucked. But hey, Nick and Harry. How were your funerals?"

I shook my head, bugging my eyes out, trying to send the signal to Declan. Their glorious tales would just be lemon juice on the walking paper cut that was Lacey. But Declan was not a genius at picking up signals.

"Nah. Funerals are for the living," Nick said, because Nick got it. "And guess what? Fiona? The girl I was with when I was shot? *She brought a date to my funeral!*" He was a little too obvious in his attempt to come up with something to complain about. But that only added to the sweetness of the moment.

Harry quickly followed Nick's lead. "The big framed photo of me that they put on an easel next to my coffin? Bald. Total hairless wonder. What were they thinking?"

But there was no darkness, no anger or sadness in his voice. He was incandescent. And anyway, Lacey obviously had a serious thing for bald Harry. The photo probably sounded yummy to her.

Lacey was nearly expressionless. "That sucks, I guess," she said quietly. Her voice lacked its usual sharp edge, and her eyes showed zero confidence. What had happened to Lacey?

But at least she spoke. We were all quiet for a bit. I think we were all searching for a way to get her to say more. Nick found it.

"Lacey, you look so pretty without all the jewelry and makeup," he said at last. "You don't need any of that stuff."

"Yeah," said Lacey. "What's the point of having diamonds if there's no one to be jealous of you? Without that, they don't mean shit."

She stared at the floor as she spoke, her face turning blotchy. "And what's the point of a funeral if hardly anybody shows up? What's the point of friends who aren't really friends? Why do they go on Facebook and make jokes about you being dead? And why do your parents have to know about that? Why do your shitty friends tell the cops that you *fell* from the roof, and then protect Jorge? What was the point of any of that?"

Her tears were falling straight to the floor. Nick gestured to Harry, who took the cue and hugged Lacey tight.

Nick spoke softly. "Let them go, Lacey. Just let them go."

She dropped her head to Harry's chest and let out a loud sob. He stroked her hair until she pulled away, almost violently. Her face was a study in pain and anger.

"Never!" she shrieked at Nick, and at all of us. "Why should I? They all suck!"

"Yeah," Nick said softly. "They do. But maybe sucking is the best they can do."

Harry hugged her again. "Now. Tell me what day you're going to revisit for your Thornton Wilder Day."

"I don't know yet." She sniffled against his shoulder. "I'm still thinking about it."

"Well, hurry up, woman!" He half-laughed as he spoke. "After Bertha takes Sarah here to her funeral, we'll be off to our old lives for a day."

Declan perked up. "I'd choose the day I did a photo shoot in Mexico. That was a great day. Hey, did you know that Mexican words and Spanish words sound a lot alike? I wonder how they tell them apart."

I bowed my head and laughed. Declan didn't seem to notice.

"I'm choosing a snow day from two years ago," Nick volunteered. "We had this massive, amazing snowstorm, and I kind of regressed to a kid and went sledding in the park with a bunch of friends. We laughed all day." He found my lost hand and squeezed it a bit as he spoke.

Lacey looked up at Harry, wiping her tears away. "What are you going to choose for your Thornton Wilder Day?"

"I'm not gonna change anything, right?" he asked.

"That's what Bertha says," Lacey confirmed.

"Oh, then it's easy. October 27, 2004. No-brainer," Harry said.

"What happened on that date?" I asked.

Nick was laughing. "Nice choice!" he said.

"The Red Sox won the World Series. I was too young to appreciate it when it happened."

"Out of all the days you could relive, you choose to go back and watch a baseball game?" I asked, absolutely incredulous.

"Not exactly. I'm going to go back and watch my parents watch the game. Which will be even more fun."

"Good choice," said a small voice. It was Lacey. "I've

decided on my day: I'll go back to my tenth birthday. My parents let me skip school. We went to Governors Island and rode bikes and had a picnic."

"That sounds like a great day," Harry said, hugging her once more. His bracelet was pale pink. Like a cherry blossom.

chapter seventeen

my. funeral. starts. now.

And for some reason, I was kind of nervous. Bertha complimented me on my blue dress. "Even though you can't be seen, isn't it nice to know that you're being appropriate?" she asked.

Yes. Yes it was. I smiled nicely, reminding myself that Bertha sacrificed herself for her sister. Be nice and don't focus on her boxy maroon pantsuit.

We entered the elevator in Bed Bath & Beyond. Before she pushed the button, Bertha arched her eyebrows. "This is the last time you'll see your family, my dear. The very last. Don't waste this time by trying to interfere. Some of them, the ones who loved you the most, may sense your presence there. See them and say goodbye. Just leave them in peace."

"I will," I lied. (What if I told her my plan and she stopped the elevator? I couldn't take that chance. See? This was why Nick, my dreams, my ability to be heard should all stay secret.)

When the elevator doors opened, we were on Bleecker Street. New York City. This was the Greenwich Village Funeral Home.

I forgot all about Bertha. I just took it all in.

"Sarah!" she called to me. "One more thing: you must come back when I say so. Do you understand? You may not stay one minute longer."

I nodded. "Yes. Understood." We were standing in front of the funeral home. Someone opened the heavy glass door, so I slipped inside and didn't look back.

I stood in the middle of the room for a long, long time. There were people arranging neat rows of folding chairs. There were people placing framed pictures of me around the room, on tables and easels. There were people arranging flowers, speaking in hushed tones.

No coffin. Yet.

Of course, Bertha had me here unfashionably early, before any guests arrived. Before my own corpse arrived. I followed the workers around and found this in the newspaper at the front desk:

TOXIC CATERER WON'T FACE CHARGES

The wedding caterer whose toxic mushrooms resulted in one fatality and four hospitalizations will not face charges. City officials found no evidence of wrongdoing or unsanitary conditions at Best Feast and have ruled that an overseas supplier is most likely to blame. The District Attorney's office issued the following statement: "We have no jurisdiction over foreign food suppliers. We urge all restaurants and caterers to inspect their imported foods with greater dili-

gence. Everyone recovered immediately following the meal, with the exception of the young
girl who took a sleeping pill. Our condolences
go out to her family."

Sarah Evans, age sixteen, died as a result of
ingesting the toxic mushrooms. Her autopsy in-
dicated a large quantity of mushrooms and the
presence of a potent sleeping pill. The city medical examiner has ruled her death an accident.

"An accident? Are you *kidding me?*" I shouted to anyone,
everyone in the room. But of course they didn't hear me. The
police were done, out, finished. No investigation. No justice.

That would have been the main topic for me, but then Dad
walked in by himself. Oh, he looked sad, serious, and so . . .
alive. Seeing his face, seeing all the features align and be
him, full-out, one hundred percent my dad was unbearable.
I rushed to his side and then just stood there, like a broken
promise. Here's a revelation of my utter and complete stupidity: Dad's grief was bigger than both of us. I wasn't supposed
to die first.

"I love you," I whispered. No reaction. That's okay. I was
just getting warmed up. He was going to hear me. Soon.

He looked around the room, and it was clear that he had no
idea what to do or where to go. He smoothed his black suit, his
gray tie, his brown hair. He blinked his brown eyes hard and
exhaled a ragged, shaky breath.

Karen was consulting with one of the hushed-voiced
strangers who worked there. She hurried over to Dad, rubbing his back. She looked super-serious. Except for her white

princessy wedding gown, she had always worn bright pastels, with her rhubarb-red hair framing her face in soft curls. Today, she wore black, with her hair pulled back and her everpresent smile erased. She looked older. Good.

"Listen, bitch. You're not going to win this," I hissed at her. She didn't hear me, but who cares? It felt so good to say it.

"Let me go see about the flowers," she whispered to him, and she was off.

Dad walked slowly toward an old picture of me playing an electronic keyboard, headphones on, totally immersed in the music. I must have been twelve years old. He had snuck the camera around my bedroom door and taken the picture without my knowledge or consent. I was so mad when I first saw that picture.

"Help me," he whispered to no one. "Please, someone. Help me."

Time for me to get to work. If strangers in the mall could hear me, my own dad just had to hear me too.

"Dad! It's Sarah! I'm here! And you're in danger. Just walk out of here and don't come back. Karen killed me, and she's going to kill you next!"

I hugged him, wrapping my arms tight around him, resting my head against his chest. But I don't think he felt it. He walked away and I shadowed him like, well, a ghost. People began streaming into the room. He shook hands with some, hugged others, and accepted everyone's comforting words.

"She's in a better place." "She's at peace now." Please. As if they knew. I spoke right over them.

"Listen to me, Dad. I don't know how she's going to do it,

but Karen is going to kill you. She tried to poison you. And she'll do it again. Get out! Get out! *Go!*"

There was an ongoing quiet murmur throughout the place but still no sign of a coffin.

I interrupted the quiet murmur every few seconds with *"Dad! Karen killed me! She's going to kill you next! Get out now!"*

There were lots of flowers. One arrangement was from my school; lots of them had cards from various companies that Dad had helped over the years. *Sorry for your loss. Condolences at this sad time. You are in our prayers.*

"Dad! Please, please! Hear me! It's your daughter. I just want to save you! Get out of here now!"

What was it going to take for him to hear me?

My friends from school were there: a decent representation of the Mathletes. They clustered together, a bit uncomfortable in the midst of so many people they didn't know. Now, in this company, they were living the stereotype. I felt a deep, almost painful longing to be around their sweet, clumsy shyness. Their conversation was stilted and kind.

"She was nice. I mean, she was always nice to me."

"That's nice."

"I know, right? So nice."

"Dad! Karen is a killer! Get out of here now!"

I shadowed him around the room, repeating myself over and over, louder and louder, angrier and angrier, until I became utterly and completely desperate. Why didn't he hear me?

My throat burned and ached in exhaustion. How long had I been screaming this at him?

And then I turned to see Karen standing off to one side, watching the day unfold with a half smile on her face and steel in her eyes. My knees buckled as I stood there looking into the eyes of my killer.

✳ ✳ ✳

I ran into a dark room off to the right, escaping the murmur and the pointlessness of my funeral. I had to. This was a mostly empty room, but all the way in the back I saw it. A coffin. I approached it slowly. Was this me? Were they keeping me here so that I could make a big entrance? And wasn't that kind of weird?

I got close enough and no, no, that wasn't me in there. I cried out and backed away in a single jump. I shouldn't have been startled. I mean, it's a funeral home, so there should be dead bodies here and there. I stepped toward the coffin once more and gazed down at an elderly man with gaunt features. He was wearing heavy makeup that failed to make him look tan and healthy. I think his lips were stitched together.

(Pull yourself together! You can't waste this day freaking out over dead old guys or wallowing in anger at Karen or in self-pity for your short little life, or mooning over your poor, grieving father. That won't help him. Did you waste a ton of time blaming him for Mom's death? *Duh. Yeah.* You already know that, *and* you regret it. Did you waste lots of opportunities while you were alive? *Hell yes.* Now don't waste this one. It's not like you have a plan B or anything. Just make him hear you. *Save your father! Now!*)

chapter eighteen
worst. funeral. ever.

I threw myself back into my stupid funeral. Dead or alive, it was up to me to save Dad. Just as I returned, Dad stood at the front of the room and cleared his throat. The quiet murmur faded to silence.

"Thank you all for gathering here today. But if I'm being truthful, I wish we weren't here," he began. His voice choked just a bit as he said, "I love my Sarah. With all my heart. And if she were here, she'd say, 'Dad, quit it, you're embarrassing me.' And I would give anything on this earth to hear her voice again, to embarrass her, to just pass the time with her."

He stopped and pressed a hand over his mouth. My heart was split in two. I rushed to his side. I wanted to scream, let him know I was near, but I wasn't able to make a sound. Maybe he could feel that I was there. "I'm sorry," he said. "I think that I should give the floor to someone else to talk about Sarah."

He sat down in the front row. He dropped his head to Karen's shoulder. She hugged him and whispered in his ear. He bowed his head and held on to her.

My school friends went up as a group and talked about me being nice. It was nice.

My cousin told the story about the time we went on a shopping spree at Bergdorf's and I only bought socks.

Karen watched him, nodding, with that half smile on her face. It sent a chill down my ghostly spine.

But then Karen stood up and spoke. Her eyes were red, and her breathing was measured. She looked exactly like someone should look at a funeral. If this were an audition for the role of Sad Lady at a Funeral, she'd get the job. Everyone stopped murmuring.

"Sarah will live on," she said in a voice that was clear and noble and *so fake*; how did I never see through her before? "Her kindness, her sweet, gentle presence—those things will be with us forever." She looked back at a large golden urn on the table behind her. I hadn't noticed it before.

"I won't say goodbye, sweet Sarah," Karen said to the urn. "You'll always be with us."

Oh. That was me in there. I'd been cremated. That had to have been Karen's idea. Dad would have had me buried next to Mom. Wow. Look, I knew I didn't need my body anymore, but that doesn't mean I wanted it burned. First I was autopsied, then cremated. It was more reason to hate Karen. As if I needed more.

That was the end of the speeches. Everyone went back to murmuring.

Now I see why people might not want to witness their own funerals. I mean, this was what my life added up to: I was nice. I liked socks. But had I ever really lived?

My funeral was over. My body was ashes. Karen was sorting out the bill for my funeral, and Dad was slumped in a chair.

Being near him was like standing in an August breeze. He was warm and alive. And I was dead. I sat down next to him and sang to him, very softly. It was the half song that I wrote for Mom, the one I slipped into her coffin, where I wrote my own words to the Beatles song "Across the Universe." As I sang, I gently shifted the words just a smidge to make it for him, and about me being the one who died.

PLEASE KNOW

Everyone keeps telling me that I am gone,
   but love lives on
I left before we finished having fun together,
   but please know
I have learned so much from you, so be at peace.
   I'll see you soon.
Be happy, please. I love you so.
Thank you for being my dad
Oh
You were a fantastic dad
You were a fantastic dad
You were a fantastic dad
You were a fantastic dad

He lifted his head. "Sarah?" he whispered in my direction.

"Yes! I'm here. I'm right beside you, Dad!" I held my breath and let him take it in.

"Oh God, I'm losing my mind!" He buried his face in his hands and began to cry.

"Dad, you're not crazy. You're hearing me. You need to get out of here. Karen is—"

Karen was stooped down in front of him, her lips pinched into some weird expression that I guess was supposed to be consoling.

"We should go home now, dear," she said gently.

I spoke louder and faster. *"Karen is a killer. Get out. Right now. Just go!"*

Dad jerked backward, holding his hands over his ears, over his head. I'd never witnessed so much pain. It took my breath away. Even Karen stopped speaking.

I heard Bertha's voice behind me. "Sarah! It's time to go."

"Just one more minute," I said without looking at her. "Dad! Get away from her. She killed me and she's going to kill you too!"

Dad finally lowered his hands, looked at Karen, and sighed.

"Oh, Karen," Dad said. "Today was too much for me. Much too much. I'm hearing things. In my head. It's like Sarah's voice, but it's an ongoing echo of pain, of anguish. Listen to me, I sound like a nut job. I'm really losing it."

"Sarah! What's going on?" Bertha commanded me. "Is he hearing you? *Is he?*"

"Karen killed me and she'll kill you too!" I shouted to Dad, ignoring Bertha completely. I heard her click-clack over to me, but I kept my focus on Dad.

"Sarah! Don't interfere with the living! It will end badly!" Bertha was pleading with me.

"Dad! Karen wants to kill you!" I yelled.

"What was that herbal tea stuff you were trying to get me to drink last night?" Dad asked.

"It's just what you need. It'll help you relax and make you sleepy." There was a tiny glint of pleasure in Karen's eyes.

Oh no. No, please no.

"I'll try anything," Dad said, shaking his head. He rose and began to follow her outside.

Dad! No! Don't do it! It's poison! I screamed with every cell, every atom of my being.

But Dad only shook his head and shuddered. "Is it strong?" he asked her.

"Oh yes," she said, helping him to his feet. "Very."

"Good," Dad mumbled.

✷ ✷ ✷

Back at the mall I was completely mute. Why? Because Bertha said exactly one thing in the elevator. And it was the single absolute worst thing she could have said:

"You know, Sarah, your father might have figured out his wife's role in your death if you just hadn't pushed him so hard. You upset him." I stumbled a bit as she added, "So if she is off poisoning him right now, alas, he is in her clutches for good. I did try to warn you."

This was the long-winded Bertha version of "I told you so."

I sprinted at top speed to Crate & Barrel, threw myself onto my bed, buried my face in my pillow, and screamed. Soon the screams transformed into endless weeping. Lacey and Alice were nearby.

"We should get Nick," Alice suggested. "He'll know what to do."

"No." Lacey overruled her. "Nobody should see her like this. Including us. Leave her alone for now."

I cried into the pillow, unable to form words in my own mind.

Somehow the deep, deep sleep of the dead overtook me. As I felt myself drift away, I made a wish: *Please. No dreams tonight. Please.*

chapter nineteen

with a song in my heart

And once again I was in a dream. I was back in my room, stretched out on my bed, surrounded by stuff that I loved. Mom came in and sat down next to me. This was starting to feel sort of normal. I pulled myself up to sitting. "Hi," I said.

"It's begun," said Mom. "He's starting to die, a little bit every day. It's going to be slow. Not like ripping off a Band-Aid."

"Can I save him?" I asked.

"Maybe. I don't know." She shrugged as she spoke.

"See? This is how bad the Knowing is. I couldn't save you. I can't save him. But I get to worry and stress and suffer about it. I hate this."

She stepped away and started sifting through my desk, which was littered with paper, pens, headphones, and odd-shaped paper clips. If I had been alive, I would have protested: come back and never let go.

"Have you moved on?" I asked. "Are you someone else now?"

"Yes. I did," Mom conceded. "I moved on a long time ago.

But some deep part of me will always be drawn back to this place. To you." She looked all around her. "I was so happy here. I wish it could have lasted. But when I wake up, this will just be another dream that I forget. And I'll be back in my new life."

"Don't forget," I urged her.

"Oh, Sarah. All those piano lessons and you could never write your own melody?" Mom asked as she studied one of my half songs. "I'm not sure Lennon and McCartney would be okay with you just borrowing theirs."

I blinked at her kind of hard. "Is that what's important right now?"

She abandoned the music on my desk and returned to the bed next to me. She took both of my hands in hers. "I just want you to fulfill your potential. And move on. I'm so glad I got to move on. I'm happy."

And then I woke up.

Death was making me nocturnal. Alice and Lacey were fast asleep as I crept out of our Crate & Barrel home and into our mall. Up on our floor, we had pretty much everything we needed. I padded around as quietly as I could and gathered my supplies. Staples: yellow paper, a ruler, black and blue pens. Brookstone: the Alfred's Teach Yourself to Play Piano keyboard and headphones.

These were pretty common items, and as I gathered them I realized that they had stuff like this downstairs, where the living could roam and shop and waste their lives. I was about to do something I could have done so easily when I was alive. What was so important that stopped me? What had I been waiting for?

And yes, I could take a hint, Mom. I needed to communicate to Dad through *music,* not just words. Wasn't that what she'd been trying to tell me? (And by the way, simple, direct, declarative sentences would work really, really well.) Okay, I did sing to him at my funeral, but maybe it had to be one hundred percent completely and totally from me. My own Beatles-free composition. Okay, then. Let's get to work.

Downstairs, in the quiet dark of the empty mall, I made myself at home in the aquarium, locking in on the gentle rhythms that surrounded me while I fashioned a few pages of blank sheet music. A school of gray fish with long snouts hung suspended in the water like floating toys. I suppose they were waiting for daylight. I hoped they liked music.

I thought that I already knew the song I would write. I had a few lyrics bouncing around in my head, and a hazy melody in there somewhere. It was going to be a song to Dad, urging him to get the hell away from Karen and naming her as my killer:

Dad, get out of here
Don't let Karen near
She will kill you, if she can

Ignore that. I was just brainstorming, okay? And anyway, the real song began to write itself, and it didn't want to be a scary warning like that. I couldn't force it, couldn't hold it in, any more than a living person could hold their breath indefinitely. It needed to breathe and be in the world. When I reached the end, I sang it start to finish.

Here it is. It's my first full song, so don't be too judgy, okay?

The Story I Tell Myself
(Music and lyrics by Sarah Evans)

Turn your face to me
Turn your gaze and see
All the pain surrounding you
Every song you hear
With a heart sincere
Brings a chance for you to do
Something more
Than
Be
Alone
Something more
Than
Be
Unknown
Be the one who does
More than she who was
Be alive in joy and hope
Be the one who does
More than she who was
Be alive in joy and hope

By the time I was finished, the stores were opening downstairs and living people were firing up super-bright lights while they gripped large cups of coffee. The night security guard walked past me. Whistling a little piece of my melody. The one that I had just written.

"Hey!" I called out. "Did you hear me?" But he kept walking, just as if he hadn't heard me at all.

The entrance was sort of jammed with a school trip, where a long row of elementary school kids were noisily filing into the mall. A teacher led the group like a mother duckling. The first girl in line had a mischievous, giggling boy behind her. He was signaling to his friends that he was going to push the girl in front of him. He was silently laughing too hard to carry it out. Yet.

As he prepared to give her a shove, I leaned into the girl's ear and said, "Duck!" She did a kind of duck and twist in my direction. Without her there, the boy shoved his teacher with all his might. "Oooooh!" the kids said in chorus. He was in trouble and they all knew it.

"Nice move!" another boy shouted to the girl who had ducked. She beamed with joy.

chapter twenty

people come and go
so quickly here

I needed to find Nick. I raced upstairs to the land of the dead, where everything was unraveling at the food court. Everybody had food, but nobody was eating. Declan was at the salad bar, filling a bowl with greens that he examined leaf by leaf. Nick was studying the ingredients in his burrito. At first, I assumed he was trying to figure out how to improve it, but then I realized that he was looking past it, not at it.

It took me a minute to figure out that something had gone horribly wrong while I was at my funeral, and it was only going to get worse.

"So? Thornton Wilder Day?" I said, helping myself to some of Nick's fries. "Did everybody choose well?"

"Yeah," Nick said. "It was . . ." He searched for the word, then looked into my eyes and found it. "Surprising."

Lacey sniffed and said, "Mine rocked." But her voice was so dark, so somber, it didn't make sense.

Alice looked like a bad Precious Moments figurine. Big eyes, solemn face.

"Okay, what's going on?" I asked, and couldn't resist adding, "Who died?"

"Harry," Alice answered in a dull, quiet voice. Her sadness was immeasurable. Was he somehow deader than the rest of us? I didn't think so. I turned to Harry, but his focus was way past me. Bertha was entering the food court.

"Now?" he asked her. Okay, clearly I was missing something, and it was big. Now what?

"Not quite yet," she said. "Declan. I'm afraid I have bad news."

Declan put down his bowl and walked toward her. "Don't make me guess," he said with a tinge of fear in his voice. "I'm not good at guessing."

"Your funeral," she began. "It isn't going to take place."

"What? You mean it's postponed?" he asked.

"No." Bertha took his hands and looked him in the eye. "It's canceled, my dear. I'm sorry. Your parents have decided not to have a funeral. I'm so sorry."

Declan's chin wobbled a bit. "But why?" He gestured to all of us. "Everybody gets a funeral. Why not me?"

"I'm so sorry, dear," Bertha said again.

"So what's going to become of my body?" Declan sounded like a child. "I wanted to have my beautiful body all laid out so people could look at me one last time."

"Yes. Well." Bertha looked at the ground. "That's a bit difficult to explain."

She hesitated for so long, Declan said, "Try!"

"Rather than have a burial or cremation, your parents have donated your body," she said at last.

Declan's eyes went wide. "What, to a museum?" You could

131

see on his face that he was picturing himself as a great stuffed statue at the Metropolitan Museum of Art. And sort of liking it.

"No," Bertha said. "To a medical school." Declan squinted in confusion, so she explained further. "Medical students need cadavers. For practice and study." He still didn't get it completely. "So. That's what they'll use your body for."

Declan fell back a step. "I get it now," he whispered. "There's nobody back there who loves me enough to bury me or even say goodbye to me. Nobody will ever visit my grave and remember me. Nobody's crying for me. And they're treating my beautiful body like garbage."

"Now, Declan, that's not true," Bertha said. She was studying his face and looked a bit panicked.

"I died all alone. And nobody loved me." Declan was staring off into the distance.

"Hey, Declan. Buddy. Don't tell yourself that," Nick said sharply.

"People loved you," Declan replied sadly. "But not me. I died all alone. And nobody loved me." Declan repeated it a few more times. Alice covered her face with both hands, unable to watch what was unfolding. I knew what was about to happen: he was slipping away from us, hypnotizing himself with his own words. He was about to become another mall walker.

"Stop it!" Nick jumped from his seat and shook Declan by the shoulders. "Declan! Look at me! Stop saying this to yourself. It isn't true!"

We surrounded him now, following Nick's lead. We commanded him to come back to us, but he didn't blink. He looked past us, his eyes going glassy. "I died all alone. And nobody loved me." His voice was dull and slow now. "I died all alone. And nobody loved me."

"Declan! Buddy! Cut it out!" We launched a chorus of shouts, but Declan was farther and farther away with every second. He went silent and took a slow step out into the mall. And then another and another.

He was lost to us.

✳ ✳ ✳

Whoever came up with the phrase "rest in peace" clearly had never died. Did I seem peaceful to you?

Harry held up his wrist. His bracelet was completely white, and it shimmered in the light.

"I'm moving on." He stopped there, letting it sink in. I tried to think of a wise, compassionate answer. But all I could think was *"Nooooooo!"* Nick put his arm around me, knowing that I'd need solid support.

"I was dying for a long time," Harry continued. "My unfinished business was about how sad I was to miss so much while I was actually alive. But I'm okay now. I can go."

"When do you go?" I asked.

"Now," he said, rising from the table.

"Noooooooo!" I called out. Just then we all turned to see Lacey sobbing loudly, covering her face with her hands. Harry walked over and knelt down beside her.

"Hey, this is a good thing, remember? And if you guys move on soon, we'll all get a chance to meet up next time around."

"I'll be looking for you," Nick said. "For all of us. We'll be together again."

Lacey lowered her hands and wiped her face with her arm, sniffling loudly. "Harry. Tell the truth: do you want to meet me and grow up with me next time?"

Harry drew an X over his heart. "I do. I swear."

Her expression shifted into something harder, and I saw the Lacey who scared the shit out of everyone back on Earth. Her angry tone didn't match her words at all. "You are the coolest person I ever met. I hate the thought of being here without you. You're moving on too soon. Wait for me."

"I'm ready now," Harry said gently.

"Then I am too. Right now." Her face, her voice, her energy were all poised for a fight.

"You will be," Harry assured her quietly. "Right now you're still kind of pissed off about Jorge. You've got to do something about that."

Lacey studied his face. Slowly, slowly the stern muscles in her face melted. "Ya think?"

Now Harry studied her face as if he needed to memorize it. And then he kissed her, ever so sweetly. They locked in a tight embrace, but then Harry spread his arms. "Bring it in, guys! Group hug!"

Our hug was joyous, loving, and all too brief. Harry stepped back and sort of saluted the group. "You're all really beautiful."

With that, he walked away from us. We stayed back, all still and silent.

Lacey gasped loudly. "Wait!" she shouted. "Harry! Wait up! I have one more question!" She ran out after him, then stopped and turned to us.

"He's gone," she said. And the finality of death drew us all together once more.

chapter twenty-one

never, never, never give up

My Bracelet Is Bright Pink Like Bubble Gum

I was alone with Nick. Finally. Sort of. We sat downstairs in the swirl of the living, who scowled, laughed, shouted, and whispered as they bought more things. It offered a kind of privacy for us. After all, everyone would have seen and heard us upstairs. It was getting kind of easy to tune out the bustle around us if I just focused on Nick.

"Nick, when I went back for my Thornton Wilder Day, something happened," I began.

"Same here," he said. "I saw you. Alive."

I froze.

"We were both about fourteen. We were in Washington Square Park. Living me almost slammed into you with my sled, but you dodged me and kept walking. But it was you, definitely you." He grinned. "I feel like I'd know you anywhere, any age."

"I saw you too," I answered breathlessly. "You were applying for a job at Think Coffee. Living me was studying at the next table."

"I remember that interview. I didn't get the job," he said. "But anyway, isn't it great?"

"It's weird how you can see any situation as good, great, or just plain nice," I said, not sure if that was a compliment or a complaint.

Nick laughed. "It's weird how you can worry about every corner of the universe."

"But, Nick, think about it: What if we had met when we were alive? What if we could have changed things so that you didn't get shot and I didn't get poisoned? What if Dad never met Karen?"

"What if, what if, what if and die." Nick laughed some more. "We didn't meet. We died. *Then* we met." He framed my face with his hands. "And here we are." He kissed me. I breathed him in and felt the weight of his body against mine. I could get lost in kissing Nick. It took all my strength to stop.

"I have to go back," I said at last. "I have to save my dad."

"And I'll help you. But how?" he asked.

"I have to sing to him. And I think it might help. I just don't know how to get through to him."

"Maybe we can help each other," Nick suggested. "My mom was so heavily medicated at my funeral, she was completely out of it. I'd give anything to see if she's actually okay."

A mom had her three kids posing for a picture with the big mall star in the background. That happened a lot, and I would never have noticed it except for one thing. We were in the path of the picture. (Dead. Not visible. No problem.)

But the mom lowered her camera and looked right at Nick. She saw him. Not me. Him. We all knew it.

"What?" she whispered. "Who?" She shook her head and

swallowed hard. "Kids! Let's take the picture somewhere else." They groaned and trudged off after her. "Come on!" she shouted, running/walking away from us. "Move it!"

"She saw you," I said.

"She saw me," Nick echoed.

✳ ✳ ✳

We went to the Lego store because Lacey bellowed for us to get there *now!* She even got Alice to come downstairs, which was quite an achievement. Lacey's face looked clean and clear after her good cry over Harry. Ever since her funeral, she had abandoned the diamonds and Oscar-worthy gowns. Instead she dressed in tight leopard prints, very low-cut. She was half human, half cat.

"Come here!" Lacey shouted over the kids, and led us to a store employee wearing an official Lego vest and name badge. He was about halfway through building a massive dinosaur sculpture in Legos. He had a small table where he had sorted his Legos by size and color.

"Watch and be amazed," Lacey said. She closed her eyes and took a few deep breaths, like she was about to do downward-facing dog. When she opened her eyes, she leaned close to the table and flicked one of the Legos to the floor.

The guy building the sculpture grunted in frustration as he picked up his lost Lego.

"What the hell?" he said to himself as he checked the table's sturdiness. "Is this thing broken?"

Lacey glowed with pride. "I've been doing this all day. All I have to do is think really hard about how much I miss

Harry or how much I hate Jorge and all my ex-friends and—"
She flicked another Lego to the floor. "Yessss!" She was
victorious.

"Oh my God! I hate my job!" the Lego guy shouted to the
ceiling. *"I hate my life!"*

Lacey snort-laughed. "The living guy hates his *life*. I
love it!"

But the parents in the store didn't seem to like this out-
burst. Oh well. Alice didn't like it either. "Lacey!" she whispered. "What if you get caught? What could happen to you?"

"Wow!" Nick said. And that was the understatement of
all time. Lacey could move things. She could touch the real
world. A little bit.

"Didn't Bertha ever explain any of this?" Alice whispered,
as if the angry Lego guy could hear her.

"Explain what?" Nick asked. "Come on, Alice. Bertha
doesn't like to talk about stuff she doesn't like to talk about.
So you explain it. Okay?"

"Oh dear. Bertha does hate all this. But here goes." Alice
took a deep breath. "The dead usually get some kind of ability for haunting. I can be heard. Harry, as you know, could be
seen. Lacey can move things."

"And I think somebody just saw me," Nick offered. He
looked at me, nudging me to speak up, so I did.

"People can hear me," I said, and it felt like a great unbur-
dening.

"So what? I can move stuff." Lacey sounded triumphant,
like she had the best gift of all.

"Just because you *can* doesn't mean that you *should*," Alice
said firmly.

"Please. No living people can see me. Bertha's not here." And then she leaned in toward Alice, lowering her voice. "And you're not gonna tell. Are you?" Right there I could see Lacey as she was when she was alive. She took no prisoners.

"But what if the Boy sees you?" Alice reasoned. "He might be here. You don't know. You never know."

"Please." Lacey sounded so confident. She closed her eyes to concentrate extra-hard, summoning the strength or the power or whatever it was. "Harry moved on too soon!" Lacey said to herself. "He's about to be a cute bald baby!" And she flicked another Lego to the floor.

The Lego guy pulled off his Lego vest, ripped off his name badge, and walked out of the store. I think he quit.

"I can move things! I have superpowers!" Lacey crowed.

Alice looked absolutely panicked. "Everyone, please, please. We've got to get out of here. We can't be doing this. Not among the living. This is so much more than dangerous!"

"Sarah!" Nick took me by the shoulders. "This is the answer you've been looking for."

Did you ever have one of those moments when the thoughts tumble in your head like elaborate dominoes? The neurons snap and fire so quickly, they don't have time to show up as words. My brain did that, and then these words came out of my mouth:

"Lacey. Will you help me? Please?"

She arched one eyebrow and smiled. She oozed power and seemed to be feeling magnanimous about it.

"What do you need?" she asked. Clearly she enjoyed this kind of moment.

"You can save my father's life."

chapter twenty-two

a girl with a plan

I wasn't exactly sure how we would do it, but I was sure that Nick was sure. It took him a whole two minutes to put the plan together, step by step. It sounded solid, and I felt aglow with hope.

We waited until the stores were closed. And if we hadn't encountered mall-walking Declan, Alice might have come with us. We all stood still and offered a respectful moment of silence as he trudged past us, unseeing and unhearing but handsome as ever. I silently apologized for all the times I'd laughed at him, even though he didn't know I was doing it. I knew. But the sight of him must have brought up horrible memories for Alice.

"That way lies madness," Alice pleaded with me. "Please don't try this insane plan. Don't interfere with the living. The Boy will be furious. Not to mention Bertha."

"Oh, Alice. If I don't try, if I don't do absolutely everything in my power to save my dad, then I'll end up like Declan. How can I move on if I know I've left him in danger?"

She looked at her feet.

"You don't have to come with us," Nick conceded. "But please don't tell Bertha, okay?"

Alice nodded, and the three of us descended to the lowest level of the mall, the land of the living. We slipped through the walls of the first store we saw—the Apple Store, which was staring down the Microsoft Store right across from it. We were stepping into the middle of a feud, I thought.

The store was bright and shiny, even in the dark. I liked it better without the Geniuses. I scanned the merchandise, all of which was useless to us dead people.

"First order of business: we need a land line," Nick said, and we all began to search in silence among the shiny toys in the store. "Found it!" Nick shouted so loudly, I sort of jumped. He found a big, fancy phone with a mass of buttons and lights right behind the sales counter. Perfect.

"We can call your dad first, because he might die and all"—Lacey pointed a finger right in my face—"but then we call Jorge and scare the shit out of him." She held a script she had scrawled for me to shout into the phone at her murderer. Okay. This was the price I had to pay, and I would gladly pay it.

"I'll say whatever you want me to say to him," I assured her. From her grin, I knew that the message on that paper must be pretty awful. Lacey turned her attention to Nick.

"It's your plan. You should get a call too," she declared. "It just seems fair."

"I want to know that my mom is okay," he began. But Lacey cut him off.

"So we'll call her and see how she's doing. Like we're taking a survey or something." Nick looked pretty uneasy with that idea. Would she really feel better after a call from a dead stranger?

"Okay. Here we go." Lacey stared down at the phone, not moving.

"Lacey, I want you to think about Harry," I said. "He's gone. And he's never coming back."

"Oh, just shut up," she grunted. "I got this. Just make sure you can do what you said you could do."

With that, she closed her eyes and went somewhere deep inside herself. It looked as if a dark cloud had passed over her and only her. And when she was ready, she pressed the Speaker button. A dial tone sang its one-note song. We changed up the tune as I fed Lacey my dad's phone number, digit by digit: 2 1 2. . . .

She was visibly tired by the time she was done dialing, but the song ended with the grand finale of a phone ringing. This was it. It clicked.

"Hello?" Dad's voice sounded so far away and so very sweet.

"Dad? Dad?" My hands were shaking so hard I couldn't focus on the sheet of paper I was holding. Nick put his hand over mine and steadied the paper. He kissed my forehead and said, "Sing."

"Hello?" Dad repeated, sounding even farther away. It is nearly impossible to sing when your throat is collapsing with salt and tears.

Turn your face to me
Turn your gaze and see
All the pain surrounding you

142

"Who is this?" Dad shouted. "Is this some kind of sick joke?"

I tried to sing some more, but I just couldn't. I felt incredibly stupid. Maybe Mom was wrong. Maybe I misunderstood Mom. *Maybe Mom was just a dream.* Maybe the song was too confusing.

"Dad! Karen is trying to poison you! Get out of there!" My voice was so loud, so shrill, I wondered if anyone could even understand my words.

"Who is this?" said a female voice. It was Karen. I gasped and had no words. In the background I thought I heard Dad. Weeping.

"My husband is ill. Don't call us again," Karen commanded in a voice made of stone. *Click.* All of the breath in me escaped into the emptiness of that sound.

Nick framed my face with his hands, looking deep into my eyes. "Time to try again." I couldn't even speak. Really? Again?

"Hell yes," he said. "Come on, you can't give up this easily. I won't let you!"

So I turned to Lacey and asked, "Please? One more time?"

Her second effort was easier (thank you, redial), but then the phone just rang and rang. No voice mail. No reply. Did Karen disconnect the phone? My lifeline to Dad was severed. I was having trouble breathing, focusing, being.

"I'll come up with a plan B," Nick said.

"That was plan B," I answered.

I wanted to fall apart, but Lacey wasn't letting me off the hook. "Jorge," she said. She dialed the number with furious intensity. Jorge picked up on the very first ring. My eyes were blurry with tears, but I managed to read what Lacey had on the page:

"You're a killer and you're going to burn in hell and nobody likes you." There was more, but he let out a cry and hung up. Lacey looked disappointed.

"You didn't get to the best part of the speech," she complained. "Where I really get nasty with him."

✳ ✳ ✳

We rode the escalator in silence. I didn't want to use my energy for anything other than working with Nick on plan C. But as we neared the top, I noticed something a bit odd about the mall walkers. Bertha was moving among them. She was talking to each of them, one by one, in a sweet, soft voice. So that's what she did at night.

As soon as we stepped onto the floor, Bertha saw us. She marched over like a drill sergeant, ready to have us drop and give her twenty.

"What, what, what, what, *what* were you doing?" she asked. She folded her arms and tapped her toes.

"Take a pill, Bertha," Lacey said casually. "We were just shopping, just hanging out. What's your problem?" Years of practice had made her into a cool liar. But Bertha had even more practice dealing with liars and seeing right through them. Literally.

"Were you interfering with the living? Sarah? Is this about your father?" she asked.

I could have played along with Lacey's lie, but no. I wouldn't. I didn't want to lie about something as important as this, especially as I saw Alice creeping toward us. She waited silently behind Bertha.

"Yes, I was trying to save my dad."

"It was my idea," Nick volunteered. He stood a little closer, and we were magnetically connected. I could do or say anything now.

"But I didn't save him. Yet. And now I'm tired, so if you're going to punish me, can it wait until tomorrow?" Okay, Bertha looked like she was not expecting quite that much truth from us. (Honesty is the best weapon.)

"Do you intend to try this sort of stunt again?" Bertha asked. "Tell the truth."

I looked at Nick before I spoke, and that was all it took to unlock all my secrets. I couldn't lie to him, or in front of him. I wouldn't be that girl.

"Yes, absolutely!" I declared. I felt like I was drunk, operating with severely impaired judgment. I couldn't stop telling the truth. Nick's eyes sparkled in my direction, and I had no filter.

"I won't repeat this exact stunt because, hello, *it didn't work.* I need to come up with a whole *new* stunt. See, here's the thing, Bertha. I'm going to save him, and you're not going to stop me. In fact, you're going to help me. I don't know how yet, but you're going to. *I will save my dad.* Because I owe him. And I'm not going to be able to move on until I know that he's safe."

That sort of made sense to Bertha, so maybe I should have stopped there. But I didn't. I linked my arm through Nick's and felt him tighten his hold on me. "And yes, I'm crazy about Nick. And I want to help him make sure his mom is okay. He deserves that. And if Lacey wants to yell at the guy who killed her, I say let her yell. Let her yell a lot. I'll help her too, if I can."

Bertha's eyes were larger than life. There might have been smoke coming from her ears as her brain burned out just a little.

Lacey broke the silence when she giggled and said, "You're the shit, you know that?"

"Yes, she is," Nick said as he kissed me. But then he looked around at the group of us and decided once again to take the lead. "Bertha? We need to go back to the living. We need to haunt. It's the only way."

Bertha looked ready to pass out.

Nick was about to say more, but then Alice spoke up in her small, still voice. "He's right."

Bertha spun around and focused on Alice, lowering her voice. "The Boy would never allow any of them to go back, to haunt. You of all people must know that. This is madness."

"Maybe so," Alice conceded. "But it's the only way. Can you arrange an audience with the Boy?" She looked up at Bertha and spoke in a different voice. She sounded sharp and determined. "Now, please."

chapter twenty-three

oh boy

We were about to see this Boy, whoever he was. I tried to pre-
dict what he'd be like. I failed big-time. Not even close.

Bertha led us into Toys"R"Us. Really. Seriously.

"Make your case to the Boy," Bertha said. With that, she
pointed.

"This can't be right," I whispered, though I hadn't intended that to be out loud.

Two children, a boy and a girl, were seated on the floor,
playing a board game: Life. They didn't look up at us but were
totally immersed in the game. The boy spun the spinner and
then moved his little toy car figure along the board.

"You will learn about life, when you play the game of Life!"
he sang to himself.

"You've had twins!" the girl declared. "That's expensive."

"But they'll love me," he replied. And then he made loud
fart sounds as he put two little plastic figures into his tiny
plastic car. They both seemed to enjoy his (very realistic)
fart sounds.

"Is he the Boy?" Lacey loud-whispered to Bertha.

The two children looked up.

"You interrupted!" the little boy whined.

"Which is rude!" The little girl echoed the boy's tone and added a tut-tut-tut.

They sighed and pushed the game pieces aside. They were suddenly miserable, sulking with a real sense of drama. The little girl pushed the board away. "Well. Now I don't care about the game anymore."

"You will learn about life, when you play the game of Life!" the boy sang, just as he had before.

They stood up and looked at Bertha. The girl cleared her throat noisily, and Bertha snapped to attention.

"Oh! Where are my manners?" Bertha asked of the air. "Everyone, this is the Boy."

The two children bowed modestly. They looked to be about six years old, maybe seven. "This is Alice, Lacey, Nick, and Sarah. They're here because they wish to go back to the living and haunt them for a time."

They looked at each of us, but before they could speak, they were distracted by the colorful, shiny objects all over the store.

"Oooh, pretty!" the girl said as some sparkly origami paper commanded her attention.

Bertha turned to us. "I've done my part. I've got you an audience with the Boy. Five minutes. If you manage to persuade them to let you haunt, well, then off you go. I'll help you get there. But."

She looked me square in the eye. "But if they say no—and

by the by, they are inclined to say no—I must insist that you follow *my* rules and do as *I* say."

The boy Boy was bouncing a slinky up and down like a yo-yo, until it got tangled. He dropped it and moved on to another toy.

Bertha looked at him, then at us.

"What are you waiting for? Tick-tock, tick-tock! Go to it," she said, and backed away from us, retreating to the store entrance. The boy Boy was staring at Lacey's boobs. I wasn't sure if it was good or bad that she was wearing such a tight, revealing top.

He asked, "Why do you want to go haunting? Do you want to frighten people? Do you want to make them go poopy in their pants?" He cracked himself up with this, but the girl Boy was not amused. She shoved him a bit, and he shoved her back.

(Are these kids ADHD? Can we get them meds at the mall?)

While they fought and accused each other of bad behavior, I took a half step back and drank this all in. This is the collective wisdom of our species? This is the Boss of Me? I flashed back to Bertha explaining the Boy, way back when I first arrived. "We are children," she'd said. Okay, yes. But I had no idea she was being *literal*.

The Boy (they) brought us all over to a toy tea party. We sat in tiny chairs, our knees jutting up uncomfortably. Everyone smiled politely. I glanced back at the store entrance, where Bertha was staring at her shoes.

Nick spoke first, of course. "So. We'd like your permission to haunt the living so that we can—"

But the girl Boy cut him off. "We don't like hauntings. We used to, but we grew up and got over it. You know how that is? The things you thought were so good and so cool when you were little don't seem so cool anymore."

The boy Boy interrupted her, sounding a little over-excited. "Plus. Also. And. In addition. Sometimes we made mistakes. We let people go back and haunt and then they were bad. They wanted to get back at people. They wanted revenge on the human race. Did you ever see *Paranormal Activity 2*? Scary!"

Suddenly he looked at Alice. "You're angry." Alice tried to speak but shook her head and looked down. Her face was reddening at great speed.

He looked at the girl Boy. (His sister? His other self? Whaa?) They spoke in perfect unison: "Why should we let you haunt?" They both looked at Lacey and the girl Boy spoke. "You. Go. What is your unfinished business?"

Lacey's voice was a bit shaky. "Here's the thing. My ex-boyfriend killed me, and everybody covered up for him. He totally got away with it, and somebody needs to—"

Before she could finish speaking, the boy Boy let out a singsong "Re-ve-enge!" comment to the girl Boy. And they seemed done with us already.

"Revengers always get stuck there. It's nasty!" the girl Boy agreed.

"Nuh-uh, I don't want revenge," Lacey began, but they dismissed her with a wave of their hands (and yes, I'm pretty sure she did want revenge).

They turned to Nick. "Why should we let you haunt?"

Nick spoke gently. And if he was nervous, it absolutely

didn't show. "It isn't about revenge. You see, we were taken so suddenly, we just need to make contact. We need to know that it's okay to close the door behind us and be done with the old life so that we can move on to the new."

I liked it. The Boy (both of them) smiled.

Nick continued. "We were young, and we just weren't ready to be gone yet."

The boy Boy jumped up and away from Nick, calling out in a teasing, singsong voice, "No, no, no, no! Too bad, so sad, lots of people die young. I'm hungry. Do they have Twister here? Let's play."

Maybe it wasn't ADHD, but he had some sort of issue. Before I could jump to a diagnosis, I realized that the girl Boy was studying me.

"She's pretty." (Me? She was pointing to me?)

That must have meant that it was my turn. "My murderer is going to kill my dad. And I can't stand by and let that happen."

The boy Boy began humming the theme to *Law & Order*. "Ch-*chung*, da da da da daaaa . . ."

"I can't get back at my murderer, and I'll have to live with that." (The boy Boy sighed, bored, bored, bored.) "But now she's poisoning my dad. He doesn't deserve to die like this. I've got to save him. Whatever the cost."

They got up and stood on either side of me, looking me down and up, down and up. The girl Boy turned and inspected Nick just as closely.

"You're different," the boy Boy said to me. I held my breath, waiting for my avalanche of secrets to be revealed. "You're wasteful. Waste not, want not, I always say. I just wish I knew what that meant."

"You like her," the girl Boy said to Nick. "A lot. A lot, a lot. Didn't Bertha tell you not to fall in love here? Dummy!"

"I couldn't help it," Nick said. "I just wish I had met her when we were alive."

"Hmmmm," the girl Boy replied. I could feel it. They were getting ready to say no and be done.

Then Alice spoke. "Don't leave her in the dark like this. Let her try."

All eyes were now on Alice. Poor Alice. "You're angry," said the girl Boy.

"I'm afraid of the dark." The boy Boy sounded on the verge of tears just thinking about darkness.

"Me too," the girl Boy agreed. "And I don't want to make the pretty girl sad. But she's making such a mess of things! Falling in love? Wanting to haunt?"

I looked up at the boy Boy, but he was squinting at something on the ceiling. I turned to the girl Boy and said, "Please?"

They laughed, sounding surprised and happy. They joined hands and began to skip away, away, out of the store. The girl Boy called over her shoulder to us, "You said the magic word! You may have one day back on Earth. Just one! A-haunting you shall go!"

The boy Boy echoed her song, and they were gone.

Did we just win?

chapter twenty-four

start spreading the news.
i'm leaving today.

Alice, Lacey, and I must have been kidding ourselves. We were going to try to sleep, knowing that we'd return to the land of the living tomorrow? Sleep was impossible. What would we do while we were there? How would I save Dad from Karen? We punctured the darkness and silence with random questions that had no answers.

Me: Is anyone else a little bit scared?

Alice: How could they tell I was angry?

Me: Have they been watching Nick and me?

Lacey: Why aren't they old and wise and stuff?

Me: When we get there, can you guys help me save my dad?

Lacey: Do I still get to kick Jorge's ass?

Me: Does the Boy know the truth about God and religion and Aztec human sacrifices?

Alice: Who looks after those two children here in the afterlife?

Me: Where is my mother right now?

Lacey: What happened to my dog after he died?

Alice: Where else does the Boy go when they're not here?

Lacey: What should I wear?

Me: What will happen to my murderer after she dies?

Lacey: Why can't we have more time to haunt?

Alice: Can I go revisit the place where I died? Can I just haunt it for a little while and be there and see all of its horrible, filthy truth? Can I just go there, just be there and see if it's wreathed in evil, connected somehow to hell and damnation? Can I go there and have a good wallow? Can I?

Lacey: Wow, Alice. Dark much? Look, just try to relax, and breakfast will be here in the morning. Okay?

A long, long silence followed. I think. I thought about Nick, looking out for his mother, protecting her one last time. And then I started wondering about Declan, walking and walking out there in the mall. What else did he know about Karen that I needed to know?

I must have finally slipped into sleep, because I was dreaming. About Declan. Seriously. Not my long-lost mother. Declan. And we were here at the mall. In the dream, he was at Ulta (his favorite store, in the absence of a Kiehl's), exfoliating with such care, you would think that he was performing open-heart surgery.

"This is a dream," I explained.

"I sort of know that," he said as he studied his face. "You kind of yanked me out of my mall-walking nightmare and into your dream."

"I did?" I asked.

"You were thinking about me. You were thinking about what I know about Karen and how to save your dad." That was true. Wow.

"Thanks." With that, he began rinsing his face over a bright stainless-steel basin. He stopped rinsing and added, "I had no idea you were so powerful, Sarah."

"But this is just a dream," I explained as patiently as I could.

"So what? Even if this is just a dream, I like it way better than mall-walking. Can we stay here long enough for me to get some hydration? My skin is so dry right now."

"Um. Sure. I guess," I said. Should I tell him that I didn't know how to control these dreams? And that this probably wasn't real, so his dry skin issues would continue? Nope.

"Look, I know you're worried about your dad, but at least somebody cared that you died," he said. "I thought Karen cared about me. But she didn't."

"Same here," I said. "What do I need to know about her if I'm going to save my dad?"

"She's really smart." Declan patted his face dry ever so gently. "Smarter than you."

"No. I don't accept that," I replied.

"She already outsmarted me," he argued. I didn't have the heart to tell him that this wasn't too challenging. "She looked me right in the eye when she was killing me. She enjoyed it. And I bet this is her idea of fun. She's probably killing your dad and enjoying every second of it. She's psychic."

"Psycho," I quietly corrected him. "And you're not exactly helping."

"Yes I am," he said as his fingers danced over his skin, applying some sort of lotion. "She knows exactly what people want to hear, and then she says it over and over again. I bet he believes everything she says. I bet he trusts her. She's going to outsmart you. Again."

My brain started to whir with a million questions for him. I was so revved up to interrogate him, I woke myself up.

Damn.

✳ ✳ ✳

Why were we even trying to eat breakfast? We were all studying the entrance to the food court, waiting impatiently for Bertha.

"I really wish they had a kitchen here," Nick said, spinning a bagel around like a toy on his finger. "I miss cooking. Cooking is life."

"*Sex* is life," Lacey corrected him. No one argued with her. She looked around at us all and figured out something

156

that should have been obvious by now. "Oh wow. You're all a bunch of virgins!" Again, no one argued with her. "You've got to be kidding me! You missed out on the best thing ever! Sex is like—"

"Bertha!" Nick shouted, and it made for a truly disturbing ending to Lacey's sentence. But there was Bertha standing two feet behind Lacey. Today's ensemble: plaid. Lots and lots of plaid. Enough said.

Nick rose, and we all followed him. "I think we're ready," he said to Bertha.

"You may think so, but I disagree." Bertha scowled at us. "The Boy has granted your wish to haunt. *Unfortunately.* When this is all over, I do hope you'll remember this warning: be careful what you wish for, for you will surely get it."

We gulped into a collective silence as she led us to Bed Bath & Beyond. We couldn't speak because we weren't really together. No. We were each of us caught in our own thoughts, plans, and fears, and all those unanswered questions.

Bertha didn't speak again until we were all in the elevator. I looked around at us, and we all looked so young. There was a kind of purity in the space that took me by surprise.

"You can all stay together or not. That's entirely up to you," Bertha instructed. "But. When the time is up, the time is up. Not five more minutes, not one more minute. At this time tomorrow, I'll collect you, and you're done."

"We'll be here," Nick assured her.

And with that, the elevator began to move. My insides felt all carbonated and jumpy. I wanted the elevator to move faster, faster, faster!

"I'm trying to help you," Bertha said quietly, and I think she was aiming her words at me. "You don't have to resort to taking this kind of risk."

It seemed like the right time to say something to Bertha. (Something kind.) But just then the doors opened and there we were. In the middle of Washington Square Park, in the middle of a freakishly too-warm late spring day. It was madly, insanely, ridiculously, unbelievably, crazily, too too extremely . . . beautiful. So beautiful. And let's be honest here, this wasn't even New York City's prettiest park. How was this even possible?

The greens and blues were so lush and intense, I tilted my head to one side, as if the colors were physically striking me. I smelled the flowers from the flower cart, and felt the breeze, and began to lean toward it all. For a moment I truly believed that this was a trick. It had to be some kind of afterlife magic/deception from Bertha. This wasn't really home, really New York, really the world, really life among the living. It was too amazing. Too vivid. Too astounding.

Was it this wondrous when I was alive? How could I have missed it?

The living swirled and danced and griped and laughed and stomped and ate and smoked and cried around us, through us, before us. We only had one day here but stayed frozen, except for blinking, for a long, long, long time.

Nick broke the silence.

"Look," he said.

"Yes," I answered.

"Wow," Lacey added.

Alice didn't speak at first. She was crying softly, almost gulping at the air. "Can we stop? And savor? Please?"

I turned around and realized that Bertha was gone. I hadn't heard the elevator close behind us. She wasn't there to tell us what fools we were or to remind us that we had such a painfully brief time here. I walked slowly toward the fountain.

The sky was absurdly, unrealistically blue, and the sun seemed a bit punishing for the living, shouting out a warning that summer would be brutal. I loved it. The sparkling gray fountain was being used today as a glorious kiddie wading pool. Half-naked toddlers splashed, crawled, swam (sort of), and dunked themselves into the cool oasis.

If Nick hadn't tugged at my arm, I might have stared at them all day.

"Hey," he said. His voice sounded sweeter here, more musical. "Look over there." He pointed east, and I squinted at a big gray cube of a building. "See that one? On Greene Street? That's where I lived—where I spent my whole life."

"I lived over there." I pointed west. I turned to him and put on my best let-me-state-the-obvious face. "We were so close together, but we never met," I said. "Not once. Not until we died. And we know that we crossed paths. We were in the same space, but how often? And why didn't we meet? Why?"

"Don't let it shake you, Sarah." He touched my chin, tipping my face up toward his. The sun and blue sky around his face were too much for me. And then his kiss sent me into a new realm of feeling. "It's only inexplicable," he added.

There was a musician in a straw hat playing guitar near the big arch at the north end of the park. His sound took over and commanded our attention. He was pretty good, covering pop tunes, converting them all into soulful ballads, and it worked. A small cluster of people watched, listened, and dropped the occasional dollar into his guitar case. There was a strawberry-blond little girl in the group, who looked to be about eight or nine years old, beaming with joy. She started singing along. She was pretty good, staying on key and in rhythm. The musician smiled as he played and urged her to take a bow when the song was done.

"Elizabeth Anne!" A harried mother yanked the girl by the arm. "Stop wandering off like that!" she cried, and rushed her out of the park; the little girl's strawberry-blond hair bounced in the breeze as she started a new song. Nick broke the spell for me.

"Guys! We have to snap out of this. We have a life to save!" he said.

"And I have an ass to kick," Lacey added.

✷ ✷ ✷

We walked, but it felt different from normal walking. We were sort of weightless. I daydreamed that we could have jumped to a treetop. I led our ghostly parade to my front door.

"Hi, Eduardo," I said to the doorman. (Habit.) He didn't hear us, see us, or look up from his newspaper.

"Lacey? Can you press the elevator button for us?" I asked. She was the designated mover-of-objects, after all.

"I don't think we'll need that," Nick said. "Look." He passed through the door to the stairs and up he went. Yes, okay. Very nice. But I lived on the seventh floor. That's a lot of climbing.

Only we didn't have to climb. We semi-floated up, tied with a lot less gravity, almost like astronauts on the moon. Sorry to be such an obvious amateur. This was my first time being dead (as far as I knew). We reached the seventh floor with the ease of an untethered balloon. And there we were.

Home. I pushed my palm against the door, and felt that itchy presence of hard reality on my skin.

I breathed in, closed my eyes, and pressed forward, enduring the overall woolly itch for just a second.

Home.

chapter twenty-five

what's the secret of life? timing.

We could all do it. We could pass through the door. I worried that it might be tougher for Lacey, since she could actually make contact with things. But she slipped right through along with the rest of us. (Never underestimate Lacey.)

"Wow. Nice place, Sarah," Nick said. "A shame you had to die and stop living in the lap of luxury."

"I take it you had your own bedroom?" Alice asked. "In my day, that was unheard-of."

"My room is upstairs," I said.

"You have an *upstairs*?" Lacey asked with a heavy dose of anger in her voice. Her arms were folded over her chest, and her face was carved with a deep scowl. "If we were alive, I'd probably hate you. And try to beat you up."

"We're here to save Sarah's father," Nick said. (Thanks for the subject change.) "We need to look for anything that might be poison. Let's destroy whatever supply she has."

"You mean me." Lacey puffed up a bit. "You mean *I* destroy the supply. After all, I'm the destroyer."

I stopped everything and smiled at her. "And I'm forever grateful. Really."

Nick clapped to get our attention. "Let's start the search in the kitchen, then the bedroom and the bathroom."

"Bathrooms," I corrected him quietly.

Lacey placed both fists on her hips. "Did you actually have your own bathroom? You would have been so easy to hate."

Before I could say a word, Alice said, "My family shared a filthy water closet down the hall with three other families. We've all had our trials. We all got ourselves killed. All right?"

"And now"—Nick picked up the thread—"we have one day here, so let's get to work."

We threw ourselves into it. Starting with the bathrooms, ending with the kitchen. Search, search, look, look. Nothing.

"I don't even know what we're looking for," I complained. "How will we know if we find it?"

Nick shook his head. "Come on, now. Think. It won't be marked with a skull and crossbones. It'll be disguised, so this won't be easy. But we'll find it."

Search, search, look, look.

The kitchen was stocked with kale, quinoa, beets, Brazil nuts, sardines, and gluten-free bran muffins. For a moment I was glad to be dead.

"It'd be easy to hide it in the vitamin supplements," Nick suggested as we studied the shelf of vitamins. She had the whole alphabet of stuff in stock.

"You said something about her offering him tea at the end of the funeral," Nick reminded me. (This boy really paid attention.) "Maybe it's already in the tea?" He pointed to a big glass jar next to the sink. It was filled with dried green and

brown tea leaves and herbs. It was labeled HEART AND SOUL
TEA.

"If this is what she's using to poison him, it either already
has the poison, or the gross taste of it disguises the poison,"
Lacey reasoned (brilliantly). "This has to go." She flicked at
the jar's side. It didn't budge. "This thing's a lot heavier than
a Lego," she explained. She looked a bit disappointed in herself.

"Lacey, you can do this," Nick urged her. "Knock this thing
down."

We all gathered around her and watched as she flicked,
pushed, nudged, and hit. For me the attention would have
been paralyzing, but Lacey fed off our energy and focus. She
loved it. She made contact twice, and we all heard it. She let
out a small grunt as she pushed against the jar again. Again.
Again. I was beginning to think that she might tell me she was
giving up. But not Lacey. She smashed against the jar and it
shattered into the sink.

Lacey was a little out of breath and a lot proud.

"Can you turn on the water? And tap that button?" I asked
her. She did, and the tea went down the garbage disposal.
Gone for good. Maybe it wasn't enough to save Dad, but it was
a start.

A really, really good one.

Where was Dad? I was waiting around for him, but I didn't
see him. Where the hell was he? And where was murderous,
lying, evil Karen?

"Maybe he's at work?" Alice suggested.

No way. If she began poisoning him at my funeral, he should be in pretty bad shape. And even my dad, the workaholic of all time, would be too sick for work.

"Okay, look," Lacey said in her take-charge voice. "We only get one day here, and no offense, but I don't want to spend it staring at you guys and waiting for somebody to come home. I have to go. I have to find Jorge. I have a message for him."

There was a dark silence after that. Lacey couldn't be heard by the living, so her message was going to be physical, I guess. I didn't want to know the details.

"It isn't all about *you*, ya know," Lacey added. "I got my own unfinished business and I gotta go finish it. So does Nick."

She was right.

"Sarah." Nick sounded so tentative. He was tiptoeing on thin ice with each word. "I need to check on my mom. I have no idea how she's doing. And there's nobody else to look after her. I have to. Really."

Here's what I didn't say: Everybody please, please stay here and help me because my unfinished business is more important than your unfinished business because mine is mine. So shut up. Sit tight. We're going to wait for my dad and evil Karen.

Here's what I did say: "Thank you, guys. All of you. You've already been so generous, using part of your haunting time to help me. Please go and do what you have to do. We'll all meet up in the park when it's time to go back." Because that's what I absolutely had to say. It nearly killed me, except that I was dead.

Nick did that half grin and wrapped me up in his arms. I

closed my eyes, grateful that his scent translated here to the real world. It was sort of like taking some kind of meds to calm me down. (Or rev me up. Not sure.) His kiss changed my body chemistry. I was convinced that joy was now part of my DNA, thanks to Nick. His face pressed against the side of my neck.

"I don't get what you see in her," Lacey said to Nick. He and I broke from our kiss with a laugh.

I must let him go (stay). I must let him go (stay). I must let him go (stay).

Lacey disappeared through the door, and Nick was next. He paused for a bit, and I sort of leapt to the fantasy that he might stay. *(Stay!)*

"See you soon!" he called. "Be strong. You can do this!" He was gone in an instant.

I stared at the door, not sure if I was looking for Nick to change his mind or for the door to unlock and reveal my dad.

"Now, now. You're not going to waste this opportunity just sitting here like a bump on a log!" said Alice.

Alice! I had completely forgotten that she was even there. She looked rather stern. For Alice.

"I can stay with you," Alice explained. "After all, the people from my time are long dead. So let's go to your father's place of work. Perhaps he's strong enough to be there."

chapter twenty-six

no no no no no no no no no no no
no no no no no no no no no no no
no no no no no sign of dad

Not at work. Not near work. Not at his favorite restaurant. Not at his doctor. And my one single solitary day here on Earth was slipping through my fingers.

"What if we're too late? What if he's dead?" I asked Alice as we floated through and among the very well-dressed population of the cool downtown Manhattan scene, searching place after place. We were adrift in Tribeca.

"He's alive. If he were dead, you'd know," Alice assured me. "There would be signs of it at home or at work. Death leaves a big footprint." And that made sense to me. "He's alive. You just don't know where he is."

"What if he's in a hospital somewhere? Which one? How would I find him?" I asked her/me. It was an impossible question.

"Oh! Did you have a vacation home?" Alice suggested. "Could he be there?"

"No. Dad worked all the time, so we weren't big on vacations," I explained. "Do you think the Boy will give me an extension? Let me have one day here *while my dad's around?*"

"No, Sarah. They won't allow that, I'm quite sure." She stopped talking. Her breathing was quick and shallow. She pointed west, but she couldn't seem to manage any more words. She came out with "Oh. Ohhhhh."

"Alice? What is it? What's over there?"

"There." She pointed to a brick and stone building that housed a chic-looking Portuguese restaurant. "That's where."

"Where what?"

She went toward it. Drawn almost (almost) against her will. And then I knew. Of course. "Is this where you died?"

She nodded, mute. "It was a factory back then. Some of the front is the same as it was. Only some."

We entered the restaurant and I said gently, "Hey, Alice. Let's get a table."

Alice looked at me as if I'd just expressed a completely revolutionary thought. We needed to search for my dad, we needed to save him. I knew that. But she needed to do this first. I owed it to her.

She followed me to a table in the back. The restaurant wasn't very busy yet. The menu was written in silver paint on an antique mirror. I couldn't pronounce any of it. But it looked pretty.

Alice was working so hard to hold herself together, that much was obvious. The place was charged with electric energy that coursed through her and only her. All I could do was watch. And listen.

"What ever became of Joe O'Hara?" I asked.

"He died," Alice said, her voice even and expressionless.

"Bertha told me. It was his liver. His death was slow. But not painful. They have drugs for that. Alas."

"Did you ever meet up with him?" I asked, sort of horrified. "In the afterlife?"

Alice shook her head. "The Boy is capricious. But not quite that cruel."

We watched the beautiful people around us as they studied the menu by flickering candlelight.

"The entrance was over there." She pointed to the left. "The stairs all the way back there. I was upstairs when it happened." She looked up at the ceiling and stared at it for so long, I wondered if she could see through it.

"This place isn't evil," she said at last. "It's just that something bad happened here. It's just that a very bad man was here. A long time ago."

She stared in silence for a while longer. There were candles flickering on every table, creating a soft, ethereal space.

"It's nice that the place is pretty now," she said. "And it's all about food. And romance. Did you ever have a beau when you were alive?"

"No," I answered. "That was for other people. Not for me."

"So. What has changed?" Alice had a small smile as she spoke.

Alice was adding to the list of impossible questions. Yes, something had changed. Actually, everything had changed.

Two very beautiful men were being escorted to our table. We hopped out of the seats and glided away.

"That may be a nice restaurant, but I think I prefer the food court," I said as we left. Back out on the sidewalk, the place lost some of its hold on Alice.

"He lives on, you know," she said, walking away from it. Not looking back. "Joe O'Hara. He had children. And grandchildren. And great-grandchildren. The world is full of Joe O'Haras." She walked a bit faster. "My family died off."

I couldn't keep walking. "Oh, Alice. I'm so sorry."

She stopped and turned to face me. Sorrow was a kind of mist all around her, melting into the dark blue of the evening light.

"Me too." She choked out the words, then gathered her strength. "Now. What are we doing here? We need to save your father from his evil wife."

My home was still empty and dark, and I thought that the cruel frustration of my plight could just possibly push me over the edge to complete insanity. Alice must have sensed it.

"Your home overlooks the park," she exclaimed. "We'll go. We can watch for him there. Would you mind?"

"Of course not. It's your haunting too." And it was a good idea. I could wait there for signs of his return. But truly, Alice and I could drink in all the light and sparkle of life around us. And maybe it would stop me from losing my mind.

chapter twenty-seven
how to kick ass

Oh, this park.

We sat still and watched as night fell, like it always did. The city lights decorated the world like they always did—crazy warm yellow lights from the windows around Washington Square, and insistent blue-white shop lights. No wonder it was so hard to see the stars in the city sky. Too much furious competition. I forced myself to look away. Watch for Dad. Watch for Karen.

I smiled and chose to ignore the sizzling lump of worry in my heart. Lucky for me, I got the perfect distraction from all thoughts, worries, or concerns in the form of Lacey. She had been gone for hours, but then her voice sailed over to us.

"Hey!" She looked absolutely triumphant. "Wait till you hear what happened to me."

I couldn't help myself. I loved Lacey's story. And she so obviously loved telling it.

LACEY'S GUIDE TO HAUNTING THE LIVING.
ESPECIALLY THE ONE WHO KILLED YOU.

So here's the thing: Most people are not okay with the memory of killing somebody. Unless there's something wrong with them. But that wasn't the case with Jorge. He pushed Lacey because he was all sad and angry and hurt and kind of drunk.

He felt bad about it. Which was good.

Lacey found him at school. He was getting his stuff from his locker. People walked right by him like he was invisible, but then they turned to check him out as soon as they got past him. They whispered to each other as soon as they were far enough away from him. It was hard to tell if he knew they were doing that.

Lacey hoped that he knew, and that it upset him. A lot.

Okay, so it sucked that Lacey's friends didn't hand him right over to the police. But they obviously didn't like having a murderer in their midst. That was a start. It just wasn't enough.

Lacey saw her so-called friends coming down the hallway. They were three giggling little bitches who looked super-happy. The moment she saw them, her fury took over. They looked way happier than she had ever seen them when she was alive and bossing them around. Their giggles sounded like fingernails on a chalkboard. How dare they giggle at all in a post-Lacey world?

No time to think (which was an overrated activity, in Lacey's opinion). Instead she just did what she really wanted to do: she shoved one of the girls. Hard. That spinning, whirling fury inside her was working perfectly. Girl One fell into the next, who fell into the next. It was Girl Dominoes, and it made Lacey happy.

Girl One pulled herself together and turned on Jorge. "Watch it, asshole!"

"What did I do?" he asked. Lacey had never noticed before how nasal his voice was. "You tripped. It wasn't my fault."

Girl One came close to him and hissed her words. "Just remember. We know something that *was* your fault. So watch it."

Jorge was practically choking with fear. Lacey clapped her hands in delight. Okay yes, she would still love to send him to prison for the rest of his miserable life. But it was awesome to see him suffer like this. Would he suffer forever and ever? How great would that be?

The girls strutted away. Lacey shouted after them, "Hey! Your butt looks flat in those jeans!" but there was no sign that anybody heard her.

Oh well. At least Jorge looked nauseous. And Lacey noticed that he was thinner than ever before. Awesomely awesome. That should make this next part even easier.

She followed him toward the stairwell. The perfect spot. The stairs were cruel, made of worn stone with metal edges. They had a heavy iron railing on one side and cinder block on the other. No place for a soft landing. She was summoning all her strength, all her rage. How could she have gotten so lucky? This was more perfect than anything she could have planned. (See? Thinking really is overrated.) She needed to find the right angle to shove him. Wouldn't it be so ironic and all kinds of perfect if she broke his neck?

He reached the top of the stairs. But instead of stepping forward, instead of lurching forward into his doom, he crumpled and collapsed. He sat on the top step and covered his face with his hands. He cried like a little girl, all high-pitched and whiny.

"I'm sorry," he whispered. "I'm sorry, I'm sorry, I'm sorry."

Lacey took a step back. His suffering looked so huge from here.

"Yeah," she said quietly. "You *should* cry. I guess you can't help being a complete and total loser. You were born that way. Loser."

He just kept crying, and eventually Lacey got sick of it. She turned to leave, but then no. Not so fast. She returned to Jorge one last time. She gave him a good swift kick in the head. It lacked the fury she needed to really hurt him, but he felt something. He paused from his girly crying to rub his head in confusion.

She crouched down next to him and said,

"Don't you ever, ever lift your hand to hurt another girl ever again, as long as you live. And the next time you're at a roof party—if anyone ever invites you to anything ever again—*stay in the living room.*"

He was staring into space, still rubbing the spot where she had kicked him.

"And I hope I just gave you a *huge* headache," Lacey said as she left.

She went straight to Harry's grave. It was adorned with a simple headstone and a spray of fresh flowers. She told him the whole story and decided that somehow he could hear her and that he thought her story was perfect. She decided he was proud of her for kicking Jorge but not killing him. She decided that he would have hugged her and kissed her and told her she was amazing.

She felt good, like she had just eaten somebody else's dessert. Lacey was, after all, still Lacey.

chapter twenty-eight
you'll never walk alone, even if you want to

We were not alone. Most of the time I kept my gaze on my apartment building entrance, looking up to our windows every now and then. Dark and still no change. Fine. I had nothing else to do, nothing better. I could wait. I just wished Dad would show up soon. Alive and well. And freshly divorced. I needed Nick here to reassure me. I wasn't really good at it.

So we three dead girls were hanging out in Washington Square Park, like you do, when I realized that some of the lingering crowd was, well, unusual.

"Look at that guy." I pointed to an iridescent-looking businessman. He was wandering aimlessly around the fountain, almost like the mall walkers. But he was talking to himself nonstop.

"He's a ghost," Alice explained. "But then again, so are we."

"Look at me!" Lacey exclaimed. "I'm all bedazzled and stuff." Sure enough, she shimmered in the night. So did I. So did Alice. So did a whole bunch of people in the park.

"When did they get here?" I asked.

"They were here already," Alice said. "Before we arrived. In fact, some of them have been dead quite a long time. They're harder to see in sunlight. But at night you can see how different they are from the living. I mean, how different *we* are."

She was right. During the day I never noticed them, as they were overpowered by all that light and life and beauty. Now they gathered around the park, like fireflies with a blue-white glow.

A middle-aged couple, brightly lit, walked hand in hand. At first, I thought they were wearing costumes, because they looked like extras from *The Great Gatsby*. She was a flapper, and he was a tuxedo dude. How the hell long had they been dead?

They didn't seem to notice us. They were caught in a conversation loop.

She: It wasn't my fault.

He: Yes, it was.

She: It wasn't my fault.

He: Yes, it was.

And on and on. Living people passed through the dead and even sat on them. A beautiful young (living) woman was sitting on a park bench, totally unaware of the disgusting pervy ghost whose lap she was on. She was talking on her phone while he laughed, enjoying the hell out of this situation. He had bad teeth and bug eyes.

"I've sat on these benches a thousand times," I said. "I wish I could take a shower right now."

"Hey!" Lacey shouted at the pervy ghost. "You! Move it! Leave her alone!"

The ghost flinched and muttered and slunk away. The girl continued her conversation, still oblivious.

We sat on a grassy knoll and watched the life and death surround us. I hugged my knees and tried not to worry about Dad or think about Nick (too much). (Welcome to my losing battle.)

"Those ghosts, they're stuck here," Alice explained. "Forever."

"Why?" Lacey asked.

"Oh, it's all too easy to get stuck here," Alice said. "Sometimes people don't come back from their funerals. Sometimes people come back to haunt, but then they stay. Sometimes it's easier, it's comfortable, being stuck with what you know. Even if it's not very nice." She took a breath and added, "Not everybody wants to move on, you know."

"But *you* do. Right?" I confirmed with Alice. She nodded, but really I wanted something much stronger from her. After all, the girl had been dead for decades and she still hadn't moved on. (Let me add this to my list of things to worry about.)

A young woman sat down right next to us. She hugged her knees, just as I was doing. It took me a moment to see the halo light of death all around her. A fellow ghost.

"Hello," I said.

"Hi, yes, hi. Hello to you! Hello!" she said with an upsetting level of eagerness. (Why had I said hello to her? I was a New Yorker. I should have known better. Besides, I really wanted to keep my eyes trained on my building.)

"Did you come from the mall?" the girl asked. "Were you there? Were you? At the mall? Were you at the mall? You were. I can tell. You were at the mall."

She was manic and painfully, skeletally thin. If I had seen her like this when I was alive, maybe she wouldn't have looked quite as frightening as she did tonight. Maybe I would have assumed she was a dancer. But seeing her in the blue glow of death in the night, she was particularly terrifying.

"Yes," I said, and then tried to start up a chat with Alice and Lacey. But the skinny manic girl wasn't letting up, and she wasn't open to hints.

"I left. I left. I left the mall. I'm here now." She repeated herself a few more times, and I tried to find a way to make a clean break from her. Lacey and Alice were no help, as they were staring at her protruding cheekbones and hollow eyes. I was hoping Lacey would come out with some smart-ass command to scare this ghost away.

But then the girl rose. "Okay. Break's over! I have to keep moving." She began to jog in place. "I have to go. I have to go," she repeated as she started to jog away. And then she added, "So close to my goal weight!"

"Wow," Lacey said. "Some people take their crazy with them when they die, huh?"

Alice nodded vigorously. "This is the one thing that's worse than mall-walking. At least I could wake up. Eventually. But these people . . ." She finished her sentence by shuddering.

Back to my vigil. Watch for Dad. Watch for Dad. Focus. Where the hell was Nick?

Off to my left, I recognized the guy in the shabby suit. Oh no. He was the one who screamed at people. All this time I thought he had just been a (scary) dream. I stared at him a little too long and caught his attention. Now he was heading right toward us, revving up for a big fat scream.

"Look down!" I shouted to Alice and Lacey.

"Why?" Lacey just *had* to ask.

"Now!" I shouted back, and we were all staring at the ground. Mr. Scream went past us and found someone else to scream at when they made the mistake of looking at him.

"Well!" Lacey had her taking-charge voice on. "Why are we hanging out here? Why don't we go someplace?"

"I can't," I said. "My dad will be back soon. I hope." That sounded a little too pessimistic. "I came here to save him. I can't miss my chance."

"Yeah, well, good luck and all," Lacey said as she stood up. "Me, I want to go find the homes of famous people and see if I can catch them naked." She was so proud of this plan she let out a little giggle.

✳ ✳ ✳

Minus Lacey, the park was amazingly quiet. My vigil continued, but my gaze drifted, just a little. I stretched out on the grass and studied the misty night sky. Then I turned onto my side and stared at the apartment entrance. Dad, where the hell could you be?

"Do you think Nick is okay?" I asked.

"Nick is the kind of boy who always manages to be okay,"

Alice said. I decided not to say, "Except for when he ended up shot to death at sixteen."

I propped myself up on my elbow. "You've haunted before." I said it as a statement, not a question.

Alice nodded. "Yes. It ended badly."

"How?"

Alice seemed to be climbing over some kind of wall to get an answer. "I . . . I nearly got stuck. I couldn't stop screaming at Joe O'Hara." I think she needed a moment to stop seeing or hearing it in her memory. "But Bertha grabbed me by the collar and took me back. I was so upset, I walked for twenty-three years. I missed World War Two."

"We won't get stuck here," I assured her. And me.

"No. We won't let that happen," Alice agreed. "We'll let go when the time comes. And let's face it, Nick would never let us get stuck." True.

We let darkness and silence wash over us.

"The sky is crazy beautiful," I said.

"Try not to love it too much, Sarah. It will end badly."

chapter twenty-nine

clues to reveal total dysfunction

Maybe it was his shoulders. Maybe it was his grin. Maybe it was the fact that he could cook and he liked to take charge. Something in me felt safe and okay when Nick was around, like I had just gotten a warm blanket wrapped around me. Any and all stomach knots untied. So when Nick finally came back to the park, I resisted the urge to yell at him and shake him for staying away so long and making me worry so hard. And it's a good thing I resisted.

He sat on the grass and ran his hands through his hair, turning his gaze to the sky. I felt like I could see him putting his story away. "Any sign of your dad?" he asked.

I shook my head. "What happened to you?"

He sighed and looked at the ground now. "It was rough," he said with some finality, as if I'd let him say so little. Something happened, and it got to him. We sat on the grass as he told the story of his haunting.

SOMETHING WENT WRONG WHEN NICK WAS TRYING TO HELP HIS MOM

Okay, so he knew she'd be a mess, but he didn't know she'd be a *mess*. He found her passed out in the living room with the lights on and the TV at full blast. The randomly scattered stuff everywhere made it look like someone had lifted the whole apartment and dropped it. He tried talking to her, but he didn't know how to make himself heard. He tried cleaning up after her, but he didn't know how to move objects here.

He studied her, the apartment, and he put together a list of the clues that it offered.

The Lean Cuisine boxes: Okay, yes, she was eating, but did she have to go for this frozen, processed crap? Did she learn nothing from him? He used to talk about what he was cooking while he was cooking it and then interrogate her about it while she ate. Right now it looked like she hadn't been listening at all.

The half-consumed Smirnoff bottle by her side, the empty one on the floor, and the full one on the kitchen counter: She was drinking way too much, drowning her grief. When Nick was alive, he had witnessed much smaller-scale bouts, usually after a bad breakup. But this one already looked worse than all of them combined.

The absence of makeup on her face: She wasn't back at work yet. When Nick was alive, he was sometimes annoyed at the time she devoted to her elaborate hair and makeup routine. "I don't go outside without my face!" she would insist. Right now she had no face.

The TV tuned to NY1, the all-day New York news channel: She was focused on finding more news about her son's murder. When Nick was alive, she only ever watched the news for the weather report, then turned to her favorite reality shows.

The absence of any signs of outside activity: She wasn't going out into the world, Nick concluded. Not even a little bit. She was having her frozen groceries and her vodka delivered, according to the receipts on the kitchen floor. When Nick was alive they went out into the world every day. The air here was stale and sad.

Poor woman. She was lost and alone. When Nick was alive he could have done something about this. Probably. Tonight he had to snap her out of this, even if it killed him. All over again.

He kept watch by her side, and then, in the middle of the night, his mom got up and stumbled to the kitchen. She stood at the sink, fished out a glass, and rinsed it for a long minute, then filled it to the top with cool water. She took a slow sip.

"Okay, Mom. I know you're incredibly sad. But you need to take better care of yourself than this. Please. For me."

And then things went kind of wrong. His mom dumped the water back into the sink and reached for the vodka. She poured a tall glass and squinted at it.

Nick watched her from the living room, half-wanting to give up and retreat out of the apartment. In all his living years, he had never ever seen her so self-destructive, so wrong, so incredibly stupid.

"Stop this! Don't do it!" he shouted, his own fury surprising him. She didn't hear him, he was sure.

She looked at the clear liquid in her dirty glass and muttered, "What's the point?"

"The *point*? What's the *point,* Mom? You're alive!" Nick berated her from across the living room. "And you're wasting it. Your life really is going to end one day. And you'd better get yourself together before then. Go somewhere and be alive! That's the point! Go out into this unbelievably beautiful world before you can't do it anymore. Stop this!"

She took a big swallow of her drink. She winced a bit as it went down. And now Nick had no pity for her, only rage.

"Are you doing this because of me? Is this your tribute to me?" he shouted. "Is this what my life meant?" He kept shouting at her, ranting at her, tearing into her, pleading with her. All right across from her. And when she opened her eyes from her post-vodka wince, she saw him. She saw her dead son, tragic and angry, right in front of her.

The glass slipped from her fingers and shattered.

She screamed and ran toward him. "Nick! Nicky! *My baby!*"

She reached for him, but just like that he disappeared. She stood in the middle of the room and turned in circles again, again, again. And then she stopped.

"Jesus," she said aloud. "Wow. This is bad."

She stood there, not speaking, just looking around her.

"I'm sorry," Nick whispered. "I didn't mean to scare you like that. I better go now. Take care of yourself, Mom. Stop all this shit, okay? I love you."

His forehead was crisscrossed with worry. Was he trying to come up with a new plan? Was he regretting this one?

"Wow," I said. "You don't have to stay here. Do you want to go check on her now?"

"No," Nick said slowly, shaking his head. "I've freaked her out enough for now. If she sees me again, I might push her over the edge. Besides, she's sleeping it off right now. I'll go back in the morning. When her head is clear."

✗ ✗ ✗

Sunlight began to slice through the night sky. It made the ghosts blend in with the living, who emerged to begin a new day. Weary parents and nannies filled the playground behind us with running, stumbling, screeching children. They were all oblivious to the ghosts surrounding them. Good.

Nick kept looking around, like maybe his mother was going to show up in the park any second now. Okay, anyone could tell that Nick wanted to break away from my soon-to-be-failed mission. (Who could blame him?)

"Go. Check on your mother," I urged him. "That's what you came here to do. Something tells me that I've wasted my haunting." I gestured toward my building. "At least one of us should get this right."

He stood up and tugged me to standing. When he kissed me goodbye, he transmitted his ever-present joy and excitement. "It's all going to be okay! You'll see." He took a few steps, then hurried back and kissed me once more.

"I promise," he whispered into my ear. I captured the scent of trees and rainstorms. I felt like a kid, wanting him to pinky-swear that it would indeed be okay. Okay would be a miracle.

He left the park, passing by two small children, a boy and a girl, playing underneath the big arch that welcomed the world to this park. He didn't seem to notice them, immersed in their own complicated game.

"You cheated! You opened one eye and saw me!" the girl accused.

"Nuh-uh! I don't know how to open just one eye!" the boy shouted back.

It was the Boy. When they saw Alice and me, they stopped playing and ran to us.

"It's the pretty girl and the angry girl!" she squealed.

"You're here?" I asked.

"Duh!" he said. "Yeah!"

"Did you save your daddy?" she asked. "Are you a ghost hero?"

"Almost," I said. The boy and girl exchanged a knowing look. "I mean, my friends and I may have destroyed the poison. I just need to give a warning to my dad. Which reminds me: I'm wondering if I could have a bit more time here? Please?"

"No way, José!" the boy Boy said.

"You have just a little bit of time left! A li-i-i-i-ttle bitty bit!" the girl Boy said.

"She seems nice," the boy Boy said. He was pointing to the little strawberry-blond girl who had been singing yesterday. Little Elizabeth Anne. She was holding her mother's hand, crossing through the park with a school backpack. She sang quietly to herself, and everything about this simple act was innocent and beautiful.

Oh no. Did the Boy's attention to her mean that Elizabeth Anne might die soon? (Oh please, please no. How many people can I save while I'm here?)

"Look!" the girl Boy said. "Pay attention, dummy! He's right there!"

I spun around to look at the building I'd been staring at all night, and there he was. Dad. I blinked hard to make sure I wasn't hallucinating. I wasn't. That was my dad. *(My dad! Alive! Right there!)* He was getting out of a taxi. With Karen.

I raced out of the park over to his side.

"You almost missed him!" the girl Boy reprimanded me. "Don't be such a dummy!"

chapter thirty

never break a promise
to a dead girl

I made a terrible, sad sound when I got next to Dad. He had
lost some hair. His skin was grayish, with a papery quality.
He looked thin, and his eyes were sunken. He didn't stand up
straight, and he moved slowly. Oh, what I would give for the
power to kick Karen into traffic.

I shadowed them in the lobby, where Karen was explaining
to Eduardo that Dad's "cardiac episode was fairly minor. But
we're not taking any chances. Bed rest for you, mister!" she
said with a *(fake)* smile.

"Glad you're feeling better," Eduardo said. But Dad just
shrugged. He opened his mouth to speak, but he was too slow.

"He's on some pretty powerful medications," Karen said.
"It's making him a little loopy." She turned to Dad. "That's
okay. I'm here to take care of you!"

Karen pressed the elevator button with pushy authority.

"This is it," I called to Alice as I floated upstairs and into
the apartment. Here we go.

As Alice slipped through the door, she assured me, "You can do this."

And then the key turned in the lock. Karen was chattering away. "Remember what the doctor said. Lots of rest. Healthy foods. Not too much salt. You've been under stress! I'm here to take care of all that. No more stress!"

Dad nodded slowly. My heart fell to my feet now that I was really able to study him. How much longer could he last? How much was he suffering right now? He looked like a mere fraction of his full self.

He slipped out of his shoes and thudded his body onto the couch. Taking hold of a pillow, he laid himself down.

"Dad! Get up! Up! Up! Up!" I sounded like a dog trainer. "Don't fall asleep here. Go outside. Now."

He closed his eyes.

"I'll just make you a nice pot of tea," Karen sang out from the kitchen. "Won't that be . . ." She paused, then marched back into the living room. She saw the damage we (Lacey) had done, and she looked pissed. Excellent.

"Charlie? Who else has keys to this place? Did Eduardo let himself in? Or that night guy, Samson?"

Dad didn't answer. He was drifting away. Karen's smile curled and expanded, like the Grinch. "Never mind," she whispered. "Where there's a will, there's me!" She laughed at her stupid, sick, awful, not-funny joke. Dad was asleep. But not peaceful.

Karen returned to the kitchen, singing to herself.

"She's bad, that one," Alice whispered to me. "She scares

me." I had no time to comfort Alice. Not now. I crouched next to Dad and took a deep breath.

Turn your face to me
Turn your face and see

(I felt like an idiot singing this song to him.)

All the pain surrounding you

It worked. His eyes were closed, but he whispered, "Sarah."

"Yes, Dad, yes! It's me! Sarah! I'm right here!" There was no word in the English language to describe the combination of joy, fear, and sheer determination that was bursting my heart with atomic power. I was doing exactly what I was meant to do.

"Dad! Get out of here! Right now! Karen is dangerous. She's killing you, and you have to get away from her."

"Sarah," he whispered again.

Karen emerged from the kitchen holding a large plastic container labeled SELENIUM and a spoon. "Did you say something?" she asked.

"Sarah," he repeated. His breathing was fast, and his face twisted in pain.

Karen smiled and bounced her eyebrows, like this was a good sign. The kettle whistled, summoning her back to her terrible task.

"You're scaring him," Alice advised. "Sing again."

There was no time to argue or debate. I dropped the song I wrote at the mall and just sang the words that I needed to say to him.

Dad, get out of here
Don't let Karen near
She will kill you, if she can

He blinked his eyes open but didn't look at me or Alice.

"She will kill me if she can," he mumbled. He sat up a bit and spoke more clearly. "Get out of here. Get out of here."

"Yes, Dad. Now. Run! Just go! Please!" I cried, trying and failing to pull him out of this place.

"Come on, Dad. Go. *Now!*" I shouted. *"Karen's going to kill you!"*

He pulled himself up from the sofa. Good. Keep going. He took a few steps toward the door, but Karen came in. "What are you trying to say, Charlie? I wish you would just speak up!"

"I'm . . . I'm tired, and I . . ." He spoke slowly. She was turning one hand in a circle, as if to say *Hurry up*. She gave up on having him finish the sentence.

"Go upstairs, then. Go. The tea is giving me trouble, but I've got some broth. That should do the job."

Karen stood and watched Dad. He looked to the front door, then to the stairs.

"Well? Go, go, go!" Karen commanded him.

I shouted "No!" over her, but she won. Dad nodded obediently and went to the stairs.

"Please! Get out of here!" I pleaded with him.

"Did you say something?" she asked, more than a little bit annoyed. It was obviously an effort for Dad to climb the stairs. She let out a groan and muttered under her breath, "Oh, you try my patience, old man, you really do." But then she raised her voice and said, "Doctor's orders: go to bed!"

She spun on her heels and went back to the kitchen.

"Alice, Sarah, Lacey, Nick. It's time." Bertha's voice boomed through me.

"Sarah?" Alice's voice was tiny and terrified. "We must go! Please! I don't want to get stuck here."

"You go." I spoke to Alice but kept my focus on Dad. He was standing perfectly still on the stairs. I couldn't tell if he was going to keep climbing, fall to the floor in a final heart attack, or turn and make his escape. I wasn't going to leave until I knew.

"Hurry!" Alice said as she disappeared through the door.

"Tell Bertha I'll be right there. Don't worry." Please note that I didn't promise. I couldn't.

"Come on, Dad." I started singing to him again. *"Dad, get out of here! Don't let Karen near!"*

That did it. He turned away from the stairs and, pretty quickly for a sick guy, moved to the door. He even checked to see if Karen saw him. She didn't.

He was out the door. And he knew that he had to escape her.

I. Saved. Dad.

"Get out here right now!" Bertha sounded furious.

I didn't have time to ride the elevator with him. He was sweating now and breathing kind of fast as he pushed the button again, again, again.

"It's going to be okay now," I promised him (and me).

chapter thirty-one
it's not going to be okay now

"Come to the park. Now!"

Bertha's voice pierced the din of the streets. I rushed and floated down to the ground, where Alice was waiting for me on the sidewalk. She tugged at my arm. "Hurry!"

We were ballet-leaping across the street to Bertha and her elevator. It seemed to tear a hole in the world. The dead noticed it and stopped to stare. Bertha looked out at the world like she was the latest cranky meme on the Internet. Lacey was leaning against the elevator door, and I think she was actually holding it open for us. Squinting through the sunlight, she seemed genuinely happy to see us.

"Orlando Bloom," she said, to explain her smile. "I saw him. Not naked, but he had his shirt off. That works for me."

Across the street, Dad was getting Eduardo to hail a taxi for him. Excellent. Go, go, go.

"Look!" I pointed him out. "I did it."

"Excellent," Lacey said. After a moment she added, "Where's Nick?"

Just hearing his name felt like a stab of fear. We all knew where he was: back home, looking after his mother, trying to make things better for her, insisting on making things right. As if he could.

"He'll be here," I said to Lacey, to Alice, to myself, to Bertha. "Nick's on his way." I tried to force a breezy tone into my voice and I thought I failed.

Bertha sighed, looking around the park, as if she were observing a den of sin. She didn't want too much of it imprinted on her eyes.

"Sarah. You know that I can't wait for him," Bertha said grimly.

"He's on his way!" I said, still failing at that casual, confident tone. "Besides, what's the rush? We're dead. It's not like we're late for something."

"Don't you understand?" she asked. "If we don't leave within the minute, we'll be stuck here. All of us."

I scanned the park for any sign of Nick. The beautiful day had brought in another boisterous crowd. He might be in there. Somewhere. (Hurry, Nick, please!)

"That means he has a whole minute to get here," I reasoned. "A minute can be a long time, if you think about it."

Bertha didn't look angry at all but terribly, terribly sad. Off to my right, I heard the *pip-pip* whistle from Eduardo, who had spotted an open taxi. Dad eased himself in and off he went. Safe. Alive. Saved.

Now all I needed was Nick. Was I asking too much?

"Everyone. Please step in the elevator now," she instructed.

Lacey stepped in. She shrugged at me, looking a bit

sheepish. "Look," she said. "I'm sorry. But did you see those people in the night? I don't want to be one of them."

I nodded. Alice stepped in. She looked at her feet and then at me.

"I'm so sorry, but I can't stay here, Sarah. You've seen how it is. I must move on." She seemed overcome with emotion.

"It's okay," I said to her, searching for Nick once more. I saw a shock of brown hair in the distance, running right toward us. "He's right over there. Just wait. Just wait for him. Please!"

"Get in the elevator, Sarah," Alice commanded me. The guy with brown hair came closer. It wasn't Nick. It was someone who was alive.

"You can't be this stupid! And he isn't that cute!" Lacey shouted. "Get in here!"

"Wait!" I begged. "I can't." The words nearly stuck in my throat. "I can't leave him here all alone. Please. One more minute!" I stayed outside the elevator, paralyzed with fear.

The doors were closing oh so slowly, and as they did they were erasing the three stricken faces that looked out at me. Plain sky and park were gradually overtaking my view of them. I edged closer, getting ready to jump in next to them.

"Sarah! I'm right here!" Nick shouted from across the park. And suddenly the world was a good place. Nick was here. I snapped around to see him zooming toward me. Yes.

"See?" I said.

But I was speaking to no one. The doors were closed, replaced by an empty patch of air.

Nick caught up to me. And here we were. Now and forever.

chapter thirty-two

click your heels three times.
try again. try again. try again.

Nick was a little out of breath when he reached me. He squinted against the sunlight, which may have explained why he didn't notice that I was equal parts furious and terrified.

"How long till they come back for us?" Nick asked, gulping for air.

"Yeah, see, that's the thing. They're not," I replied.

He laughed and shook his head. "Oh, come on. They won't just leave us here. Stranded. What are we supposed to do?"

"Haunt. Walk around. Get used to being a ghost." That was all I could say. For the moment. We walked around the perimeter of the park, just like the *Great Gatsby* couple I had seen last night.

"Where were you?" I asked, trying like mad to dial down any accusing tone in my voice, just in case we were creating the dialogue we'd be stuck with for all eternity. "Why didn't you get back here on time?"

"My mom was in bad shape," he explained. "I couldn't just leave her."

"Yeah. I get that. But now we're stuck here." The accusing tone in my voice morphed into the sound of fear and grief. (That's what the truth sounded like.)

"Sarah, don't worry so much. They'll be back for us. You'll see. Bertha's just trying to teach us a lesson."

(We were stuck. We were stuck. We were stuck.)

(We walked. We walked. We walked.)

(All day. All day. All day.)

✺ ✺ ✺

Technically it was all just as blindingly beautiful as it had been yesterday. The crazy pastels of dusk were starting to give way to the metallic shades of early evening. And right now I saw it as my pretty, pretty prison.

"So." Nick spoke with a perky optimism that was hard for me to believe in. "Starting now I think we should stay together. We can look out for each other. Things go wrong when we separate."

I only half-listened to him. We had been walking, walking, walking. Was this going to be our crazy thing as we haunted Manhattan? What was to become of us?

"Where do you think your dad went?"

"No idea. But he heard me. I know that for sure. He knows the truth about Karen. That's pretty good," I reasoned.

"Pretty good? That's excellent! He's safe! You saved him. See? I told you things would work out." He hugged me as we walked.

"Um, hang on," I said. "He's still sick, and it isn't like she's in jail or anything. As long as she's free, he's in danger. I don't even know where he went."

"Well, that's what's so good about us still being here. You can find him and see what your stepmother is up to. And I can see if my mom is making some progress. This'll be good. You'll see."

I stopped walking, which stopped Nick. I looked him in the eye and he smiled the crazy crooked seductive grin that I loved so much.

"Are you *smiling*?" I asked. "Seriously? For real? Are you actually happy? Because, if you are, that might mean that you're insane."

Nick grinned more broadly and may even have laughed a little bit. At me. In this situation. (Bad timing for laughs or smiles.)

"You worry too much, Sarah."

"You don't worry enough, Nick."

"We'll be fine." He sounded unreasonably confident. "Look at it this way: we're getting more time here to see everything through. How is that bad?"

It was dark enough now.

I pointed to the figures in blue glow all around us. They walked, laughed, cried, and fluttered from place to place. The *Great Gatsby* couple came by.

He: Yes, it was.

She: It wasn't my fault.

He: Yes, it was.

"What the hell?" Nick whispered. "Who are they?"

"Those are all people who got stuck here," I explained. "They all seem a little bit crazy. Or a lot bit crazy. And that's going to be us. Someday." My face was such a tangle of worry it nearly hurt.

For once, Nick's unshakeable confidence shook. Just a tremor. I studied him as if my life depended on it because, really, it kind of did. If *he* lost hope now, we were officially lost for all time. He took his damn time, surveying the luminous creatures roaming the park and beyond.

"No. That won't be us," he concluded. "We'll be fine."

It was such a definitive statement, I felt my forehead ease up. Just a little. I needed to hear those words the way that living people need to breathe. He knew that somehow.

Nick took my hands in his. "Sarah, I know you. I see you, and I know who you are. You worry too much, but you look out for other people. You have a wicked sense of humor that makes me always want to be next to you and hear what you have to say. You're strong and you're crazy smart. You have music in everything you do," he said, moving closer. "And you have a great heart."

We kissed, and I felt the tangle of worry come loose and fall away. (Was this his true superpower?)

"You could have left without me. Why are you still here?" he asked.

"I couldn't. I don't want to be there without you," I said. It was so true it hurt my eyes to say it out loud.

Nick held me close. "I want to be with you. Always." But I had to pull away and look him in the eye.

"Where the hell were you, then? Why didn't you get there

when Bertha called? Tell me what happened." I needed to
know. Needed.

WHERE NICK WAS

Nick's mom was sleeping it off, which took a
while. But then she awoke, at last, and made coffee. She sat in all that mess and drank it. Nick
tried to speak to her:

"Mom. You've got to get it together. Live the
life you have." And then: "Mom. Clean yourself
up. Take a shower and put on clean clothes.

For the twelfth time: "Mom. Brush your teeth."

She heard none of it. She sipped her coffee
and browsed Facebook. They were cloaked in silence for such a long time. Nick knew what he was
waiting for: a glimmer of hope. A sign of life. And
better hygiene.

When she finished the pot of coffee, she
looked around the apartment and seemed to notice for the first time that it was kind of a wreck.
It surprised her, but not enough to fix it. Ah well.
She sat on the sofa and stared at the ceiling for a
long time.

She took a deep breath and focused intently on
that ceiling. "Nicky. I thought I saw you last night.
I'd sell my soul if I could see you or hear you—"

"Alice, Sarah, Lacey, Nick. It's time." Bertha's
voice boomed through Nick.

"I'd hug you every single day. I'd forget about

all the stupid stuff that distracted me while you were alive."

She looked down at the floor.

"Go on," Nick urged her. "I'm listening."

She turned her gaze to the ceiling once more, as if Nick were up there somewhere.

"See, here's the thing." Her voice was singed with tears. It was hard for her to speak, to breathe, to do anything other than cry. But she had something to say.

"Get out here right now!" Bertha sounded furious.

"I worked out a plan to kill myself. Just after your funeral, I figured out how to do it. I was such a wreck, a bunch of doctors gave me a boatload of pills to calm me down. If I took enough of them, I could calm myself *all the way down,* you know? But I didn't. Not yet, anyway." She lowered her head and laughed at herself a little. "Obviously," she added.

"Don't do it, Mom," Nick whispered. "I know you can't hear me. But please tell me you won't do it."

"Come to the park. Now!"

Mom sniffled, wiping her nose on her sleeve.

"But last night, I realized: a part of you will always be alive, as long as I'm alive." She was whispering now. "I can't kill that off. So. I guess I'll have to keep living."

Nick tried to hug her as she buried her face in her hands.

"And now I'm a crazy lady, talking to dead people. Great."

He smiled. "Keep talking. Keep living. You can do this, Mom."

From a distance, you might think Nick and I were just one person. With a blue glow. We wrapped our arms around each other and breathed in unison.

"I don't want to be here in the park all night," I said at last.

"It's kind of beautiful here," Nick replied. "But if you want a home, then we'll make a home. Together."

Neither of us spoke for a long while, basking in the luminous diamond that was us. Nick moved us gently, slowly, out of the park to the building where he lived when he still lived. Honestly, he could have promised me that we'd spend the night on the moon and I would have followed him there.

chapter thirty-three

life is wasted on the living

Nick led us to his apartment building on Greene Street and through the door of a vacant apartment. Even though nobody lived there, it was furnished like a page out of an IKEA catalogue. Everything matched everything else's rectangular shape and was kelly green or navy blue. It looked so cozy and fake.

"It's for visiting professors at NYU," Nick explained. "It's usually empty all summer."

"Well. We're not visiting all summer. Right?" I asked Nick, as if he would absolutely know.

"Of course not!" Nick spoke with absolute confidence. "Hey. This is sort of random, but I'm not hungry. Are you?" Nick asked. Smooth subject change.

"No. When's the last time we ate?" I wondered aloud. "And hey, are we even able to eat? I mean, can we eat the food that's here? Are we going to starve? Is that even possible, since we're already dead? Why didn't Bertha talk to us about food here?"

"We're dead. We can't starve. But this is so annoying: I finally have a kitchen and I can't cook," Nick complained. "I so want to cook for us."

This funny feeling settled over me. Like we were kids playing house in some model apartment. Look! Here's our modular furniture. Look! Here's our bland, generic book collection. Look! Here's our barely used cookware. And look! Here's us.

We ended up in the (only) bedroom.

Okay. Deep breath. This was a whole new chapter in our relationship. Was this just sleep? Or was this sex? Or was this sex followed by sleep? What exactly was about to happen? Most important, *what did I want to have happen?* (I had no answers to any of these questions. And that seemed like kind of a deal breaker right there.)

"I'm totally exhausted," Nick said quietly. "You?"

I nodded and interpreted that as *We're just going to sleep now. No sex.*

Some small part of me felt relieved that I didn't have to make any decision right here, right now. If I were alive, I would have felt disappointed or rejected. But now everything about me was ready to collapse and disintegrate. If I had bones, they were weary.

We lay down on the bed, perfectly synchronized. We were drawn together like the puzzle pieces we really were. My head fit perfectly against his neck and I breathed him in. Our legs and arms wrapped around us. Our breathing aligned in an easy rhythm. Sleep was pulling me down like heavy, heavy gravity. I let silence contain us for a while. My brain slid backward to Lacey and her shock that Nick and I were both virgins. Assuming he was telling the truth.

"Nick? Did you really never have sex when you were alive?" I asked.

"I always meant to. But no, I never did," he said in a half whisper. "You?"

"No. Didn't even get around to having a boyfriend." My voice grew softer and smaller. Nick turned his head to look at me in disbelief, then drew me back in against his neck, where I inhaled trees and rainstorms once more.

"Well. That's final proof that life is wasted on the living," he said. "Because we're both kind of fantastically desirable."

He may have said more, but I wouldn't know. I left. My mind slipped away, into the cool darkness, relinquishing language and emotion. My mind, my spirit, my whatever-I-was might have slipped into Nick, into his body/nonbody. We were too connected just then for anyone in the universe to consider us separate people.

I was safe. I was whole. I was real.

Wait. No. Forget all that. I was happy. I took all my fear and worry and put it to bed for the night.

I smiled a tiny smile as I drifted into a dreamless sleep. I was where I was meant to be.

✻ ✻ ✻

"Wake up!" Nick was smiling over me. "Come on, we've got a busy day of haunting ahead of us."

I sat up, slowly coming to full consciousness. Yes, we were still here. No, it wasn't all a dream. "Well," I said. "I want to make sure my dad is definitely out of there—that Karen didn't find him and drag him back so she could finish him off."

"I bet he's filed for divorce and thrown her in jail by now! As for my mom, she's probably still asleep. But we'll see."

Nick stayed obstinately optimistic as we made our way through the world. This morning the crowds seemed denser and a lot less beautiful. The sky was gun-metal gray. But that was okay. It didn't need to be pretty to be beautiful. And even if it turned dreary and ugly, just plain being in the world was nothing short of glorious. We could see people, hear music, and witness life in all its madness. The artificial mall world stood as a stark contrast to real, messy, crazy, beautiful, ugly life in the outside world.

Elizabeth Anne, the strawberry blonde, was still singing and therefore still alive, despite the Boy's attentions. Good.

It began raining lightly, and the raindrops passed right through us with a cool, refreshing sparkle. The bruise-colored sky made it easier to see the dead among the living. Wow. New York was already crowded and bustling. Add all these ghosts slipping through and around the living and Manhattan was a glowing patchwork of humanity.

Karen was alone in the apartment. Throwing a tantrum. She was on the sofa, punching a pillow. Her makeup was half cried off. It was early morning, and she was finishing off an expensive bottle of chardonnay.

"This is excellent!" I practically sang to Nick. "She's going ballistic because she's been thwarted. He's gone. She's screwed."

Karen was working hard at pulling herself together. She

wiped the mascara tracks away, sniffling, shaking her arms and head like a runner about to start a race. She cleared her throat, picked up the phone, and dialed.

"What's she doing now?" I asked, as if Nick would know.

"Hi, sweetheart. So, what is this, voicemail number fifteen? I don't mean to nag, but, Charlie, I'm really super-worried about you, so just call me back to let me know you're okay, okay? Remember the doctor said to avoid stress, but I don't think that he meant that you should stress *me* out!" She tried to laugh.

After she hung up, she looked at the phone as if it had betrayed her. "You bastard!" And then she was punching a pillow again. "No, no, no!" She seemed to be losing steam, though.

"Wow," Nick said. "Now, that's impressive."

"No," said a small voice. I wheeled around and there they were. The Boy. They stood in the middle of the living room, arms folded over their chests. They scowled at us, at each other, then back at us.

The girl Boy shook her head and asked me, "Are you trying to get revenge on her? Just so you know, we don't like that."

"No!" I insisted. "I just wanted to be sure my dad was safe. That's all! I'll leave her alone now."

The boy Boy looked up at the ceiling and sang, "I don't belie-e-eve herrrrr."

Nick took a step toward them, which seemed insanely brave.

"You're here," he said. "Among the living."

The boy Boy smiled and said, "Oh yes. We go where we want. We're the Boss of You!" He laughed pretty hard at this, as if he had just thought it up.

Karen began to snore softly in the background.

The girl Boy said, "You two think you can do anything, but you can't. We can. Would it be easier for you to take us seriously if we looked"—in an instant, they changed into a wise-looking old man with a long white beard, who wore flowing robes and leaned on a staff— "like this?"

Actually, yes. Now they looked like a deity worthy of the big screen and Charlton Heston. I sort of wanted to bow or kneel or something.

"Sarah," he said in a deep, kind voice. I think it had a built-in echo. "What do you seek here?"

"I seek . . ." (Oh, I had to come up with an answer that was worthy.) "Peace."

"See?" he said, still in the deep, serious voice. "This totally works." The words were jarring coming from this Old Testament star. "So does this."

Right before my eyes he transformed into Mother Teresa.

"Please be sure that your actions lead to peace, my child," she said. Her voice was frail and strong at the same time. "Alive or dead, your actions will have consequences." She smiled sweetly and said, "This version of me is pretty cool too."

I wasn't sure if I should laugh or cry. Nick let out a breathy kind of laugh that made me think that he was in the same place I was.

"Can we go back?" Nick asked. "To the mall, I mean. *Should* we go back? And you're probably the one person, or persons, or whatever you are . . . You can get us back there."

Mother Teresa smiled at him benevolently. And then she transformed. (I'm really reluctant to reveal this next transformation. As incredible as everything else had been, this was the one that blew my mind.)

She transformed into Oprah. (I swear.) She was wearing a glamorous pale pink dress and diamonds in her ears. She was made up and ready for television.

"You want to go back?" she half-laughed, and walked over to Nick. "Tell me something. You had the chance to go back and you didn't take it. Why is that? I think we all want to know." She nodded in my direction.

"I—I couldn't leave her. I felt responsible. I had to fix things," he answered. (He was doing a better job at keeping up with these transformations than I was.)

"Mmm-mm-mm. Son, you don't know the first thing about addiction. But you might know a little bit about co-dependence!" She turned to me. "And what about you? You were there. At the park. You could have gone back. But you stood perfectly still when your friends were begging you to leave. I know. I was swinging on the swings nearby. Why did you stay? Why are you still here?"

"You already know why I stayed," I said. "Don't you?" (Seriously, was Oprah going to make me declare my feelings for Nick? Right here? Right now? Rude.)

Oprah (really? Oprah?!) smiled warmly and shook her head. "You should have watched my show when you had the chance."

"Sorry!" I said quickly. Nick was still in some kind of shock.

"Well. That's all we have time for today," she said, as if signing off from a show. "See you next time!"

We walked/glided our way into the building where we were (sort of) living. (Should I call it *home*?) His mother remained in some unknown state of being behind this heavy metal door. Nick's face was ever so slightly taut with worry.

"Should I—can I come with you?" I asked him. I wouldn't blame him if he didn't want me to see her like this, but then his face melted into a little smile.

"Thanks. Yes," he replied. And we didn't speak again until we were inside.

CLUES ABOUT NICK'S MOM'S STATE OF BEING:
GOOD VS. BAD

The place was still a mess = Bad

The television was still playing in the background, loud and largely ignored = Bad

The television was showing an entertainment gossip show, instead of all-day New York news = Good (but questionable taste?)

The vodka was put away on a shelf = Good (it would have been Excellent if she had gotten rid of it all)

There was a wet towel on the bathroom floor = Good (to hell with neatness—she was clean!)

She was sitting at a small table, drinking coffee = Excellent

She was eating an organic burrito = Pretty Good

She was dressed = Good (it would have been
    Excellent if she had also put on her "face")

She was talking on the phone = Excellent

The conversation sounded like it was escalating
    into an argument = Bad

"I need work! You gotta find me something," she insisted.

"Mom works for a bunch of temp agencies," Nick explained while we studied her. "She does secretarial stuff, babysitting, dog-walking, all sorts of things."

"Yes, I'll hold!" she shouted into the phone, then sighed loudly, drumming her fingers against the table. The television took her attention as the host prepared to break for a commercial. She watched the commercials attentively, phone to her ear, waiting for the call or the show to resume.

Nick was roaming the apartment, but he returned as soon as his mother spoke again.

"Yes?" She sat up straight as she turned her attention back to her phone. "Where is it?" She brightened up. "Easy commute. Okay, what are the hours? What's the pay?"

She shook her head and folded herself down a bit.

"That's part-time. I'm going to need more." She listened. "No, no, no! I'll take it. I mean hey, it's a start, right?" She listened. "Thanks. And keep trying to find me something? Maybe another part-time gig and I'll be in good shape." She looked around the apartment. "Well. I'll be in *better* shape than I am right now."

She hung up, shut off the TV, and went to the refrigerator. She stared at its contents for a long, hard minute.

Without a word, she grabbed her phone, her keys, and her purse and went outside.

Progress = Good

✷ ✷ ✷

New Yorkers have excellent peripheral vision. We need it. We need to know, at all times, who's getting close enough to grab our stuff and run. We need to turn on the lights and check for anything scurrying across the floor. We need to be aware of the world around us. Always.

That didn't change after we were dead.

Nick and I were passing through scaffolding on a side street where it was extra-dark. Our own blue glow showed us the way, and it put a spotlight on a sudden movement up ahead to our left. Nick and I both halted all movement and sound.

"Hey! Let go!" a woman's voice cried out. "Help me!"

"Shut up, bitch!" a man's voice growled at her. It didn't take long for us to find them, enclosed in this wooden alley-way. She was putting up a hell of a fight for her purse. She scratched his face, which really pissed him off. So he punched her in the jaw, knocking her to the ground.

She looked like somebody's grandmother. She was whimpering in pain.

"Stop!" I shouted as loud as I could. The guy jumped and looked around for the source of the sound. When he didn't see me, he went back to work.

He kicked the woman in the stomach. She moaned, curling

her body into a tight ball. He took her purse, he took her jewelry. He looked ready to kick her in the head, when Nick put himself between the two of them.

The man froze for a few long seconds. He saw Nick, but he didn't understand. His face was a map of fear and confusion. (Good.)

"Police!" I shouted. And that was it. The guy took off at top speed, holding tight to everything he had stolen. I followed after him. "Police! Police! Police!" I shouted into the night.

We couldn't, we wouldn't leave until the ambulance worker wrapped her in blankets and bandages and took her to safety. She was crying as they wheeled her out of the scaffolding. And then the siren took over, crying on her behalf.

The quiet that followed was thunderous.

"We helped," Nick said.

"Not enough," I answered. I was stuck on the image of her curled up on the sidewalk.

The land of the living had turned unlovely just now, and I desperately wished to go back to the lush greens and blues of the park or the hushed warm earth tones of home.

chapter thirty-four
sunday in the park with nick

Nick and I were relaxing, sort of, on a bench in Washington Square Park. The light rain had gained some power and it showered through us. As it passed through me, it offered a gentle silver feeling of endless cool. We sat in our cool silence together for a long while.

The ghosts of Washington Square slowed down. Some of them stopped and opened their arms to welcome the rain passing through them. Maybe the rain was flattered, because it grew even more intense.

The super-skinny ghost sat down next to me. "You blew it, didn't you? I knew you would. I knew it. I saw you and I thought, 'Oh, she's here to do something important. And she's gonna blow it.'" Her voice picked up speed, pitch, and mania. "I knew it. I called it. I was right."

"As a matter of fact, I didn't blow it. I saved my dad's life. Nick's mom is getting better. So even if we get stuck here with . . . people like you . . . we did what we came here to do." And I just had to add, "So there."

She didn't acknowledge a word I'd said. Instead she jumped up from the bench. "I have to keep moving," she said. She began to jog in place. "I have to go. I have to go," she repeated as she jogged away. "So close to my goal weight."

"Can you kill someone who's already dead?" I asked Nick.

Lightning woke up the park, punctuated by a satisfying clap of thunder. The ghosts around us made sounds like they were excited. But their movements slowed even more.

"This is so weird," I said to Nick. "Do you mind if we stay here? For just a bit?"

Part of me knew that this was a dangerous question. But most of me felt slow and thick, sort of the way I'd felt the night I died. Could someone have drugged me?

"Let's enjoy this," Nick said, leaning back on the bench, arms outstretched, turning his face to the rain. I rested my head against his shoulder.

"We have all the time in the world," he called out over the heavy sheet of rain that enchanted us both. "They'll be okay. We'll make sure."

He took my hand in his, and that's when I saw it. Both of our bracelets were a heavy brick red. I thought about saying something, but the rain was gentle and mesmerizing.

✳ ✳ ✳

Tomorrow morning, set your alarm and get up before dawn. Then get yourself outside, or to a window or to a rooftop, and face east. But be careful. It's so unreasonably beautiful, it might kill you.

"This was here every day when I was alive?" Nick asked

as he shook his head. We leaned forward and studied it, like we were witnessing magic. "I had how many thousands of chances to see this—and I missed most of them?"

We had been in the park all night, and we both stayed awake for most of it. The gorgeous sensation of rain was something we didn't want to miss. Not one drop. It was too amazing.

I felt it, and I let my mind drift. When I tried to suggest that we go home, the rain hypnotized me into silence. It washed everything clean. My forehead was unknotted and my breathing was even. Now the damp ground glittered in the sun, and the city eased into life (and into death, for some of us). The noise increased—in the world, and in my thoughts:

"It wasn't my fault."

"Yes it was."

"It wasn't my fault."

Ah yes. The sounds of the living and dead were starting to fill any blank spaces. The strawberry-blond singing girl was show-tuning her way through a thicket of ghosts (I was so glad she couldn't see us), while that heartfelt troubadour with the guitar and the hat overpowered her with a tragic ballad. A garbage truck honked and challenged them both but didn't stop either of them for a beat.

Yes, it was true that the city could be brutally ugly, I knew that before I died and got reminded of it when I saw a man kick an elderly woman in the stomach. So why was I so entranced with it? Why couldn't I let go of its beauty?

"Sarah," Nick said softly. "Is it so bad—being here among the living—with me?"

(Another dangerous question.)

I couldn't lie, not even a little, but I couldn't answer right away. Sunlight was passing through me, and I felt as if I might be a ghostly rainbow of refracted light. I looked in Nick's eyes and saw something I'd never noticed before. The gold flecks in his irises were old (arresting) news. What I saw was that Nick was right for me.

It flashed inside me as a two-word heartbeat: Nick. Right. Nick. Right.

Here is the story that I think I was telling myself: being with Nick couldn't possibly be wrong. It didn't matter where we were. If we were together, we were exactly where we were supposed to be.

I smiled at Nick, reached over, and kissed him. He touched my face and smiled sweetly.

"I'm happy," I said at last. It made no sense. And it may have been the first time I'd ever spoken those words in that order. "Thank you."

"For what?" he asked.

I grinned and said, "Oh. You know."

(Oh. He knew.)

✻ ✻ ✻

It was happening. The kind of hypnotizing sense of belonging here, even though we knew we could never belong here. We were dead. Let's leave this stuff for the living. Come on. Seriously. It was time to move. But we didn't. We couldn't. Maybe the rain had washed away our strength, along with our fear or any trace of worry. (That would be a miracle.) Maybe the sunrise had ushered in peace or calm or acceptance. Being here was changing us.

We both rose and I took three steps forward. Nick still had my hand in his, and he tugged me toward him. He didn't have to try very hard, did he? I sort of twirled back to him, into his arms and into a kiss. Even here, kissing Nick made my heart dance. It was chemical, it was physical, and it was ethereal. Maybe it was even magical.

Maybe this was happily ever after, as in "forever and ever."

We broke from the kiss when we heard the voices of the dead all around us. They saw us, of course, and felt the need to comment. Nick and I just smiled and listened.

"Hey! Get a room!"

"Oh, isn't it romantic?"

"Come on, you guys!"

Nick flinched at that last one, and so did I. It was a woman's voice. No, it was a girl's voice. And we both recognized it. Lacey was shouting at us.

"Come *on*, you guys!" she repeated, louder and with less patience. I needed to turn around to see her, but the expression on Nick's face slowed me for just a second. He seemed disappointed to see her.

Lacey was excited and very, very, extremely proud of herself. She stood in the elevator, in the middle of the park. She peered around and then announced, "I'm here to rescue you! I can't believe I *did it*!" she crowed. "Okay, it was Alice's plan, but I'm the one who actually *did it*!"

Nick and I stayed still. I waited for him to move toward the elevator. Maybe he was waiting for me to move. Lacey was too caught up in her tale of triumph to notice.

"So, Alice has Bertha all distracted, making her have a big heart-to-heart," she continued. "And yes, you're welcome,

I'm so strong, I actually got the elevator to work for me. And here we are! And yes. I. Am. Fabulous."

A small swarm of the dead had gathered around to watch and listen. They seemed in awe of her story, and Lacey seemed delighted to be the object of their awe. She was standing still and strutting at the same time. Only Lacey could do that.

"Wow, Lacey," Nick said. "You got the elevator to work for you? That's incredible!"

"I know, right?" She glowed. "Now, come on, already. Get in." She looked around the park at the gathering dead. "You guys!" she squealed in notes and tones I had never heard from her before. "Look! Look who it is! Best celebrity sighting ever!"

It was Oprah. But only our little audience of the dead noticed her. The living walked right past her. This was the Boy, of course.

"Not so fast," Oprah said.

"Oh wow! Oh wow!" Lacey gushed. "Are you talking to me? Can you see me? Oh, of course you can! You're Oprah! You can do anything. I love you! I really love you!"

Nick and I wore matching smiles as Lacey fell all over herself in tribute and admiration.

"Thank you," Oprah said graciously. "Now. Have you actually asked these two people what they want to do? I have a funny feeling they'd rather stay here. And I'm all about free will, you know."

That was insane. Of course we wanted to get back to the mall. *Didn't we?*

"Can we have a minute to think about it?" Nick asked. I felt a chill and thought I was about to be sick.

"No. We can't have a minute to think about this," I insisted. "Let's go."

"Why do you want to stay, Nick?" Oprah asked. Our audience of the dead was growing larger. Nick looked at the crowd, and his speech slowed down a bit.

"If we stay here, we can, you know, finish our unfinished business," he said.

"Mmm-hmm, mmm-hmm . . . ," Oprah hummed as she nodded and took that in.

Lacey crooked her finger in our direction, saying, "Come here." We obeyed but stayed just outside the threshold of the elevator.

Lacey reached out and slapped Nick, kind of hard. "Wake up! You're dead. Come back to the mall so you can *move the hell on!*"

"I don't think we need to resort to physical violence," Oprah chided her, but she was laughing as she shook her head.

"I'll go!" a male voice called out from the crowd. It was the pervy ghost who sat underneath young girls on park benches. He lunged for the elevator, but Lacey scared him off.

"Get back, sicko!" she shouted.

"What about me? And her?" shouted one of the *Gatsby* ghosts.

"Do they still have the food court?" asked the super-skinny ghost. "Take me! I wanna go and look at all the food. I promise not to eat any! I just wanna look!"

The dead yelled among themselves. "Not her! Take me!" Mr. Screamer stood in the center of it all and, guess what, screamed. Nick turned me toward him and held my shoulders to bring me into focus.

"We can be together. Here. We can look out for our families. Here. We can see the sun and feel the rain. We can live wherever we want, with nobody telling us what to do. Forever. *Here.*"

"But look at them." I pointed to the dead crazies around us. "What if we become like them? They're so messed up!"

"Hey! I heard that!" a dead guy called out to me, but I ignored him.

"Stay with me," Nick said. Those were all the words he used. But inside those three words, I heard an eternity of love and caring, of rain and sun (I wondered what snow would feel like as it passed through us!), of being together and alive in our own way. Here on Earth.

"Oooh, girl. He's a romantic!" Oprah cooed. (Could she hear what was underneath all his words too?) She turned her attention to the dead who were bickering for a chance to ride that elevator.

"Enough!" she commanded them, and they obeyed with shocking speed.

"I can't hold this elevator much longer, you guys," Lacey said plaintively. "Don't you want to move on?"

Nick framed my face in his hands and said it. He said it. He said it.

"I love you."

I took his hands in mine, and smiled. "I love you." The words felt perfect as they unfolded between us.

That's what made this next part so painful.

"Nick. Please. I have to move on. And so do you. Please," I said quietly, so quietly and slowly, because a well of emotion was stopping half of my voice. Nick was shaking his head. Tears sliced their way down my cheeks.

"We can move on together," I whispered. "We can. Please, Nick. Come with me."

"No. We belong here. We're already together," he whispered back. "This is perfect. Let's not change it."

Oprah spoke to her audience. "Our lives, and even our afterlives, are made from the stories we tell each other. We are the stories we tell ourselves."

"Oh, just shut up!" I cried. The crowd let out an "Ooooh" in response. "I don't know what to do!"

"Now!" Lacey sounded frantic.

My heart, or something like it, pounded through my rib cage. I took a step toward Nick, then jerked backward, hard. Lacey had grabbed me by the hair and yanked me into the elevator.

I was still in shock at the pain, violence, and swiftness of her actions as she reached out and did the exact same thing to Nick. We fell back against the wall of the elevator, a mere second before the door closed.

"You two are such idiots," she said. "You sort of deserve each other."

chapter thirty-five
it's as if i never left

Don't Look at My Bracelet

Nick loved me. He said so. I tried to remember that during the elevator ride, and after. But it just kept slipping away.

He wasn't speaking to any of us. He bolted off the elevator, headed for parts unknown. His face was locked up, totally expressionless, like a sculpture of Nick but not the real Nick.

This all sounds pretty bad, but I told myself that he'd get over it, and he'd see reason. I also told myself that Lacey was the one who had pulled him in. Not me. So he had no reason to be mad at me. (Of course, I was grateful to Lacey, and I wished I had done what she did. I maybe had to factor that in.)

Our part of the mall was a different universe; it was so clear to me now. This was no place for the living. The air felt different, and so did the light. There was a cool, clean simplicity here and it chilled me. But the warm, pulsating, mad beauty of life among the living was officially my drug of choice. It took me less than one minute to start missing it all. Oh no. No.

I wanted to go back. What if Nick was right and we should

have stayed back there? What if we belonged there, together? I shook that thought out of my heart.

"Sarah!" Alice called out from the entrance to Staples. "You're back!"

Bertha soon appeared by her side.

"Oh my, oh, oh, oh my . . . ," she said slo-o-ow-ly. "You've returned. You've actually returned. How did you . . . ?" But then she looked at Lacey. Math completed, she did one of her cluck-sighs (still hate them) and said, "Of course. I should have known."

"I saved my dad!" I announced to her. Her smile was tinged with a bit of sadness.

"Good for you, my dear. Good for you." She looked around. "And Nick? Where is he?"

(Yeah, I didn't want to go into all that. Not yet.) "He's here," I said. "Somewhere. In the mall. Here."

She shook her head. "Incredible," she murmured. But then she looked at me and pushed the sadness out of her smile. "Welcome back, Sarah. You're welcome here, indeed. And you must be hungry."

As soon as she said it, I was. In fact, I was ravenous.

"Go. Eat. Let me see about Nick. We'll reconvene anon."

I wasn't sure when "anon" would be. But it sounded ominous.

✳ ✳ ✳

We three girls were at the food court, having a huge dinner. I was wondering about the story I would tell myself/tell them about the time with Nick. Lacey cut right to it.

"So." Lacey elbowed me. "You and Nick. All alone. All night. Two nights. Did you do it?"

"What?" I asked, as in *How can you ask me that?* not *Whatever do you mean?*

"You're *so* pathetic," Lacey said. "Wasted opportunity. That's you! Go find him, girl. What the hell are you waiting for?"

"He seemed terribly upset," Alice said tentatively.

"Yeah," Lacey agreed. "But he'll get over it when he realizes that I saved the day. And he has a girlfriend who's kind of hot. In a nerd/skinny-white-girl kind of way."

"Thank you," I said, genuinely surprised at her kindness. (Note to me: never underestimate Lacey.)

"Hooray for Lacey," Alice added.

I hadn't checked my bracelet since we had returned. It was Disney Princess pink.

✷ ✷ ✷

My dad had a cousin who was profoundly deaf and talked in his sleep. See? No matter our circumstances, we've simply got to tell our stories. Do you know why Earth is never quiet? It's because the whole place is teeming with life, and life itself is so noisy. The heavy silence in our section of the mall came from that absence of life, and it took (almost) all of my attention. Almost. The thing is: I needed to talk. To Nick.

There he was. Nick. Fast asleep in a bed in the middle of a cluster of beds, in Sleepy's. I hurried to him. I wanted to kiss him, hold him, touch him, and breathe him in. I climbed into the bed and found my rightful place, right by his heart. He stirred.

"Sarah," he whispered. "I'm sorry about before. And I'm sorry about—"

"Me first," I interrupted him. "I'm sorry you didn't get to choose for yourself. And I'm sorry that I'm *not* sorry that we're here together."

He laughed a little bit. "Come here," he said. But I was already here. Very here.

He leaned over me and kissed me. Maybe it was because of the victory of the day, I wasn't sure, but this kiss held more passion, more subatomic energy, more life than any kiss before it in the history of kisses.

And just like that everything changed. The energy between us shifted. We both knew that this was the end of us talking and the beginning of us taking off our clothes. We blinked at each other and that said it all. Me first. I didn't hesitate, but I did move kind of slowly, deliberately. In that small moment when I was separate from him, shirt traveling up and over my head, I thought one single word: yes.

Yes. It was time. Nick. Sarah. Now.

And as the shirt fell to the floor, I became aware of every nerve ending in my skin (and was deeply glad to be wearing the cute bra with the lace). My heartbeat accelerated but stayed true. Nick. Right. Nick. Right.

His hands traced a line across my back. And it felt like I was a black-and-white photo magically rippling into color wherever he touched me.

"Sarah?" he said softly. "Are you sure?"

Okay, maybe we weren't on the exact same page here. I faded to black, white, and gray.

"Aren't you?" I asked, without looking back at him.

He kissed my back, and then my neck and my shoulder. I was transforming into color once more. His hands wrapped around my waist and almost made me laugh. Was I joyful or ticklish? Not sure. I turned to face him. He smiled and breathed me in.

I tugged at his shirt a bit. "You," I said. And his shirt fell over mine.

I touched his shoulders, which were even more amazing up close. When our bodies pressed together, I felt like I owned him, I possessed him. He was mine. In living color.

I got the feeling that I was the one initiating this, continuing this, building it up to greater heights. For a girl who'd had zero boyfriends when she was alive, it was a little strange. Maybe even disappointing.

"We should use protection," Nick whispered after a while. He slowed us down.

"Can the dead get an STD? Or pregnant?" I asked, not really expecting an answer.

But he sat back. He stopped. And my heart fell through the floor. Oh no. Oh no. He didn't want me. That's all I could feel, and it felt utterly wrong and painful and totally humiliating.

"What's wrong?" I asked, dreading the answer, hiding the pain (I hoped).

"Before we do anything more, I think you should know something." He paused, and my mind raced to figure out that something before he could say it. And then he said it.

"I'm leaving," he said. "I'm leaving the mall."

(My brain turned into a pile of lint, because this made no sense.)

He continued. "I died saving Fiona. Remember?"

"Just for future reference," I interrupted, "it's not cool to talk about some girl when it looks like you're about to have sex with a completely different girl. I'm just sayin'." I curled my body up tight, wishing I didn't feel so totally exposed.

He smiled. "Point taken. But here's the thing. Saving her means that I died a hero. That's why Bertha offered to let me go to that spa place. It's totally different there. You can move on a whole lot faster, or . . ."

He was leaving. He was leaving the mall. He was leaving me. Something in my brain was exploding. I was losing the ability to speak or understand words of any kind.

"I'll find out tomorrow. Bertha is talking with the Boy tonight," he concluded.

Where to begin? Well. I began by putting my shirt back on. Fast. I stuffed my bra into my pocket. Just like that, passion transformed into blind anger. And I was ready to start swinging.

"First of all, you didn't die a hero. You guys were trying to run away. You told me yourself: you didn't take a bullet for her. You just got in the way of one." My voice was like metal.

"Let's not get technical. I was getting her away from—"

Nope. I wasn't letting him finish.

"Second, we're almost ready to move on, and we could move on *together*. You're going to run away now? *Now?*"

He shook his head. Maybe he wanted to speak, but I wasn't done yet.

"Third, yeah, maybe you get to return a little sooner, but

that won't help your mom. You'll come back as a new life. A new baby! And you won't even know her."

"See, that's the thing. It's different for them," he began, but I wasn't listening. I was half-aware that my face was burning, and I was shaking just a little.

Nick waited a decent interval.

"Over there it's different. You can move on. Or become an angel. You can look out for people. And after that whole haunting experience, I know for sure that's what I want to do."

If I spoke now, I'd cry, so I just breathed. Damn those trees and rainstorms. He held me close, which I loved and hated, which stressed me out beyond measure.

"Let's get this straight. You're leaving me. For your mother."

"This isn't about her, or any one person. This is my mission, my fate, Sarah." His voice was cotton-soft, but it hurt like hell. "I don't need to move on."

"Don't go."

"I'm sorry."

"Don't go."

chapter thirty-six
the billion stages of grief

We were all at breakfast, but I wasn't hungry. I opted to be really pissed off at Nick, instead of sad or scared that I might be losing him now and for the rest of time. My jaw was clenched so hard it hurt.

"Could you pass the salt?" Nick asked.

"I don't know," I replied. "Will it disappear forever and never come back, in the afterlife or the next life?" I asked before I handed it over. "Does it have serious mother issues?"

"Thank you," he said.

"Is this how you two flirt?" Lacey asked. "Because if it is, you kind of suck at it."

I gave Nick a look that said: *Well. Tell them.* But he didn't figure it out, so I said, "Well. Tell them." Out loud.

"No. Not till I hear from Bertha. I should wait," he said.

"Great idea. Wait until everyone feels really exposed and vulnerable. *Then* tell them." The words came out a lot harsher than I had intended.

"Wait for what?" Alice asked. "What's going on?"

Yes, I was being kind of bratty. Sorry. But no one had ever broken my heart before. I didn't know how to behave. And then it got worse.

We trudged our way to Bertha at Staples. She was waiting by the entrance, which wasn't her usual thing. My heart was in a permanent state of broken panic. This was it.

Bertha took Nick aside for a private chat. They spoke quietly, but I heard bits and horrible pieces.

Bertha: somethingsomething honor system. That's why I offered you the choice to somethingsomething.

Nick: It's only right that I somethingsomething.

Bertha: It's rather late for such a somethingsomething.

Nick: Before I go, tell me who brings all the somethingsomething.

Bertha: Ah, those are somethingsomething. They do it because they somethingsomething. And now . . .

She reached out her hand and he removed his bracelet. She took it from him. Oh no.

Done. I could hear blood rushing through my ears. It overpowered me. Every possible emotion was flowing through it.

Bertha and Nick remained together, separate from the rest of us. Bertha began a little speech. I didn't hear most of it. I didn't want to. "Somethingsomething heroes belong in another somethingsomething." And "Angels are something-something."

It was real. They all knew now. Nick was leaving us, and it would be just as sudden and as permanent as death itself. Maybe even more permanent. We stood in mournful silence in the absolute emptiness of the mall.

Alice stepped forward. Her voice sounded younger than ever.

"You'll look out for us all, won't you, Nick?" And then her voice broke. "We need angels. The world is a dangerous place." And with that she threw her arms around his neck and hugged him. She cried on his shoulder.

After a bit he gently removed her arms. She let them fall as she stepped back. He looked at Lacey, whose gaze was locked to the floor. He said, "Hey, Lacey. You're already in charge of the afterlife. Next time around I think you'll run the world."

When she looked up at him, her face was streaming with tears. She shook her head, unable to speak. So Nick stepped over to her and held her tight. She cried, rather loudly, then took a sudden step back.

"This hurts," she said. "This kind of goodbye. It isn't right. Are we actually supposed to be happy for you?"

Nick had no answer for that.

Lacey looked in my direction. "Oh, Sarah. Holy shit, girl." But I didn't say a word. I didn't have any. I was past language at that point anyway. I looked at Nick, and he looked at me. Nobody else existed.

When he scooped me into his arms, I couldn't move a muscle. My arms dangled at my sides. Useless. I tried to turn away from the trees and the rainstorms, but they were inescapable. Wherever he wasn't touching me, I felt the hard-edged fluorescence of the mall.

Deep in my heart (or my brain or my stomach) I knew that this was my one, final, only opportunity to speak to Nick and say my goodbye to him. To give him my love in language. But my central nervous system (if I still had one) had shut down. No words came. No movement either. I was missing my chance and I knew it.

"Sarah," Nick whispered to me. "I love you. That will never change."

My arms moved upward and rested on those shoulders that had captured my attention when I first saw him.

"I'll find you," he assured me. "I'll look out for you."

My arms tightened around him and his around me. He studied my face and kissed me, then kissed me again. "Please," he urged me. "Please tell me you forgive me."

"Nick." Bertha tugged at his arm. "We must go."

Nick held me tighter. "Please tell me you love me." But I had no words, no sound. Something inside me was gone and I couldn't find it. Come on. Open your mouth. Open your heart. Say it. Speak. Connect. Now. I was missing my chance and I knew it.

He began to let go. "Please. Let me take that with me. Sarah!"

When he stepped away from me I crumbled to the ground and dissolved into a fog of grief. And when I looked up, he was gone.

I had missed my chance, and I knew it.

My bracelet was the color of blood. I was enjoying the irony in that.

Could everyone see that I was walking around with a gaping hole in my heart? Did it run straight through my body, like a cannonball had shot through me? Did they know that I now, finally, felt like I had actually stopped living?

I refused to join Lacey and Alice as they scurried off to participate in Bertha's brand of group therapy. No thank you. Was it okay to blame Bertha for taking Nick away? For falling for his "I died a hero" bit? Please. If you wanted to get technical about it, when I died, I saved my dad. And then I went back and really, really saved him. So there.

I eavesdropped on Bertha's group therapy sessions but stayed on the outside, invisible like a (say it with me) ghost.

"We very nearly had a new arrival!" she crowed. "A young man in a coma was near dead, following a gang-related shooting. But he pulled through. Another modern medical miracle." She sounded really bummed that the kid survived.

Besides feeling allergic to Bertha, I really didn't need to hear her do a whole song-and-dance number entitled "If You Fall in Love at the Mall, You'll Ruin Your Life and I Told You So."

I lingered outside, peeking around the corner whenever I could. Lacey and Alice sat, obedient and attentive, on folding chairs. With any luck that coma boy would give up the ghost and help fill up the room. Meanwhile, Bertha happily instructed poor Lacey and Alice.

"Today I want you to write the story of your life, if you hadn't died when you did."

Writing assignments in the afterlife. Talk about irresistible!

The next day I listened as Bertha joyfully preached at poor Lacey and Alice.

"Today I want you to immerse yourself in your anger about your murder until you can't stand the taste of it any longer. Alice, we'll start with you. If you could speak to your murderer, what would you say?"

Suddenly Alice let loose a tirade that just couldn't be coming from such a small girl. She screeched, *"I hate you! I hate you! I hate you!"* She said it again and again until her voice went raw. I recoiled from the doorway, blown back by the sound and the fury.

"Yes. Well. Very good!" Bertha sounded a bit shocked at the volume little Alice had reached. "Now. Lacey, your turn."

But Lacey spoke quietly. "I don't think Alice is done yet. Are you? Alice?"

She was silent for a long time. Then: "I'm ever so done. I'm so tired of hating him and hating Ma and hating Da. I'm so tired of it. It's a satchel full of stones and I want to put it down. I need to put it down. I choose to put it down."

I peeked around the corner. Alice was crying softly, as Lacey and Bertha sat on the floor with her. Finally Bertha pulled herself up and straightened her clothes.

"Well then, Alice. I think that you should . . ." But something about Alice's expression must have stopped her.

When Alice finally said something, it felt like she was

speaking to herself. "It's done. No more. I'm laying it all to rest."

She breathed. She smiled. Her eyes were clear. Her bracelet was pale pink.

I slithered away.

chapter thirty-seven

and then this happened

The Mall of America is hugely big. There was no reason for me to stay on the fifth level and hang with the dead when there was plenty of room for me down here. Give me the living, any day of the week. I would stay down here and just haunt.

There was a gaggle of little girls, all carrying American Girl dolls, each girl dressed to match her doll. Their mothers abandoned them (temporarily) for caffeine at Caribou Coffee. One of the little girls was the clear leader of the group. She was giving a speech to her smallest follower, while the others looked on.

"Well. Zoe told me that Seana never liked you." Her words hit the small girl right between the eyes. She clutched her doll a little closer. The leader girl seemed pleased, so she continued. "She only *pretended* to like you because you had a trampoline and she wanted to do trampoline Olympics someday. But now she knows there's no such thing, so she doesn't need to be nice to you ever again."

The small girl was crying now. The leader girl grinned.

"I'm telling you this because I'm your friend and I think you should know the truth."

I leaned close to the leader girl and said, "You're a terrible human being. You're going to die someday. And you will be haunted by regrets."

Just like that, the leader girl started to cry. The followers followed and started crying too. Their mothers emerged, coffee in hand, to comfort them.

"What's wrong?" one of the mothers asked.

"I don't kno-o-o-ow!" the leader girl wailed.

Great. I just made a bunch of children cry. What an achievement. For the record, I was not proud of myself. And I was now getting really good at slithering away. There were lots of places to see.

I smiled as a pair of (living) senior citizens in tracksuits power walked through a cluster of dead mall walkers. None of them saw each other. Can we all pause to enjoy this moment a little bit? The living were mall-walking to fend off death.

"What a good idea. I think I'll go for a walk," I said to myself. I laughed just a little, but it felt like acid in my throat. I walked among the living on this level. And then I walked on the next level. And the next. And the next. I went upstairs among the dead, where I wouldn't make anybody cry. When I got to Crate & Barrel, I stopped. Really, I should have gone inside, but I just didn't want to. Not yet.

I made a turn and decided to keep walking. So yeah. I walked. Not fast. I walked. Just steady. I walked. The rhythm of my walk began to cast a spell on me. I walked. It was calming. I walked. It was rhythmic and seductive. So I walked some more. Keep going. I walked. I walked. I walked. I . . .

chapter thirty-eight
sisyphus had it easy

I'm at the wedding. The lights are too bright and the music is too loud. I know what's going to happen and I'm powerless to stop myself. All I have is pure terror at going through this again. Again. Again.

There I am. I'm eating way too much. I steal a glass of champagne from the dais table. Its sharp taste bites at my mouth. And then I eat some more. The food is meaty and savory, and I feel sort of cruel eating it. And then I'm feeling sick, so sick. Now I'm on the bathroom floor in my mango bridesmaid gown. I'm going under. I'm being torn from my body, thread by thread by thread by thread. It hurts like hell. And then . . .

At the wedding. Eating. Drinking. At the wedding. On the bathroom floor. Going under. Hurts like hell. Start over. At the wedding. Eating. Drinking. At the wedding. On the bathroom floor. Going under. Hurts. Start over.

(Stop, please stop. I hate this. Make it stop!)

At the wedding. Eating. Drinking. At the wedding. On the

bathroom floor. Going under. Hurts. Start over. At the wedding. Eating. Drinking. At the wedding. On the bathroom floor. Going under. Hurts. Start over.

(How long have I been doing this? How many times do I have to do this? Somebody? Anybody?)

At the wedding. Eating. Drinking. At the wedding. On the bathroom floor. Hurts.

(Please! I'm begging you! Nick! Bertha! Alice! Lacey! Boy! God! Oprah! Anybody! I'm in here, and I'm stuck watching myself die over and over again. Make it stop! Please, please, please. No more. Nick!)

The lights went big, loud, super-bright. Blinding. Piercing through my eyelids. But then it was over. There was a calm darkness around me.

Was this me giving up? Was I done now? No more? Had I exploded into ash? What comes after all this afterlife, after all? I supposed that it was safe to open my eyes.

I was at home. I was sort of breathless and confused. (Aren't *you*?)

Still. Any kind of change from that awful, endless loop of dying and death was a good thing. I'd overlook the fact that I was standing in the middle of my living room dressed once more in the hideous mango bridesmaid gown because, hey, at least I wasn't watching myself die again.

Because the real problem was, I wasn't just watching myself die. I was *feeling* it. I was in it. And that horrible sick feeling of being extracted from my body was bad enough the first time. The repetition was unbearable.

So I'd wear anything as long as that stopped.

In fact, home looked sweeter and more precious than ever

before. I smiled with more joy than I may ever have felt when I was alive. I was here! In the land of the living!

I finally took a step and felt the carpet give way just a bit beneath my feet. Wow. That felt excellent. I looked around and saw Dad, sitting on the sofa.

And Karen.

She was holding his hand in both of hers. And he was tolerating that. She was smiling.

"Dad!" I yelled. "It's Sarah! Please don't trust Karen!"

He didn't hear me. Not even a little. And then my skin started to feel funny. Sort of like a sunburn that somebody was pushing and twisting. Oh no. The lights changed and flashed. They hurt my eyes. No, no, no. (Maybe it's just a dream? Just a dream. Stop worrying. Just breathe.)

At the wedding. Eating. Drinking. At the wedding. On the bathroom floor. Hurts.

At the wedding. Eating. Drinking. At the wedding. On the bathroom floor. Hurts.

At the wedding. Eating. Drinking. At the wedding. On the bathroom floor. Hurts.

If you watch yourself die enough times, you get *just* a little bit numb to it. The awful feeling becomes tolerable because you know just how bad it will feel and how long it will last. It becomes a repetitive story with a predictable ending, even though you care enormously about the protagonist. That's what was happening with me.

I was a little bit aware of some stray intrusions on this

cycle, but I didn't manage to dream (or haunt?) again. And I mostly knew that yes, I was now a mall walker. There were sounds on the breeze now and then, and they may have come from the people at the mall, but I couldn't be sure. I was safely uncomfortable repeating the story of my death over and over and over again. My legs and feet were serving as the motor that ran the story again, once more from the top.

I could swear I heard Bertha a few times, saying, "Wake yourself up, dear. You can do it. Haven't you suffered enough?"

But I couldn't answer her. (BTW, the answer would have been *No. I need to suffer more.*)

Or maybe I was just being awful. To her and to me. Just try waking up. Just try. Just for a change. I summoned strength/courage/free will/fury/love/chutzpah/and anything else I could find. Wake up. Wake up. *Now.*

I didn't see the wedding, the bathroom, or my home. Things were sort of darkish. And then I heard a new voice. A male voice speaking right to me. It was Declan.

"Wow. This sucks," he said. I had to agree. I could see him, sort of blurry, like he'd been photographed with the wrong filter, but it was definitely Declan. Walking right by my side. We were in rhythm.

"Are we awake now?" I asked him.

"I don't think so," he said. "I don't feel awake. Maybe this is like a dream. Or haunting. Or something." Clearly he didn't know the answer. "Whatever this is, you just made it happen, Sarah."

Me?

The lights were medium-bright, showing us that we were now in a hallway. "Where are we?" I asked.

"We're in a hallway," Declan answered, helpful as ever.

Up ahead of us was a mahogany-brown door that I had never seen before. Of course we opened it. Of course we walked through it. Of course.

So far, every dream had happened in a familiar place. But I didn't recognize where I was now. This looked like a kind of living room, with pretentious art masks on the walls and a big desk on one side. Everything was brown or olive green. Sort of like the floor of a forest. I had definitely never seen this place before.

And there was my mother. (It wasn't fair that I was dead and people were haunting *me*.)

"Now what, Mom?" I asked her. "Is this an intervention? Is this about Nick? Because I'm not done being upset about him, so don't bother yelling at me to get over it. And have you actually returned from the dead to nag me? Really?"

"Yeah, I don't think I'm the one making this happen," Mom interrupted. "You are."

"Um," Declan began. "Okay then, Sarah, first of all, thank you. Even though things still do kind of suck, and I may have to go back to reliving my death over and over again, I'm really thankful for getting drawn into this break. Thank you."

"You're welcome," I replied, even though I wasn't sure that I was the reason for any of this. But hey, he was saying it to me, so I accepted it.

"What's going on? Are you trying to wake us up?" I asked Mom.

"Here's the thing." Mom sounded very confident, like a TV news anchor. "You've got a big problem. Besides mall-walking. You didn't finish what you were supposed to do.

Karen's winning. I mean, I hate to sound like a jealous first wife, but she's really awful."

"But Dad left her. I saw him leave," I insisted, trying really hard not to panic. "I'm the one who got him to leave, and I know, I *know* he understood what I was saying."

"Uh-oh," said Declan. "Remember what I told you: she's smarter than you."

The door to this ugly room opened once more. In came some man I didn't recognize, followed by Karen. Followed by Dad. Oh, Dad. Oh no.

Dad and Karen were seated, all prim and proper on the khaki-green couch. The man sat in a big brown chair. He was studying a folder full of papers and sharing them with Dad. They were full of medical jargon, plus some colorful charts and graphs.

"Your blood work came back perfect, though your cholesterol is on the high side. No toxicology to report," the guy said. *Translation: I didn't find any arsenic or poisonous mushrooms or any other poison in your bloodstream. You are not being poisoned.*

Well. Maybe she hid it. Maybe it's somewhere else. What was she up to?

Dad and Karen smiled at each other (*stop!*). "Well, that's good news," he said.

"You do have a serious heart condition, probably exacerbated by the unbelievable stress you've experienced recently."

The guy (I'll assume he was some sort of doctor) gave Dad a bunch of pamphlets about diet, lifestyle changes, stress relief, and heart medications.

"Why are you showing me this?" I asked Mom in the deepest, angriest tone I could summon.

"I'm not showing you anything!" Mom insisted.

"The Knowing is stupid, pointless, and mean! I can't save him. Whatever she's doing, she's going to finish it. Him. She's going to kill him. And having to watch is just cruel."

"Pay attention," Mom said, directing me back to Dad, Karen, and the doctor.

"It's been awful. I was kind of losing my mind for a while there," Dad confided. "I was hearing things. Or thinking things. It didn't make any sense. I thought"—he gulped before he could continue—"I thought I heard my daughter's voice. In my mind."

"Oh, you poor thing!" Karen cooed at him, rubbing his hands as if they were cold. (She was cold. That's what was cold. And her coo-voice sounded to me now like a car with bad breaks.)

The doctor smiled kindly. "That's perfectly understandable. The mind can play tricks, especially when you're trying to cope with something that's beyond your reach."

"Great! Now I'm a hallucination. Even if I could speak to him again, now *he'll never believe that he's hearing me!*" I shouted.

Dad kissed Karen. (Ew.) "I'm so sorry," he said. "I went a little haywire there."

Karen smiled too sweetly for my taste. "Don't be sorry. Everything is fine now."

I couldn't believe I ever fell for her lies. And Dad was still falling for them.

"Since when does Dad have a heart condition? Can you give somebody a heart condition?" I asked Mom. "How? And how do I stop her now?"

But my vision began to blur. Mom was speaking, but I couldn't hear her.

"Mom! Please don't go! Tell me what to do!" I could feel tears stinging my eyes.

Mom was already gone. So was Declan. The room faded to a mossy blur of nothing. No voices, no Karen, no Dad.

Everything changed. Familiar cool light surrounded me. My feet stopped. I was standing still for the first time in I have no idea how long. My eyes were open, but I couldn't figure out what I was seeing. The mall. I was back. And the silence made for an almost painful transition. But I blinked and I waited.

"Sarah? Are you awake? Are you in there?" the male voice asked me. The voice was quiet, but it penetrated deep into my rib cage. This voice mattered, I thought. I had to pay attention to this voice. So I did.

"Nick?" I asked.

He wasn't Nick. He was Declan. I blinked again. Still Declan.

"I think you woke me up," he said. "That was really weird." (And wasn't that the understatement of all time?)

I sat on the floor. My feet hurt.

chapter thirty-nine

oh, but it wasn't a dream. you were there, and you were there. and you.

Alice came running to me first, practically screaming with delight and launching a hug-fest here in the Mall of the Dead. But when she hugged me, she whispered in my ear, "It's over now. You must never go back."

"You're awake! Excellent!" Lacey cried as she hugged me so hard I thought she might crack my ribs. If someone had told me on our first day in the mall that Lacey and I would end up completely overjoyed to see each other, I would have drowned that person in sarcasm. But here we were.

Lacey's face was different than I remembered it, or at least the look in her eyes was completely changed. They were open and curious, and her facial muscles were a lot more relaxed. She looked younger than ever. This must be what letting go looks like. Lacey was a new Lacey.

Bertha welcomed me (and my now rose-pink bracelet) back with open arms. And to her credit she didn't utter the phrase "I told you so" once. At least, not yet. Each and every time I stretched my tired muscles, I smiled. And I meant it.

Alice understood everything, rushing us all to the food court, where Declan and I could put our feet up and recover.

The taste of bread and salty butter was so simple, perfect, and complete, I nearly started crying. The sound of conversation had magic in it, even when it was Declan complaining that his bracelet was not a flattering shade of pink. ("I'm an Autumn. I need something with more yellow!")

"Sarah." Bertha spoke gently. "I'm certain that the group would benefit from hearing about your recent walking experience. You know, it's highly unusual for someone to walk for such a brief time."

Time. I had forgotten about time.

"How long was I walking?" I asked. "A few hours?"

"Five days." Bertha said it like it was nothing. Five days of nonstop walking. I was right on the cusp of complaining about this when Alice caught my eye. She had been in the afterlife since 1933. She had walked for years at a shot. I should maybe shut the hell up. So I did.

"The really fun part was how I got to relive my death over and over again. There are lots of unpleasant ways to die, and puking your guts up is somewhere on that list. Probably near the top. Anyway, I relived it a lot. Probably from the moment I first took the poison to the moment I left my body. Over and over again."

"Gross," Lacey said under her breath, which was louder than most people's normal volume.

"Yeah, gross," I agreed. "But then I had these other dreams. I think I was haunting. Just a little. First I was at my home, and my dad was there—"

Bertha was all aflutter. I think she twitched whenever anybody used the word "haunting."

"No, no, no, no, no, no!" Bertha corrected me. "You were not dreaming, and you were certainly not haunting. That's quite impossible. You never left the mall, I assure you."

"Trust me. I was haunting," I replied.

"I'm sure you *think* you were haunting." She spoke to me like I was an idiot child. "But you weren't. It's impossible."

I took my feet off the table and leaned toward her.

"Oh, I was haunting, all right," I said, but she shook her head. "And you know what else? I've haunted before. At night. When I went to sleep, I had dreams, but the dreams were real. And while I was mall-walking, I dreamed that I saw my dad and Karen at a doctor's office. He totally trusts her now."

"You're just tired, dear." She was in full-on I'm-talking-to-a-fool mode.

"Hey! Did we just have the exact same dream?" Declan asked. "There was a lady talking to you. And you know what? I had another dream where I got to hydrate my skin at Ulta."

"That was my mother you saw," I explained. "And it wasn't a dream. I don't know why it happens, but I have these weird haunting episodes with people who are connected to my old life."

"Wow. Yeah. I could feel like you were pulling me into these dreams. I went to Ulta." Declan touched his face gently. "It really happened. So I was haunting," he said.

"Impossible!" Bertha declared, in what was clearly a losing battle. "The dead don't dream!"

Declan ignored her, leaning across the table like he was

sharing juicy gossip with me. "Wasn't it creepy when she was rubbing his hands like that?" he asked.

"I know, right? And the way *he* apologized to *her*!" I added. "I wish I could deck her, I really do."

"You're making this up," Bertha insisted, but Declan talked over her.

"This was real," he said. (A moment of insecurity: Declan is the person supporting my argument. Is that good?) "Karen is most definitely trying to kill Sarah's father. And now he thinks that if he hears Sarah, it's all in his head, like she's an illusionation. Sarah and I saw the whole thing."

(Okay. Vocabulary issues aside, go Declan.)

Bertha's mouth fell open as I spoke. "And I'm going to save him. Just you watch. Where can I find the Boy? I need to go back. Again."

This was Bertha speechless: mouth open, eyes wide, perfectly still.

I kind of enjoyed it.

✽ ✽ ✽

Bertha refused to help me. "It was a mistake the first time. Why would you want to repeat a bad mistake?" And other stuff. For me, her words all dissolved into "blah blah blah."

Lacey, Alice, and Declan looked at each other. They were the picture of reluctance.

"I don't want to go see them," Lacey blurted out. "I think the Boy is a little bit crazy. And besides, when they look at me I feel like they know all my secrets. Even the ones I don't know myself. They scare me."

"They terrify me," Alice whispered.

"I'll go with you," Declan offered with a shrug. "Who's the Boy, again?"

"That's okay, you guys," I conceded. "I'll go and talk to them alone."

I went to Toys"R"Us. And just started talking. To myself. (Remember how we're not judging?)

"Are you here? Boy? Oprah? Old Testament Guy? Mother Teresa? Oprah?"

There was no answer, but that wasn't stopping me. "Here's the thing. I need to go back to Earth one more time. I need to finish saving my dad. So. Would you please tell Bertha to get that elevator going and send me back?" And then I remembered to add "Please?"

And then they appeared.

They just sort of ambled around a shelf of coloring books. The girl Boy was starting to get the hang of the yo-yo, while the boy Boy was shaking a Magic Eight Ball.

"Should I add a bowling alley to this floor?" he asked it.

"Excuse me?" I tried to interrupt.

" 'Reply hazy. Try again later,' " he read from the ball. He looked up at me and said, "What does that mean?"

"Please," I began, leaning heavily on that magic word, "I don't have much time, and I need a favor. A request. Please!"

The girl Boy dropped her yo-yo, and the boy Boy dropped his Magic Eight Ball with a great thud. I had their attention. Here goes.

"My stepmother is going to kill my father," I began.

"We know that already. But. Are you Snow White or Cinderella?" the girl Boy asked. And she looked like she was serious.

"Neither. I'm Sarah. And I need to find a way to stop this woman." The girl Boy laughed at me.

"How are you going to do it?" the boy Boy asked.

"I have no idea," I said, assuming that they might know if I was lying.

"Didn't you already save him?" the girl Boy said. "Isn't that why we sent you back before?"

"Reve-enge!" the boy Boy sang out to the sky. "She wants reve-enge!"

"Please!" My voice began to break. "I just want to save him. That's all."

"Why?" the boy Boy asked.

"Because. He's going to die." I had to choke out the words. "Please."

"So?" the girl Boy answered, reexamining her yo-yo. "Dying isn't so bad. Sometimes it's messy, and sometimes it hurts. But lots of things are messy and hurty." Then she stopped eyeing the yo-yo and said, "Isn't it nice here? You have nice food and nice things, right? Wouldn't you want something like that for your daddy?"

That felt like a trick question, so in my desperation I ignored it. Besides, I knew I was much too emotional to handle a debate with the Boy, so I just kept begging.

"Please. When I haunt them in my dreams, I can't get them to hear me. But if you send me there, I can tell him he's in danger." I added an extra "Please!" just in case it would help.

The Boy stopped playing.

"What else can you do?" they asked in unison.

"I have dreams that might be more than just dreams. I draw people to me. I sort of haunt them, I think. And when I talk to living people, they sort of hear me. They do as I say. At least, here at the mall they do." I watched as this revelation landed on them. They checked in with each other silently. It looked like this might work in my favor.

"And what about when you were alive?" the boy Boy asked. "Did you have special abilities?"

"She did!" the girl Boy loud-whispered. "You just know she did! She probably knew things or saw things that most people can't."

"That's true. I did have that ability," I said. They were both so delighted at being right, they clapped their hands.

"Told you!" the girl Boy squealed.

"But I said it first!" the boy Boy whined. "I knew she was different. I called it the first time we saw her." He stomped his feet and seemed ready to lose it.

"But I made it stop." I interrupted the tantrum. "I only had it when I was little. I didn't keep it with me when I got older."

"What?" The boy Boy was sort of outraged. "You gave up on being special?"

I knelt down on the floor, so that I was eye to eye with him. He was deadly serious.

"Yes." I was (finally) owning it as I was saying it. "I didn't want to be special. I just wanted my mother back. And I'm sorry. If this was a gift that you gave me, and I didn't appreciate it when I was alive, I'm truly sorry. Please don't punish my father for my mistake."

"Waste not, want not," the boy Boy mused. "I don't know what that means."

"You threw it away. And now you found it again. You had to die to find what you wanted and needed. I think that's funny," said the girl Boy. They looked at each other, and then she came close to me.

The girl Boy took my hand in hers. "You're a special one. You need to break away from your old life as soon as you can. Your daddy is very close to death. Very. It will come for him soon. Let him die. Let him go."

chapter forty

um, no

So apparently I was all specially special. Woo-hoo! There was a voice inside me that let me know when things were going to happen. I was able to save the lady in the green coat, but I couldn't save my own mom. I didn't understand it and I didn't want to. Okay, let's be honest: I retreated from a *lot* of stuff after she died. But this special sauce that was me, well, it had followed me into the afterlife. It's why people could hear me the way that they did. It's why I had these dreams where I was haunting. Special, special me. Whatever.

When I'd been alive, this gift didn't help me save my mother. And now that I was dead, it couldn't help me save my father from my wicked stepmother.

I would like to exchange this gift for something more useful, please.

The Boy refused to let me go haunt. My bracelet held the faintest traces of pale pink. I'd be moving on soon. So would Alice and Lacey. Declan had a tiny drop more color in his bracelet. Bertha was more determined than ever to see us all move on. Maybe she was sick of us? Anyway, she did her classic cluck-sigh as she forced a smile and invited us all to her affirmations session. Yep. That's right. She had everyone repeating affirmations into a mirror.

"I will move on to a beautiful new life."

"I deserve a life of joy and service."

"I will appreciate the gift of life when I have it again."

Declan was a little distracted by his reflection, but he joined in. Not me. I looked past the mirror, past this afterlife. What could I do?

✳ ✳ ✳

We were back among the Legos, drifting among living people and brightly colored toys, where the high-pitched screams from the roller coaster began to feel like my favorite song. I thought of Nick, of Harry and those crazy first days of death. A little boy dropped a Lego down his mother's pants, which started a loud, kind of ugly scene.

I stayed out of it.

"This place makes me think of Harry," Lacey said. She was on my right and Alice on my left. "I wonder what he'll be like in his next life. I hope we meet. I hope we get married and have beautiful bald babies!" I think she had given this fantasy some thought.

"When I go back, I'm going to be an independent woman," Alice declared. "No man will be master of me!"

"Good for you." I smiled. "I can't begin to think about what I want next time around. I can't accept that my dad has to die like this. He deserves better."

"Yeah, your stepmother sounds like one scary bitch," Lacey said. And as she spoke, she flicked a Lego into the crowd. No one noticed it. But I stared at the empty space where the Lego had been. There was a kind of supernova explosion in my mind.

"Lacey! It's you! I need your help," I said breathlessly. And yes, I realized that I seemed a little too frantic to be taken seriously. I did my best impersonation of a calm person.

"The elevator," I explained. "I bet you could work it again. And you could get me back there." I tugged at her sleeve. "Come on! Why didn't I think of this before? You can do this. I need to go. Right now." But Alice and Lacey didn't move, didn't speak. It was maddening. "Now!" I repeated, and I may have sounded like I was ordering them around. Because I was.

"Whoa," Lacey began. "First of all: chill. You don't want to be the girl who tries to tell me what to do. Bertha says we're like a day away from moving on. My bracelet is nice and light. I want to keep it that way. Don't you want to move on?"

My bracelet was nearly white. It showed faint signs of shimmer. I was nearly ready.

"I don't care about that!" I half-lied. "She's going to kill my father. I'm running out of time."

"How will you stop her?" Alice asked. Okay, maybe that was a reasonable question any other day, any other time, but *not now*! I needed a way to explain this whole mess in ten seconds or less. It didn't exist.

"Please," I said simply. "You two know me. Just trust me, please. This is important."

I looked at Alice and then at Lacey. They looked at each other and nodded.

"If I end up mall-walking, I'm going to kill you," Lacey whispered.

✻ ✻ ✻

"Declan, I need you to use your acting skills," I said to him.

He nodded sagely, as if he were the wise old man on a mountaintop and he'd been expecting us to come to him eventually with this very request.

"Hey. Sure. After all, I do sort of owe you one," he said.

I shouldn't have asked. But I did. "What do you mean?"

"Well. I put the mushrooms on your plate. How could I have been so stupid? I trusted Karen, and you ended up dead. And you act like you pretty much forgive me. You even woke me up, I think. So. Ya know."

"Oh, Declan." I took his hand as I spoke. "It wasn't your fault. She tricked all of us. And now you're going to help me save my dad."

"How?" He looked so young and eager.

"Distract Bertha. Keep her in Staples. Ask for more affirmations. Or talk about something from your life. Do one of her therapy exercises. Anything!"

Declan looked off into the distance, picturing the scene. "Improv. I can do that." But then he refocused on Lacey, Alice, and me. "What are you going to do?"

"Maybe it's best if you don't know," I replied. "That way you won't have to lie."

"But I'm an actor!" He seemed a bit hurt. "I can totally act my way through it. Please? Tell me?"

Lacey interrupted us. "We're taking the elevator back to the living so Sarah can save her dad. Somehow."

"Cool." Declan nodded, smiled, and went off in search of Bertha.

✳ ✳ ✳

Lacey focused on the elevator button. She focused for a long minute, and nothing happened. I knew it wouldn't help to shake her by the shoulders and yell, so I locked myself and my fears into silence.

After a while, Lacey blew out a breath. "I'm out of practice. Losing my touch. Sorry!"

"It's okay," I said. "You've got this. I know it."

Alice smiled. "You've got all that life and fury and passion inside you, Lacey. Just tap into it. You can do this."

Lacey nodded. The pressure must have been awful, because she shook her head, as if she wanted to pretend none of this was happening and none of us were here. She closed her eyes and then, *bump*. The elevator moved. Then the door opened.

Go, Lacey!

I stepped through it and turned to thank her. But she and Alice were right beside me. "Hey!" I called out as the door closed behind us. (How were we going to get back now?)

"Where should we start?" Lacey asked. "I'm ready to kick a little ass."

I reeeeally should have explained what little plan I had.

I was the only who was supposed to go back. Lacey, at the very least, needed to return and run the elevator to come back for me. Clearly she hadn't figured out that we were now stranded here. Neither had Alice.

"Let's start at my place," I said.

✳ ✳ ✳

The apartment was dark and quiet as I went from room to room to room. No sign of Dad or Karen so far. The place was perfectly clean and spare. Barely lived in.

Could they be at his office? Was he well enough to be at work? Was he sick enough to be in a hospital somewhere?

"Are we too late?" I wondered aloud. "Did she already kill him?"

"How do you know that he's in mortal danger?" Alice asked.

"When I was mall-walking, I saw them at a doctor's office. He has a heart condition now. All of a sudden. And his hair is falling out and he looks terrible."

"Oh, Sarah," Alice said. "Maybe that's just life, just nature."

"Declan knew her, and her whole terrible history. She killed him, I'm sure of that. She killed me by mistake, and now she wants to finish what she set out to do." I had absolutely no doubt. Alice, on the other hand, looked full of doubt. She drifted off to the window.

I kept searching for any sign of where they might be.

"You know, we never did find any actual, definite poison," Lacey reasoned.

"Girls! Come here at once!" Alice commanded, and we obeyed.

She was pointing out the window to a bench on the other side of the fountain. I spotted Karen's red hair right away. The salt/pepper/balding man next to her on the bench was Dad. Alive. At least for now. He was leaning forward a bit, and I knew that he was in danger. Zero doubts.

"Wow," Lacey said. "How did he get there?"

"She must have walked him out there," I reasoned. "Maybe it's better for her if he dies in public? I bet that helps her look less guilty. Or maybe he was trying to get away from her!" I set my jaw a little too tightly and began to make my way to the door. "Either way, I'm stopping her now!"

Alice and Lacey stayed by the window.

"Come on!" I beckoned, and couldn't quite believe that I had to rush them.

"Not your dad," Alice said. "Look."

I didn't want to look. I wanted to go. *Now.* But okay, fine. I would probably need their help, and maybe they knew something I didn't. So I looked. Dad and Karen were still there, on the bench. It was early morning, and the population was still fairly light: workers going to work. That same street musician getting set up to perform near the Washington arch. And an assortment of dead people who were stuck here. The usual suspects. Just another day.

"Look," Lacey said with more urgency. There was a guy doing jumping jacks near the bench. Or he was waving his arms. Karen and Dad acted like they didn't notice him. Maybe they were being true New Yorkers, ignoring the crazies, or maybe the guy was dead and therefore invisible to them.

When my eyes rested on that figure, he clicked into focus, and the earth seemed to shake. Nick. Absolutely Nick. Unmistakably Nick. My Nick.

I didn't pass through the door or the wall to get down there to that scene. I passed through the window, sailed through the air, and landed in front of Nick. And Dad.

chapter forty-one

it takes a village

"Sarah!" Nick called. "Your dad—he's in danger!"

"I know!" I said. Seeing Nick, hearing his voice, being near him again, it all conspired to throw me off and slow me down. And I couldn't afford to be slow. Not now.

"She's been giving him selenium. It's destroying his heart. And if he dies from a heart attack, *she'll get away with it.*" He was waving his arms in front of them, and I realized that he was trying desperately for them to see him.

"What are you doing?" I asked, and okay, there was just a hint of hostility in my voice.

"I'm trying to help. I'm trying to become an angel, and that's what angels do." It was his turn to sound hostile. "We help!"

"So they'll see you, and then what?" I asked. "My dad sees a ghost and has an *instant* heart attack? Is that the plan?"

"No!" Dad gasped. His red face was contorted in pain. He was sweating and fighting for air as he clutched his left arm. I knelt before him. "Dad. Get your phone. Call nine-one-one. You need an ambulance. Right now!"

There were at least a dozen dead people all around us. They broke from their usual routine to watch what was unfolding here. "He doesn't have long now," one of them said.

"Dad!" I shouted as hard as I could. A few ghosts echoed me. "Dad! Dad!" The ghost who screamed at people let out a banshee howl. The *Gatsby* couple stopped their endless bickering and joined in the chorus.

"Listen to her!" *Gatsby* guy shouted.

"Your daughter is trying to save you!" *Gatsby* girl urged him.

"Call nine-one-one!" My voice was a ragged shriek above the rising chorus of screams, shouts, and moans from the dead encircling us.

Maybe he heard me. He reached toward the inside pocket of his jacket. Or was he reaching for his chest? His trembling hands rested against his heart. The dead went silent, waiting for him to do something, anything.

"Help," he whispered.

"Finally," Karen said. "I have to hand it to you, Evans, you have endurance. I mean, the stress of Sarah's death should have pushed you to a coronary by now. But no, you had to make me earn it. Fine."

And now, all around us, the voices of the dead rose up—shouting, moaning, shrieking, and screaming—at him, her, me, and the sky. It was an ever-expanding, deafening chorus of alarm, like someone had started a rebellion in the ape house.

Dad turned to face her. The pain was magnified now with fear and bone-deep sadness. I moved in even closer, to hear and be heard above the madness.

"*Dad! Don't listen to her. Listen to me! Call nine-one-one right now!*" I practically bellowed.

Karen leaned close to Dad. I could barely hear her over the madness all around us. "Just let it happen. It's better if you don't fight it. You'll have to take my word on that."

Dad groaned and tried to move, but the pain in his chest and his arm stopped him.

And now the dead were scrambling outward, shouting warnings all over the park to the police and every living person who passed by. "*Nine-one-one right now! Somebody call nine-one-one! Murder! Murder! Death! This man is having a heart attack!*" But the living tuned us out.

Karen scanned all around her, a momentary look of confusion on her face. But she quickly returned to Dad. "Maybe this'll help," she said with false sweetness. "I never loved you. But I'm mad about your money. I've been waiting for this day since we met. And now I'll go over there." She pointed to a distant bench with a good view of this one. "So I can come back and discover you. And I'll be shocked and sad and all that. Whatever. I'll give you a dramatic send-off with lots of witnesses. Would you please move this along?"

"*Nine-one-one. Please! Hear my voice and call nine-one-one!*" My throat was raw and painful. A few living people looked up for the source of the voice, but then instantly, maddeningly turned away. Karen looked around, a flicker of worry overtaking her.

"Weird," she said. She checked her watch, impatient for Dad to die, no doubt. She whispered once more into his ear. "How about this? I killed Sarah. Or at least I arranged it. Here's the punch line: *You* were supposed to die that day, but my idiot caterer screwed up. Sarah died in your place."

That did it. Dad's head dropped forward. His struggle against the pain was over. I could feel it. He was losing the fight. Soon he would be in that thread-by-thread part of dying.

Karen rose slowly, casually, not calling any attention to herself. She walked away to that distant bench. She sat and she watched. The cries of the dead rose in pitch and volume and felt like a physical wall around us.

Alice and Lacey were by my side. "We're too late," Alice said. "He's gone."

"Not yet," Lacey said. "I'll get his phone. I'll dial. You'll shout into the phone," she ordered me. I was ready to obey.

She reached into his jacket for the phone, but she couldn't grasp it. Three tries. Four tries. Finally she had it and began to ease it to the bench. But it fell from her hand and crashed to the ground, facedown.

"I'm trying." She was nearly weeping as she reached for that phone over and over again.

"Sing," Nick said. "Sing and somebody will really hear you."

It sounded like the stupidest idea ever. But it was the only idea we had left. I scanned the park for someone who might hear me and respond. The musician? Maybe. And then I saw that little strawberry-blond girl, the one who liked to sing.

She was walking through the park with her mother, humming a tune to herself. Elizabeth Anne. I had to pin all my hopes on a random kid. So, I sang out as hard as I could.

Turn your face to me
Turn your gaze and see
All the pain surrounding you

She stopped walking and stopped humming. Good. Her mother tugged at her hand to start up again. "Elizabeth Anne, we have to go," her mother urged. But Elizabeth Anne stood still and listened. Good girl.

Every song you hear
With a heart sincere
Brings a chance for you to do

"Sweetheart, don't stare at that man on the bench. It's rude to stare," the mother advised.

Something more

"I think he's sick. I think he's in an emergency," she said. The mother shook her head, but she studied the man on the bench, the man who was beginning to leave his body, thread by thread.

Turn your face to me
Turn your gaze and see
All the pain surrounding you

epilogue
free will

Dad was alive. Whatever was to come after this, I knew I'd be at peace with it.

As the ambulance was loading him onto the stretcher, I saw him blink his eyes open, and I could swear that he saw me. He reached his hand forward, and I reached mine. I heard the word "stable" and that would have to do.

In the distance, I saw Karen rise and leave the park. Maybe she had some sort of getaway plan. Or maybe she'd be caught and spend the rest of her miserable living days in prison. Either way it was fine. Despite the Boy's predictions, I didn't need revenge. She'd find hell right here on earth. I was certain of that.

Little Elizabeth Anne stood all alone, crying, as she watched the adults in a state of emergency around her. So I crouched next to her and sang softly into her ear.

Be the girl who does
More than she who was
Be alive in joy and hope

Just as her weeping quieted, a familiar, faintly Irish voice sputtered, "Honestly!"

Bertha. I was never so happy to see that little face, even though it was twisted into an old-lady scowl.

"How did you know we were here?" I asked. And all at once, I knew. Declan couldn't act his way through this one. (Good.)

Bertha did her classic cluck-sigh combo and said, "Come on, you lot. Get in."

"Hey," Lacey said, with a realization dawning on her. "How were we going to get back to the mall?"

"Oh, I would have found a way to help you," Nick said. He was there by my side as the elevator bumped to a start.

"Yay for Nick," said Lacey.

"Yay indeed," Alice echoed.

He took my hand and warmed me through and through. Was he staying? Was he just passing through? Were these our true final moments together? I looked up at the gold flecks in his eyes and that crazy smile. This was my chance at a do-over for our goodbye. I kissed him and let us both get caught in the dream of that kiss. Bertha wasn't shy about interrupting us.

"Ah-hem!" she shouted, and we all followed Bertha to the Toys"R"Us. Nick kept hold of my hand. I felt like I was watching a movie of us walking together. I was the smiling girl. The one holding hands with the boy who had the crooked grin. I was the girl filled with light.

Bertha came to a sudden stop at the Toys"R"Us entrance and said, "I wonder, really, at what point I lost control of this group. Just this once, do as I ask and wait here. Do not go to the elevator. Do not go anywhere!"

She didn't wait for an answer.

"You were trying to save him," I said to Nick. "Thank you." I couldn't believe what I was feeling. Could I really be happy that Nick had left me and become an angel?

"I was failing." Nick shook his head and grinned as he spoke. "You saved him."

"We all did," I said to Nick, to Lacey, to Alice. "Thank you." Bertha screeched to us from the store, "Come inside!" That was our Bertha, forever stepping on the pretty moments.

We found her at the back. "And now . . ." She raised an eyebrow at me and said, "It's time." The Boy was waiting for us. Declan was cowering off to one side.

The girl Boy jumped up and cheered, "Bravo for you! You did it!"

"But I thought you didn't want me to interfere—it sounded like you wanted me to let him die," I answered.

"You never told us that," Alice whispered to me.

"We *did*!" the boy Boy said. "Only angels are supposed to interfere. But you were naughty, and you went there anyway, and now your daddy's going to live."

"He is?" Oh, I was too full of joy. I had to share some of it, give it away. Dad would live through all of this. Victory.

"Well," the girl Boy corrected the boy Boy, "he won't live forever!"

"I'm really sorry I told on you guys," poor Declan said. "She just kept asking me. And I cracked. I'm really sorry!"

"It's fine, Declan," I assured him. "All is forgiven. Truly."

Bertha muttered, "I asked him twice. Hardly the third degree."

"Hey, Bertha?" Declan asked. "Are those new shoes?" She

was wearing ballerina flats. No clunk whatsoever. And they were—how can I say this?—cute.

"Oh. Well. I felt the need for a change. A few changes." She was blushing hard.

Suddenly Lacey shouted out, "Hey! My bracelet! It's all white and shimmery! Like Harry's was." She was giggling with delight. And then I realized that Alice and I were both wearing white shimmery bracelets too.

"Even me!" Declan crowed.

"Time to move on," Bertha said quietly. "And not a moment too soon."

Nick squeezed my hand and I let myself lean against his arm and his shoulder. I had nearly forgotten how intoxicating trees and rainstorms could be. I had to inhale it and enjoy it while I could.

The Boy transformed into an old man, complete with the white beard, the flowing robes.

"We seem way more important like this. And this is an important moment," he said. He was in a serious mood now, peering down at Declan, saying, "You can now move on, if you believe you are ready."

"Yes, sir!" Declan seemed completely intimidated by this version of the Boy. "Yes, Your Lordship. I would be honored." And with that he gave a deep bow.

The Boy turned to Lacey but didn't get a chance to speak. She looked at all of us and said, "Are you kidding? Let's go! Right now! I want to have a whole life. I want to be a person, have some kids. I want to get old and not die till I'm totally ready."

The Boy looked at Alice.

"Yes, I'm completely ready to move on," she said eagerly. "My life was too brief and too dark. My afterlife has been too long, too arduous. I'm ready. I want some life. Some joy."

He looked at me. I wanted to find some poetic way to say, "I'm ready!" But he said this instead:

"Sarah. You aren't an ordinary girl. You've always known that, even if you pretended otherwise. If you so choose, you could become an angel," he boomed. "You could stay in the afterlife. You could help the living and help the dead. You would be immortal. But you would not be alive."

I couldn't speak. Was I about to choose between life and death? For all time?

Bertha stepped forward. "When you were able to haunt in your dreams, it was a clear sign that you're an angel. If not this time, eventually, Sarah, you will be an angel."

When I looked back at the Boy, he had transformed into Oprah.

"Don't make this decision because of him." She pointed to Nick. "He's not much of an angel, I have to tell you! He couldn't help an old lady across the street. But he helped you and your dad. And he is kind of heroic, so there you go."

I looked straight at Nick. "Thank you. Not just for this, but for everything that went before. Thank you."

Oprah laughed to herself. "He's a sweetheart. True. But. As angels go, this one needs help!"

Nick nodded and answered Oprah. "Okay, yes, I have a lot to learn. It's true." He turned to me. "If you want to move on, I'll understand. It's sort of maddening to be among the living and see them not get it. Life is this amazing gift. Who would turn it down? And, Sarah, if you move on, I'll watch out for you. Hopefully by then I'll be good at it."

"Sarah," Bertha said. "When I found you in the park, you were singing to a little girl. Why?"

"I had seen her a few times before. She was almost always singing. I needed someone to hear me, and somehow I knew this little singing girl would hear me," I answered. And now that I was saying it out loud, it sounded crazy. Why didn't I go to the policeman, like Nick did? Why did my instincts propel me toward the strawberry-blond singing girl, Elizabeth Anne?

"Yes, of course she could hear you. Oh, Sarah. You and she are deeply connected. You knew her in her last life." Bertha stepped toward me and took my hands in hers. "She was your mother. She's returned."

I gasped and fell back a step. Nick put an arm around me.

"How did you know, Sarah?" he asked. But I had no answer.

"I believe you would make an excellent angel." Bertha spoke with quiet confidence. "Even if you have a lot to learn." (She just had to add that. Then again, it was true.) "And I, for one, am ready to move on. I need someone else to be in charge here." Bertha was looking at me and half-smiling.

Lacey and Alice shook their heads with a violent, determined "no" on their faces. "You were just a kid when you died," Lacey said. "You should get to have a real life."

"And we could all meet up together," Alice reminded me. "Alive."

Life, in all its noisy, messy glory, pulled at me like an undertow. At the same time, a silver voice inside me tilted toward being an angel. And oh, I didn't dare even look at Nick.

Have you ever had to make a choice that would last beyond time?

✳ ✳ ✳

I woke up dead. At the mall. And while I was there I fell in love, found out who killed me, haunted the living, made friends, and saved my dad's life. Not a bad afterlife.

I was a daughter, a friend, a lover, a singer, a Mathlete, a New Yorker, a girl. All of my stories were woven together.

I have a new story now. I'm the girl, the angel, who helps you move on. I'm the girl, the angel, who lives here at the mall. I'm the girl, the angel, who loves Nick. He's the boy, the angel, who helps you move on too. Who loves me. Here at the mall.

We both hope that you stay safe and well. But if something should happen to you, we'll be here for you. We want to know your story.

But first, stop and listen. Can you hear that? It's the sound of life and afterlife. And it sounds exactly like music.

acknowledgments

Thank you, thank you, thank you, in no particular order, to:

Wendy Loggia, for multitasking as an editor/deity

Dan Lazar and Victoria Doherty-Munro of Writers' House, for being scary smart and endlessly patient

Myra Donnelley, for being a staunch supporter, an evil twin, and a goddess among mothers

Ryan, Kirsten, Donna, Erin, Phil, and Dandan, for being such a delightful work family

Diane Lambert Dixon, for all that early encouragement

Edward Zabala and the friendly baristas on Bond, for providing me with my personal writer's colony, plus tea

Jeanne and Mur, for being like sisters to me

Annie, for being my favorite human

And a group hug to Fred Sullivan, my Senior Seven sisters, Dream Moms, Justine Lambert and Kenneth Nowell of Looking Glass Theatre, the PS130, MAT, and Baruch gangs. Go, Blue Devils!